THE ENTERTAINMENT NEWSPAPERS WENT BERSERK.

International pop diva Saxony had been seen naked chasing a man through an L.A. restaurant, begging loudly for sex. There were a hundred witnesses.

Remo felt someone kick him in the shoulder a little before 6:00 a.m.

Chiun was glowering at him in the orange sunlight coming into the RV. "What agitates you, Remo?"

"Little Koreans."

"In your sleep you were disturbed. Were you dreaming of fowl flesh?"

"No. Can I go back to sleep now?"

"You have done something." Chiun walked slowly toward the glass patio window, then he turned swiftly, hiding in the shadow. "You have sullied yourself."

"I didn't sully."

D1307462

CREATED BY MURPHY & SAPIR

THE DESTROYER

NO CONTEST

A GOLD EAGLE BOOK FROM
WORLDWIDE.

TORONTO • NEW YORK • LONDON
AMSTERDAM • PARIS • SYDNEY • HAMBURG
STOCKHOLM • ATHENS • TOKYO • MILAN
MADRID • WARSAW • BUDAPEST • AUCKLAND

First edition January 2005

ISBN 0-373-63253-3

Special thanks and acknowledgment to
Tim Somheil for his contribution to this work.

NO CONTEST

Copyright © 2005 by Warren Murphy.

Printed in U.S.A.

And for the Glorious House of Sinanju,
sinanjucentral@hotmail.com

Dee Ligit didn't care anymore about being a champion. All he cared about was staying alive.

Two competitors were dead already, and the evidence was right there in front of him. Blood-black smears stained the plywood catch basin that was jokingly called "the Moat."

Getting hurt was one thing—in the sport of rail surfing you broke bones all the time. But these guys were dead. And not just any two rail surfers. They had been two of the greats.

Antonio the Terrible was a legend. Around from the beginning, when kids first started standing atop trains as a sport, these days he was to rail surfing what Michael Jordan was to basketball. He'd been on a hundred magazine covers in his native Brazil. He had his own line of helmets and knee pads. And now he was dead.

Francis the Fran Man had been around almost as long. He was old, like, in his thirties, and he'd been a star of the sport since he was twelve. It was the Fran Man, the grandfather of American rail surfers, who inspired Dee Ligit to stand on top of a speeding train for the first time. And now the Fran Man was dead, too.

"The show *will* go on," declared the vice president of programming for the Extreme Sports Network, sponsor of the first North American extreme rail surfing competition called Pro Train Surf I. "It would be an insult to these brave athletes to stop it now."

The network gave the media prerecorded videotapes of Antonio the Terrible and the Fran Man. "We all face death every time we strap a locomotive to our sneakers," Antonio said in his heavily accented English. "I don't want the sport to stop if something happens to me. Carry on—let the world see the bravery of all professional rail surfers."

The Fran Man's video said pretty much the same thing. In fact Dee Ligit had made a tape just like it, which was a requirement of the games. You couldn't compete in Pro Train Surf I until you'd made a tape like that and handed it over to ESN.

Dee said pretty much the same words on his tape and he felt oh so sincere at the time. Now he was miserable and afraid. Sure, he was a professional rail surfer, but he wasn't one of the superstars of the sport. Tony and the Fran Man—they were in a league of their own, right. If they couldn't surf this course, how could he?

But he had no choice. If he backed out now, his career was over. He'd lose all credibility. He'd never get another promotional fee. Landing his own branded line of surf shoes would be out of the question—who'd want surf shoes from a guy who was afraid to surf? And for sure he'd lose the fifty-thousand-dollar check from the cereal company that was sponsoring him. He really needed that money.

Dee *had* to surf the course, but that didn't mean he

had to kill himself in the process. He'd take it easy, go casual. As he stood out on the launch platform, he examined the track and tried not to see the plywood gutters.

When he was a kid, he rail surfed for fun. He didn't let high school or his parents interfere with his passion. He was expelled from school three months before graduation and kicked out of the house the same day, but it was right about that time he won his first big rail surf competition. He couldn't even count how many contests he had won since then.

Back then the competitions were strictly underground and illegal. A few hundred devotees would meet in the middle of the night to watch the launch. The launch pad was a truck, a parked boxcar or anything else that was close enough to make a jump possible. The surf train would roll alongside, and the surfers would leap aboard. They were always passenger trains, which traveled regular schedules and offered curved, challenging roofs.

After the surfers leaped aboard, the crowds would drive to the finish line. The best contests involved high-speed trains traveling track with a lot of twists and turns.

Sure, it was hard to stay on. Especially on a sharp curve with a speeding engineer. Dee took his share of tumbles and broke his arms and legs, but he had natural talent, and his cut of the wagering pots was more than he'd make at any job he could think of.

A few months ago he had his biggest win. It was in South Dakota, or maybe the other Dakota. The contest started out as nothing special until Dee heard that the sponsors, a bunch of small-time hoods from Fargo, had invited friends from Las Vegas. The friends from Vegas had never seen train surfing before, but they had cash to wager. The stakes grew to astronomical levels.

The train came and the players leaped onto it. One first-timer misjudged his leap and tumbled right off. Dee chuckled when he witnessed the snap of bones as the kid landed. He heard the kid was a Texan. Hell, they surfed on boxcars down there. His grandmother could surf a boxcar!

When the rain started Dee thought he was a goner, but at least he knew how to take a fall. And yet, as the surface of the passenger car grew slick and the other contestants flew off one after another, Dee managed to stay on.

A rain out became official if all the contestants slid off before the halfway point. Everybody assumed this early downpour would be a rain out for sure—and yet the train came into the finish line with Dee Ligit still surfing the top.

Dee was already well-known on the underground train-surfing circuit, and that win made him famous. He got his first cover on *LocoSurfer* magazine. Then he heard plans for the first legitimate, legal rail-surfing event in the U.S.

The new Extreme Sports Network was behind it, and their people wanted Dee Ligit to compete. "We have all the permits we need to make it legal," the producer told Dee on the phone. "Now all we need is the athletes."

Dee said sure, he was interested. Minutes later, the cereal magnate called. The man offered to sponsor him in Pro Train Surf I, including expenses and a hefty fee. Dee got fifty grand just to compete, and a lucrative promotional contract if he won.

Dee Ligit felt everything was going right in his world. He dumped his girlfriend to take advantage of his growing base of adoring rail surf groupies. He got all new gear. He did a photo shoot and felt like a star. He flew first class to California, where the cereal company put him up in a nice room in Bishop Hills, the setting for Pro Train Surf. Then he went out to have a look at the track.

"What is this?" he asked the ESN crew. It was like no track he had ever surfed—a torturously twisted stretch of narrow-gauge rail in the hills the town was named for. One of the producers from the Extreme Sports Network described the history of the steam engine. The train consisted of an antique steam engine and a single old-fashioned passenger car with an ornate, curved roof, refinished to a slippery shine. But Dee didn't care about the train.

"What's with this track?" he demanded.

The producer explained that it was a two-mile stretch of mining rail left over from the Wild West days of Bishop Hills.

"Rail surfers don't surf track like this," Dee protested. "We have to have a lot longer curves—these are way too sharp. And we surf for miles and miles—two miles is too short."

The producer gave him a superior look and tried to explain a little bit of reality to Dee Ligit.

"Who's going to want to watch you boys standing there while you go on a Sunday surf through the cornfields? And how would we go about filming it, anyway. See, this way we have a short, exciting event and we capture every second of it. We have cameras mounted all over these hills."

He pointed out the steel camera platforms dotting the hills around the track. They had been expertly camouflaged to blend in with the dried shrubs and rock.

"They look permanent," Dee said.

"They are. ESN is in this business for the long haul, so to speak. We bought the land, bought the track and bought the engine. We own Pro Train Surf, the only professional rail surfing event in the world."

Dee got the message. Either get onboard with ESN or get out of the sport. "But what's with the walls around the track?"

Alongside the entire two-mile tangle of rail was the plywood catch basin, also painted in the browns and tans of desert camouflage.

"That's the Moat," the producer said with an ear-to-ear grin. "Legal made us put it in. Got to look like we have safety measures in place."

"We're pros," Dee said. "We can take a fall from a train, dude. It's what we do. This isn't gonna help."

The producer shrugged. "It was either a catcher like this or some sort of netting or cushions, which would make you all look like a bunch of pussies."

So Dee didn't argue. The competition began. He made it through the first few elimination rounds, which were tough on all the surfers. Nobody was used to this kind of rail. It was the most challenging track ever train-surfed, and competitors were falling off all over the place. Lots of bones broke in the Moat. With every round of the contest, the speed of the train increased, and when they entered the finals the speed became deadly.

Antonio the Terrible lost his footing at the first sharp turn, called Hanged Man's Curve. Dee thought he leaned into the turn just right, but his feet went out from under him at the apex of the curve. He flew off the train like a rocket and slammed into the Moat at one of the support braces. His impact cracked the wood like plate glass, but the steel reinforcing rods held it in place. The coroner said there were at least fourteen major bones broken inside Antonio the Terrible's body—not counting multiple spinal cord fractures.

Extreme Sports Network made the most of the delay. They stayed live, reporting every few minutes on the latest developments and replaying video of the catastrophe twenty times an hour. Abbreviated video clips were released to news networks around the world, which channeled more viewers to ESN. By afternoon, as the on-site investigation wrapped up, the network was registering its highest viewership ever—and the next contestant was ready to compete.

Francis the Fran Man commented briefly on the sad loss of his longtime friend and professional rival Antonio the Terrible. He told the ESN anchor that, God forbid, should he die while competing, he would certainly want the glorious game to continue.

After which he promptly died.

The Fran Man had to have been overcompensating. He leaned less on Hanged Man's Curve and nearly fell headlong at the same spot Tony had died, but the Fran Man held his balance with a lot of wild arm waving. At the second sharp curve on the track, the Forty-five Degrees of Doom, he leaned too far. He lost his balance. His feet flew up, and the Fran Man slithered over the edge of the passenger train car. He pushed away from the car; one of the first tricks you learned as a train surfer was to get clear of the train if you fell. He started to roll into the fall, but the fall was already over. The speed and sharpness of the curve basically slingshot the Fran Man into the plywood. His head battered through the wood so far that his upper body penetrated.

"At this point, Fran's body mass loses its forward momentum," the ESN anchor explained during his three dozen slow-motion analyses of the accident. "His body weight is pretty evenly balanced between the two sides of the catch basin wall, so gravity drags him down onto the broken wood. Fran is still struggling to get his hands free, but he is literally being knifed open by no less than twenty sharp wooden splinters. Wow—now, that's an extreme way to die!"

Impromptu protests began across the country after ESN announced that it would continue the high-speed finals the next day, despite the two fatal accidents. A coalition of media conglomerates hurriedly asked for an emergency injunction against ESN.

"In the interest of public safety, we cannot in good conscience allow the reputation of professional sports to be sullied by this reckless upstart network. It would be irresponsible of us as a broadcasting community to allow viewers to see barbaric and violent activity. We broadcasters want to be known for safe, family-oriented sports programs such as professional football and professional baseball."

The judges didn't side with the networks, noting that every member of the coalition was threatened with large revenue losses when they lost viewership and dipped below the audience they had promised their advertisers.

A middle-of-the-night meeting between the networks and the governor of California was unproductive.

"I don't haff duh audority to stop dis contest," the governor said sleepily. "Besides, why would I want to?"

"It's anticompetitive," one of the lawyers explained. "They are exploiting man's fascination with the grotesque."

"So call your guhberment rebresendadives. They can pass legislajhun. Leave me oud of it."

"The governor has refused to terminate the activity of these barbarians," the coalition lawyer told the media. "It is a sad day for civilization."

It was a Sunday, and football broadcasts were trying to hold on to viewership by adding their "Profiles in Felony" feature. During a lull in the game, viewers saw a segment with a star football player's statistical profile of accused, pending and convicted felonies. They took a cue from college football and outfitted all cheerleaders in pasties and thongs.

Even these improvements couldn't keep viewers from deserting football that Sunday. Nothing could stop the inevitable continuation of Pro Train Surf I and its locomotive ratings.

The first contestant on the last day of finals was Dee Ligit, who felt sick in spirit and sick in body—he was permanently constipated these days.

He should just walk away. But the eyes of the world were on him, and the train was getting nearer. When Dee Ligit heard the steam engine rumble underneath the launch platform, almost without thinking about it he stepped off into space.

He landed on the top of the passenger car and screamed inside as the train whistled and rumbled around Hanged Man's Curve. The dark red blot on the inside of the Moat was like the cyclopean eye of Satan.

But it wasn't that bad, really. The train was moving fast, but he could work with G-forces like this. Dee rode through the Curve.

Next came the Forty-five Degrees of Doom, and Dee raised his arms wide and descended into a bouncy crouch, letting his instincts guide him through the vicious twist in the track. He felt good. His feet felt glued to the train car.

Before he knew it, Dee Ligit stepped off the train onto the landing platform. Everybody was cheering, for *him.* He had surfed the Pro Train Surf finals and survived.

He was taken into a private booth for an ESN interview, and read his responses sincerely to the camera, then tried not to watch the other surfers take their best shot at the high-speed finals. Every time he heard the gasps from the bleachers he knotted up inside. Competitors dropped every time. Dee realized *nobody* else was making it to the finish line.

"The final contestant is about to surf," he heard an ESN anchor telling a camera. "If he falls, this competition is over. If he reaches the finish line, then we head into the superfinal competition."

Dee watched on the monitors as Luke Hey Wayne prepared to surf. "Please fall. Please fall," Dee prayed silently. He just couldn't face the superfinals.

Luke Hey stepped onto the train car and surfed down the straightaway. The engineer cam got a close-up of the teenager's face—terror drew his large mouth into grinch lips as he approached Hanged Man's Curve.

As he came into the curve, Luke Hey's arms began spinning and one of his feet flew out from under him. The boy screamed plaintively and somehow managed to stay atop the car as the track straightened again.

Luke Hey was crying like a baby. A hundred million people around the world watched it in close-up, and then they saw Luke do something unthinkable.

He jumped off the train. He bailed. He bowed out. He took a big dive. He slid off the train car, slid into the Moat and slid on his behind for a hundred feet. The boy clambered out of the Moat, crashed to the earth outside it and ran away sobbing.

Luke Hey was never heard from again.

Could have been me, Dee thought.

There was more hubbub. The crowds were cheering for *him* again. The reason, as far as he could understand it, was that he had won.

He was the first extreme rail surfing champion of the world.

2

His name was Remo, and he felt just as stupid as he looked.

"You look fantastic," said the Romanian image consultant.

"You're just saying that."

"I am a professional. I'd never say it if it weren't true. Simply put, it is the most natural-looking fake mustache I've ever seen."

"You're trying to butter me up so I don't splat you." Remo gripped the Romanian by the belt and dangled him out the eighth-floor window of the Albuquerque Salon of Image Consultation.

"That wasn't even a consideration," the image consultant lied.

Remo could smell a lie a mile away, with or without the fake mustache tickling his nostrils. He wrenched off the mustache and flung it out into space. It tumbled to the street like a skydiving caterpillar. The image consultant watched it disappear.

"Long way down," Remo pointed out.

"Yes, it sure is."

"My arm's getting tired."

"Sorry to hear that." The Romanian, named Flower-rescue, or something similar that Remo couldn't pronounce, examined the arm in question. It wasn't terribly muscular, but the wrists were thick and hard. The important consideration was how long it could hold a 170-pound Romanian image consultant by the belt.

"I believe my trousers are giving way," Vlad Florescu said.

"Maybe you should try answering the first question again," Remo suggested. "Maybe you should think carefully about your answer. The question is about Meredith Fordham. Where is she?"

"Meredith is dead. Dead and gone." No lies this time.

"How do you know?"

"I helped, well, get rid of her, so to speak."

There was a rip and yelp as the man's pants failed at the seams. The image consultant fell.

But not for long. Something locked on his hand, and when he opened his eyes again he was standing inside his salon on the eighth floor of a historic building in downtown Albuquerque, New Mexico.

"What's the story on Meredith Fordham?" Remo prodded.

Vlad Florescu adjusted his trousers and didn't seem embarrassed that the inseam had ripped open to the shins. "I did it for her son, Jack. The boy was in trouble."

"So you helped him kill his mother?"

"She was dead already. The poor woman was a heroin addict. How she managed to hide it from me for all these years I will never know. She was my best friend."

"What about Jack?"

"Jack is…very intelligent."

"Yes?"

"And reckless. Irresponsible. But so smart. Anyway, I came to the house to have dinner. We cooked dinner together once a week, Meredith and I. Usually on Mondays but occasionally on Tuesdays. I let myself in, and there was Meredith, dead on the living-room carpet. Jack was in a panic. He was devastated about his mother. She had overdosed herself, you see."

"Oh boy," Remo said. "You were doing okay until the end." The image consultant went out the window again, this time dangling by his ankle. His shout echoed among the high-rises.

"If I let you back inside, do you think you can stick to the truth?"

"Yes, I believe so," said Florescu, who didn't look at all like a Vlad.

"I got to hand it to you, Vlad, you are one cool customer."

"Thank you," Vlad Florescu said, although he was rather winded. He tried to adjust his trousers, but his trousers were now draped on a No Parking sign in the street below.

"Where was I?"

"Telling me how Meredith Fordham died and why you went along with it," Remo said.

Vlad Florescu told the truth this time. "The boy did it. He never said so, and I think he wanted me to believe she killed herself, but I know he did it. I helped him get her into an incineration shaft in a local landfill."

"And in exchange you got…"

"My life! I was sure he was going to kill me, too! Plus, er, he gave me fifty thousand dollars from the life insurance."

Remo rolled his eyes.

"From her savings account. I meant savings account."

"Ever see Jack again?"

"No. Should I?"

"How long ago was this?"

"A year, maybe a year and a half. How is Jack?"

"Rotting in hell."

"Jack's dead?" Vlad gasped.

"I didn't say that."

Vlad was confused.

"Now, go over one part of the story again," Remo said. "You walked into the apartment and Meredith was dead. Right?"

"Right. Well, maybe not quite dead. But she was dead soon after that."

Remo looked expectant.

"She was out cold. Her head was bashed in, you see. But she was still alive. I told Jack she was still alive. He said he didn't believe me, but I think he did. She, you know, screamed. When she was, you know, burned up."

Remo nodded. "Now, just so I have it straight, Vlad, you burned your best friend alive for fifty grand."

"Well," Vlad said slowly, "yes. I do feel bad about it now."

Remo nodded and glanced out the window. "Oh, look. There's your pants."

"Oh."

"Don't you want to see them?"

"No. They're torn. I have no use for them."

"But it's kind of funny. They landed on a No Parking sign."

"Heh," Vlad said.

"Have a look." Remo gave Vlad a nice close look at the pants. As Vlad plummeted toward the pants, he kept his eyes closed until, at the last moment, he opened them and saw the pants. He saw the No Parking sign they were draped over, then Vlad became as one with the No Parking sign and the torn pants.

Much later that evening as the coroner labored to separate man, pants and sign, he was amused to discover a fake mustache, which had apparently become stuck to the No Parking sign by some prankster shortly before the pants and the image consultant were skewered on it.

3

"I think that about wraps it up for Remo," said Remo, standing at an Albuquerque pay phone at a sprawling Happy Go Gas Service, Snacks & Shopping Hub. If he wanted to, he could have purchased gasoline, magazines, fast food, canned beverages, home remodeling equipment, travel insurance and bronze cowboy sculptures, all at this one place. He could get his oil changed, get his hair cut and buy tiny hamburgers by the sackful. As if that weren't enough, several vendors hawked their wares in the grass along the street.

The feature that most attracted Remo to Happy Go Gas, however, was the vast asphalt. He needed at least three acres to make a U-turn in the vehicle he was driving.

"I don't think we have wrapped up anything." The man on the other end sounded calm but sour, as if he had been sucking a lemon just before he picked up the receiver.

"I made a to-do list." Remo fished in the pockets of his tan Chinos, retrieving a FedEx receipt with a scrawled note on the back. "Here it is. Remo's to-do list. Item one—wrap up Jack Fast loose ends. I'll just scratch that one off right now."

"Remo—"

"Hold on." Remo used his Vlad Florescu, Image Consultant pen to scratch off item one. "Okay, so much for that. Item two. Oh, look, no item two. I guess I'm finished."

"There is much more to be done."

"Not according to my paperwork. Let me look again." Remo scanned the page, then turned it over and scanned the front, where the receipt detailed the delivery of fifteen pairs of handmade Italian shoes to a Connecticut address. It was dated two days previous. The declared value of the shipment was half the price of a midsize sedan. "Nope. That's it. *Finito.*"

"Do not hang up the phone."

"Hanging up now."

Remo hung up and found himself surrounded. He wasn't surprised. He had heard the attackers as they approached.

"Some lovely flowers?" asked a swarthy man with a greasy bucket labeled Bokays.

"No, thanks."

"T-shirts, tree for ten doh-lar." A damp cigarette dangled from the second man's lips.

"No, thanks."

The third man had come over with his entire cart, which was a wheeled contraption with a pole across the top for rugs on hangers. "Look, *señor.* Beautiful wall hangings. Use them as a beautiful rug, too." The rug he displayed was jet-black and illustrated with a brilliant orange life-size jaguar in midsnarl.

"Naw."

"I have many beautiful pictures. You like ladies?"

The rug seller whipped out another black sample, this one showing a model in the midst of taking off her denim shorts. Her top half was bare, her breasts were buoyant, her blond hair billowed out like yellow mist. Big pink letters declared that Swedes Are Superb.

"Not Swedish."

"I haff more!" He was now wheeling his rack along-side Remo and he lifted out another picture of the same woman, now a redhead and wearing a kilt. "Scottish, see?"

"Got anything Korean?" Remo asked, but he didn't stop walking.

"*Sí!* See?"

Remo glanced at a black rug illustrated with a life-size Bruce Lee in his famous *Enter the Dragon* kick pose.

"If that's Korean then you're Puerto Rican."

The rug seller stopped smiling. "I'm not a fucking Puerto Rican."

"Exactly."

A fat, short man in a child-size T-shirt waddled out the front of the convenience store of Happy Go Gas and headed straight at Remo. "Son, what the hell you think you're doing?"

Remo looked around.

"That's right, I'm talking to you, son," the fat man bellowed. "What are you doin'?"

"Leaving."

"Stealing's more like it. Come in here and buy not a damn thing."

"I used your phone."

"I know. I was watching you."

"That's why I moved over. Didn't want you watching me dial."

"Uh-huh. I saw enough to know you didn't even put in any durn money. I'm not running no free phone service, son."

"You're standing between me and my...thing that I'm driving."

"That thing you're driving is taking up fifty percent of my square footage, son. That means half my paying customers are being denied entry. I dropped one-point-three million dollars into this-here establishment. You think I can afford to let folks come in and rob me blind?"

"I notice the other half of your square footage is empty, too," Remo pointed out. "What was it I stole exactly?"

"I think you best make some sort of a purchase before you be on your way," the fat man said threateningly.

"I'm guessing the minimart doesn't have rice or fresh fish," Remo asked. The fat man looked at him as if he were insane. "That's what I thought. Sorry, I gotta go."

Remo started walking again. The fat man folded his arms defiantly and stepped between Remo and his vehicle—then found himself doing an energetic whirl, as light and graceful as the little girls doing the ice-skating twirlies on ESPN2. His arms flew out and the centrifugal force even lifted and stretched his belly away from his body. Then he collapsed and threw up.

"Hey, smart-ass," the rug seller said. "You think you tough, huh?" The rug, flower and T-shirt sellers were closing in on Remo. A mechanic from the Lube-U-Kwik garage was striding out to give them a hand, wielding a wrench.

The fat man wiped his mouth with his arm. "Work him over while I call the cops."

"Yeesh," Remo complained, and then began whistling while he worked. It was an old Disney tune about whistling while you worked.

The red-faced flower seller threw a punch, then found himself airborne. The smart-ass had him by the collar and moved him quick. Just then the mechanic brought his oily wrench down on the smart-ass's head.

The mechanic saw the switch happen faster than he could believe, and for sure too fast for him to react to. His wrench collapsed the flower seller's head instead of the smart-ass's, and then the wrench zipped out of his hands. The next thing the mechanic knew, the oily wrench handle was in his mouth and going down, down until the fat head lodged between his teeth. The mechanic gagged and clawed at the wrench.

The T-shirt seller found himself tied up. Had he lost consciousness? Because getting his hands knotted up in T-shirts had to have taken five, ten minutes, right? His ankles were bound up, and a second later the whistling man tied his ankles and hands together around the pole of the rug rack. The T-shirt seller dangled like dead game being carried home for dressing.

The rug seller was snarling and growling like the jaguar on his rug, and he danced and dodged around all the activity, and he still couldn't seem to get his hands on the whistling smart-ass. The smart-ass ignored him, and the rug seller kept seeing his blows and lunges just miss the guy. All at once his snarls became mewling and whimpering, much as he used to imagine the Swedish babe on the other rug mewled and whimpered.

He found himself rolled inside one of his own rugs, but it wasn't the one with the Swedish girl. He found his face pressed into the face of the Dragon himself, Bruce Lee.

"Consider yourself lucky," the smart-ass said. "You try that sales pitch on some Koreans I know, and you'd be dead already."

The rug seller felt the wind pushed out of his lungs when he was draped over the rug rack. He couldn't see the gagging, limp mechanic flopped over the bar next to him, followed by the unconscious flower seller.

"I thought you had a phone call to make?" Remo said to the astonished proprietor of Happy Go Gas. The fat man struggled to his feet and headed inside, craning his head over his shoulder. He pushed himself into a jog for the first time in years as Remo wheeled the rug rack and lined it up on the proprietor.

The proprietor knew what was going to happen. It was impossible to get the rug rack moving that fast, especially top-heavy with all those bodies, but none of what happened in the past minute was possible.

The fat proprietor yanked open the door and thudded inside and thought he might be safe. Outside, Remo shoved the rug rack.

The rack wobbled but somehow stayed upright. The casters sheered off and the underside sent up a shower of sparks, but the rack never veered off course. It hit the glass minimart doors and plowed through them with a noisy explosion of glass, then slammed into the fat man and kept right on going. The rack didn't stop until the fat man was shoved through the cooler doors and pinned among racks of soda. The rug rack was still upright. It hadn't lost even one passenger.

An assistant manager was screaming. The fat proprietor was wriggling the body parts that still worked, pudgy fingers and bulging eyes, when Remo came through the gaping hole.

"This is really going to make you laugh. I just remembered that I *do* need something." Remo snatched a small magazine from a rack and slapped a dollar on the counter. Then he left.

4

In the passenger seat of the rig Remo was driving was a small man so ancient he should have been in the record books. So aged he shouldn't have been alive. But he was alive, and kicking.

"You spared them all?" the old man demanded in a squeaky voice.

"Start," Remo said to the dashboard. "Stut. Stert. Stort. Stump." He frowned. "Trump?"

The vehicle came to life clattering of the massive diesel engine. A bewildering array of lights and displays flashed to life on the dashboard. They reminded Remo of the exterior of a cheesy casino. "They're just jerks," Remo said. "You can't go killing every jerk you run into."

"I heard what the filthy one said about me," the ancient man added.

"He was talking about Koreans in general."

"When one insults one's heritage, he deserves to be silenced, especially when he insults the superior heritage of the Korean peoples."

The old man was Korean, and perhaps the Asiatic features helped him appear less old than he was—but there were other factors at work, too.

"It is your heritage, too," the old Korean said. "You are Korean. You allow yourself to be insulted without reprisal?"

Remo thought the dumb jerks at the gas station had been subjected to plenty of reprisal, but before the old man decided to jog back and murder them himself, Remo handed over the magazine. "Got you something."

The old man sneered. "*TV Guide?* Why do you think I should want this?" He flipped it out the open window.

Remo reached for it. Even as he was steering his steamship-size vehicle onto the street he stretched across the old man and caught the flying magazine, which he tucked into a storage console between the front seats.

The old man squinted. Not that he had trouble seeing. It was his suspicious look. "Why do *you* want this *TV Guide,* Remo Williams?"

"Eh. You know. Just interested in seeing what kind of programming is being offered these days. Reading about it is less frightening than actually turning on the TV."

"Hmph."

The old man lapsed into silence, and being obstinately silent was just one of his many talents.

His name was Chiun; his title was Master of Sinanju Emeritus. There was just one other living Master of Sinanju—the man who was driving the oversize, super-customized travel trailer and trying to figure out the meaning of the electronic displays on the dashboard.

Chiun had trained Remo Williams in the art of Sinanju during their many years together. Even for Remo, who possessed an uncanny talent, Sinanju was not easy to learn.

There were those who looked at Sinanju as a martial art; indeed, almost every martial art had its origin in Sinanju. Scraps of wayward Sinanju knowledge, stolen splinters of Sinanju technique, overheard whispers of Sinanju wisdom, these were the basis for all the great fighting arts. Ninja, karate, kung fu and even modern judo had all descended directly or indirectly from the ancient practice of Sinanju.

The House of Sinanju had trained assassins for five thousand years. They left the tiny Korean fishing village of Sinanju and traveled the world, taking employment with emperors and kings. During five thousand years of world travel, a few secrets were bound to leak out.

But none of the derivative arts came close to the magnificence of the true Sinanju assassin. The Sinanju used their breath and their bodies to expand the use of their minds. With this great well of instinct guiding them, the Sinanju masters could perform physical feats that defied the understanding of the average human being.

This instinct and understanding didn't always translate to twenty-first-century electronics, or even of post–World War II mechanics. This Remo proved, for the umpteenth time, as the rear wheels dragged over the curb with an unpleasant scraping sound. It wasn't as unpleasant as the look in Chiun's eyes.

"For the record, I was against getting a travel trailer from the beginning," Remo stated. "I was especially against me driving a travel trailer."

"This gives you license to destroy my home?" Chiun demanded.

"Course not. Another thing I don't have a license for—this *Lusitania*-on-wheels."

"It is the home of the Master of Sinanju and should be treated with respect."

Remo's eyebrows weighed down as he maneuvered the school-bus-style steering wheel to swing the vehicle onto the interstate ramp. "Masters of Sinanju, plural, don't you mean? Or is this not my home, too?"

"That remains to be seen," Chiun sniffed.

"Really? So what am I doing driving this thing around if I don't even get to live in it? Not that I want to live in it. I don't even know what it is. What is this thing, anyway? Wait. I don't need to know. I'll just shut up and drive."

"Is this a promise?"

Except for the clattering of the diesel power plant, the cab of the travel trailer was darkly silent as it rolled out of Albuquerque and headed west.

"All those nice castles," Remo muttered.

"You are breaking your promise," Chiun retorted. "What castles?"

"In Boston."

Chiun stiffened. He and Remo had once dwelled in a Boston castle. It had been their home for years, until an arsonist destroyed it. "Explain yourself."

"I begged you. The Boston Catholics have lawsuits up the yin yang. The archdiocese is selling off real estate at prices so low, they're insane. We can get a nice old church, rip the guts out and remodel it into a new Castle Sinanju, better than the last one."

Remo had always thought the first Castle Sinanju, which was itself a converted church, was as ugly as sin.

Still, it had been home for longer than any other place since he and Chiun began working together, and he missed it.

"I have no wish to live again in the city of beans and bad drivers," Chiun said. "Besides, there were Vietnamese in the neighborhood. And Japanese."

"You drove them all out eventually," Remo added.

"In this mobile castle we may set up house in any place, then depart again if we sense unsavory neighbors."

"Where you gonna park this in L.A.?"

"You shall park it," Chiun said dismissively.

Remo was going to decline the offer, then considered the alternative. Briefly his mind's eye saw the old Korean behind the wheel of the travel trailer on the streets of Los Angeles. "For the good of Southern California, I'll park it." He sighed. "Now, where did this light come from? It wasn't there a second ago."

Chiun ignored Remo and the new dashboard blinker.

"Now it's beeping," Remo said. "Why's it beeping?"

Chiun snapped the blinking, beeping device off the dashboard and jettisoned it into the desert.

"Hey, what if that was the oil gauge or something?" Remo demanded.

"It was a radar detector," Chiun explained wearily.

"Huh?"

"You are driving at more than 100 miles per hour." As if to bear him out a pair of flashing emergency lights blossomed a mile behind them.

"How'm I supposed to know that?" Remo demanded. "Is there even a speedometer on this thing?"

Chiun tapped the dashboard LCD that read 167.

"Your swollen white digits reset the display to kilometers per hour when you started the vehicle." Chiun touched the glass, where Remo was certain there wasn't even a button, and the 167 transformed to a 101 miles per hour and dropping.

"Criminy. Think I can lose the trooper?"

"Please do not try to lose him in my new home. What if you killed the last great Master of Sinanju and were forced to live out your existence with this enduring shame?"

Remo pulled over and the trooper parked behind him, emerged and strode up alongside the travel trailer with deliberately heavy steps. Remo grinned, trying to look friendly.

"Evening, Trooper. I deserve a ticket. Please give it to me."

The trooper's suspicions notched up. "What all are you driving here, son?"

Remo had enough of people calling him son, but he ignored it. "I have no idea. All I know is she's as big as a house and she steers like an overloaded river barge."

"Okay, then, I will tell you what you're driving there, son. What it is, is a circa-1954 thirty-foot Airstream Sovereign of the Road. That's what she started out as, anyway. Somebody made her all pretty and new again, added a whole new heavy-duty suspension by the looks of it. Then I guess whoever it was sawed off her front end and stuck on that there flexible hallway thingy to attach it on the back of this here SUV. Then it looks like the somebody nickel-plated the SUV and polished it all up to match the Airstream. An amazing piece of work. One of a kind. Worth a couple hundred grand easy. Even more amazing that you don't seem to know jack about it."

Remo shrugged. "Not mine."

"That's what I figgered."

"It's his."

The trooper rose up on his toes, giving him a view of the passenger, who stared straight ahead. "That a real man or's he taxidermied?"

"My father. He's antisocial. This camper, whatever it is, belongs to him. He commissioned it from a dealer who restores vintage RVs. We just took delivery."

"But, son, this ain't restored. It's *mutated.*"

"I had no say in the matter. Please give me the ticket so I can get back on the road."

Chiun sighed heavily and slipped out the passenger door, unnoticed by the trooper.

"I don't like folks telling me how to do my job, son."

"Fine, Dad. Give me a ticket or not. You decide."

"What if I decide to haul you in, smart boy?"

Remo knew there were good, honest cops out there. There were also some belligerent cops who liked the power that came with the badge more than they liked serving and protecting the citizens. This one was strictly in the second category.

Remo smiled.

"What's so funny, son?"

"My lips are sealed."

"You're acting mighty suspicious, son."

"He is always this way," called Chiun, now back in the passenger seat. "All of life is just one entertainment after another to him. My son, he is a jokester."

"A joker?" the trooper asked.

"He laughs at other people's mistakes."

"So why is he so damn overjoyed now, old man? You trying to say I made some sort of mistake?"

Remo flicked his eyes to the rear. The trooper glanced back just in time to witness his car roll backward off the road and into a ravine with a crunch. All that was left to see were the headlight beams aiming up into the stars.

"See? You would have let the obstinate constable fine you," Chiun chided as they pulled away from the trooper, who shouted for them to come back or be arrested. "You need me to save you from yourself."

"I get along without you for days at a time, Chiun."

"Still."

"What are you talking about, anyway? Are you threatening to leave me because I'm on strike?"

"Masters of Sinanju do not go on strike."

"I do."

"Masters of Sinanju honor their contracts."

"We've been over this so many times I'm sick of it. I'm on strike, or I quit, whatever you want to call it. Until I get my contract renegotiated, I'm out of the picture. CURE can get along without me."

After many miles they heard cars coming toward them fast, and Remo pulled into the desert to avoid being spotted. The convoy of troopers, without their emergency lights, tore down the highway. A few stragglers were probing off the road for hiding vehicles. They were too far off to be spotted. Chiun said, "Will you tell me yet why we're going to California?"

"Job interview."

"You seek employment with the terminating iron

pumper? Working for governors is beneath the dignity of a Master of Sinanju. Another bad choice, Remo Williams."

"Maybe not. I read somewhere that California had a bigger economy than most of the nations on Earth. And Ahnuhld's never going to sit still for just being governor. He's going to want to be President. Anyway, it's not him I'm trying to get a job with and it's not assassin work I'm applying for."

"What, then?" Chiun demanded. "All other occupations are beneath you."

Remo refused to say. He enjoyed putting Chiun in the position of not knowing what they were up to. Chiun did it to Remo constantly. The problem was that Chiun, while he could dish out the silent treatment, couldn't take it. Remo knew that the old Master would lose patience and demand to know what Remo was keeping from him. Remo couldn't withstand an assault from Chiun.

No human could.

"I will tell you about Master Yeou Gang," Chiun said after much time had passed. "He is known as Yeou Gang the Fool."

"No, he's not. He's known as Yeou Gang. There's no 'Fool' after his name."

"You pretend to know the history of all the Masters?"

"Of course not, but I've done my homework. I know a lot of names, even if there's nothing particular worth knowing about some of the Masters," Remo said. "There's about a thousand of them, and most of them were just your average, run-of-the-mill Master of Sinanju. That's the point."

"You have no point. You may have memorized the names on the scrolls, but the entire story is not transcribed. Some history is remembered only through our spoken tradition. Such is the tale of Yeou Gang the Fool."

"This is where I start thinking you're making it up as you go."

"Yeou Gang was like you in some ways, Remo."

"A sharp-dressed Caucasian?"

"Moody. Disinclined to accept advice. Headstrong and arrogant. Like you, he was young and immature when the Rite of Succession made him Reigning Master. Like you, he kept the companionship of his mentor, Master Ghu Ung, but did not give heed to Ghu Ung's wisdom."

"Why?" Remo asked.

"It does not matter why." Chiun waved at the air, as if wafting the question away like floating dust.

"Why does matter. Maybe Ghu Ung wasn't so smart himself. It's possible Yeou Gang was a genius but Ghu Ung made him the scapegoat for his mistakes."

"Unthinkable. The Korean Masters are not petty egoists, because they were not raised in The Land of Not-Me and the Home of the Blame."

"I get it. The Korean Masters as in everyone but me, right? Remo, the American Master, is one peg lower than all the other Masters because he's an American?"

"Cease your prattle and pay attention."

"Cease my prattle? Shouldn't a Master of Sinanju deserve better than 'cease your prattle'? Or do only non-Korean Masters rate a 'cease your prattle'? What's prattle, anyway?"

Chiun shook his head tightly. "Prattle is rambling speech devoid of meaning. For example, everything that comes from your gargantuan mouth qualifies as prattle."

"My gargantuan American mouth, you mean?"

"Correct," Chiun said.

"Go to hell."

5

In Rye, New York, a sour-looking old man was immensely perturbed.

Harold W. Smith was the director of a private hospital in Rye. Folcroft Sanitarium was an exclusive facility that took care of the well-to-do when they required private recuperation, and it handled special medical cases in an eclectic mix of obscure fields. Likewise, Folcroft doctors were considered first-rate, if not always mainstream. The facility went out of its way to maintain its reclusive demeanor, because that's what the patients wanted.

Folcroft Sanitarium was also home to an agency of the federal government—probably the smallest agency in terms of total employees. Named CURE, it was so secret that even the United States President—who had oversight over the agency—knew little of its methods or resources. Former Presidents, who had previously had oversight over CURE, no longer thought about it. The memory was erased from their minds.

Since being formed by an idealistic young President decades before, there had been just one director of the agency, and he was the same man who served as director of Folcroft Sanitarium.

Harold W. Smith, retiring from a career in U.S. intelligence, was ready to enter academic life when he received a request from the young President that he lead the new agency. Instead of becoming a university professor he took the reins of CURE. These days Smith found himself wondering what life would have been like if he had turned down the young President.

Such thoughts were unproductive, but they came more often than he would have liked.

For its first years CURE was an intelligence-gathering agency, but with a huge difference. It ignored the laws of the United States.

CURE violated the privacy of its citizens. It spied on innocent people. It planted bugs without probable cause. It was accountable to no set of rules, least of all the Constitution of the United States.

CURE was created with the intention of violating the Constitution. That great document had a downside in that it created loopholes for the criminal world to exploit. The worst murderers and thieves and mobsters were often the very ones with slick lawyers and lots of dollars for buying off justice.

CURE used dirty tricks, too, which worked much of the time. It rooted out the lies behind the Mafia countersuits. It exposed judicial bribe taking. It ferreted out evidence other law-enforcement agencies couldn't get their hands on. In the end, the good it did wasn't enough, and Smith decided to take on an enforcement arm.

He intended to hire one man, an assassin, working beyond the laws of the land. Through a strange series of events, one of the trainers hired for the new CURE assassin was an old Korean man, Master of an obscure martial art named after his home village of Sinanju. The old Master proved to be extraordinarily skilled, and in the end the other trainers were dismissed. The old Korean, Chiun, became the sole trainer of Remo Williams, the CURE assassin.

Remo did well under Chiun's tutelage. Harold W. Smith was surprised, and even Chiun was surprised at Remo's aptitude. Smith learned, much later, that no adult and no non-Korean had ever absorbed the full scope of the teaching of Sinanju in all the long history of the village. Somehow, Remo Williams did absorb the full scope of it. He became a Master of Sinanju himself.

Smith should have seen years ago just how odd this was, but he turned a blind eye—and he stayed blind for decades.

Remo was in fact a descendent of Sinanju himself. Although raised an orphan in New Jersey, chosen seemingly at random by CURE for this assignment, there was nothing random about it. Remo was eventually proved to be the son of a Hollywood stuntman who came from a small Native American tribe that dwelt near Yuma, Arizona. The tribe had been founded centuries ago—before the European incursion into North America—by a self-exiled Sinanju Master.

Smith learned this very recently, and he was still troubled deeply by the implication. CURE was not what brought Chiun and Remo together; CURE was the mechanism used to bring Remo and Chiun together.

The question that echoed like thunder in Smith's head was this: *who, or what, had used CURE?*

The agency was so secure and Smith's confidence was so absolute that he knew, incontrovertibly, that no human being or organization could have made it happen without him knowing. That pointed to something bigger and less easily explained. Smith's mind retreated when he ventured into those shifting, unsettling mists of conjecture.

Now it looked as though it might all unravel. The supersecret agency was seemingly being exposed in some new way every time Smith turned around. The blame for most of it lay squarely on the shoulders of Remo Williams, who had become as obstinate and rebellious as a teenager in recent months. And right now, with anti-American sentiment at its highest peak in decades, somebody was adding fuel to the fire. These ridiculous sporting events were damaging U.S. relations around the world.

Smith had never been too big on the sports section of the newspaper. He was concerned with crisis, not games. He did not have the time to follow sports.

But these days there seemed to be a real crisis in the world of competitive sports—a crisis above and beyond the drug addiction, egotism, sexism, racism and wholesale greed that was endemic in all sports, starting with Little League.

These days there seemed to be a lot of murder.

At least, it looked like murder. A lot of people were dying, anyway, and Dr. Smith's probability models indicated they were too numerous to be coincidence.

It started with yacht races. A series of deaths on a transatlantic kayak race had wiped out the five front-runners just hours before the race was won by the sixth-place contestant, who was now a familiar face on boxes of breakfast cereal across the country.

When person or persons unknown began picking off the leaders of a round-the-world sailboat race, Smith dispatched Remo Williams to the very tip of South America to join up with the sailor who was now leading the race. Within hours the sailboat was attacked by well-equipped, professional assassins. Unlucky for them they ran into the most skilled assassin on the planet. None of the three survived their meeting with Remo Williams.

But neither did Remo come home with a wealth of data on the killers. Smith was not even convinced that they had been connected to the killers in the kayak race. Maybe they were just copycats.

Other times in recent months Smith had noticed a peculiar frequency of deaths during high-purse sporting events, but he simply couldn't tell if there was cause for alarm. These were, after all, risky sports, which was why they were all carried on the fledgling cable television network, the Extreme Sports Network. That link was obvious.

But it didn't mean ESN was the cause of the deaths. After all, it was a twenty-four-hour-a-day operation running hundreds of sports shows a month. Many of them it produced, but most it didn't. The kayak race and the round-the-world sailboat race weren't organized by ESN.

Deaths also occurred during events that were ESN organized. The network organized and broadcast a Rocky Mountain States Extreme Unassisted Freestyling Association competition, which involved competitive rock climbing without the use of rock-climbing gear. The climbers ascended barehanded and barefoot, and the competition always occurred on rock faces where safety harnesses were impossible to deploy. The association lost something like ten percent of its active membership to fatal rock climbing falls every year. It was an absurd sport.

Smith would have assumed the sport would fade away quickly, losing enthusiasts to death or common sense, and yet the total membership numbers climbed each year. As long as there were people willing to take the risks, there were certainly audiences willing to watch, and extreme sports programming was becoming big business. ESN was slurping up audience share from sports viewers and reality TV programming. Advertising dollars were skyrocketing, and extreme games were now high-stakes competitions. That meant more newcomers to the sports, hoping for a share of the pie. The growth and the influx of amateurs meant even more spectacular injuries and deaths, which was caught on video more frequently, which drove up ratings....

And the death toll mounted.

This evening, Smith intended to clarify one of his many security issues. He knocked on the door of the suite in a private wing of Folcroft Sanitarium. He knocked again. There was no answer. It was three in the morning, so he gave the occupant time to get up and come to the door, but the occupant didn't materialize.

Smith cocked his head, considered the next door down the hall and walked to it. He glanced at the chart next to the door and read it, just to stall for time. This was getting more awkward by the minute.

The chart showed the patient was doing well. Responding to therapy. Unless he overdid it again, the patient would be able to permanently discard his wheelchair in a week or so.

Smith finally knocked and waited.

Smith's assistant, Mark Howard, opened the door. "Dr. Smith. What's wrong? Why didn't you call?" The young man was standing there in a pair of jogging shorts and a hastily donned pajama shirt, buttoned incorrectly.

"I'm sorry to disturb you, Mark," Dr. Smith said. "May I have a word with Ms. Slate?"

"Dr. Smith, what's going on?"

"I must speak with Ms. Slate in private."

Mark reluctantly nodded and ducked into the private hospital suite—he had not been back to his Rye apartment since he was wounded on the job months before. A hurt leg put him in a wheelchair. He escaped the wheelchair briefly only to aggravate the injury by overdoing his physical therapy exercises. Now he was walking again, a few steps at a time, and taking it slow.

"Oh, don't worry about it, Mark." Sarah Slate slipped out of Mark's room with an easy smile for Dr. Smith.

"Ms. Slate."

"Call me Sarah."

"Sarah," Smith said officiously, and nodded, and then realized that the young woman was buttoning a man's shirt that was so oversize that he could see... He looked away, then he looked back, his eyes glued to the small ornament around her neck.

"Like it? It's from Chiun."

"It's very pretty," he said gloomily.

They strolled down the hall together. Smith was trying to recall if he had ever known Chiun to give a gift to anyone—especially something as invaluable as a symbol of the House of Sinanju. Sarah was not perturbed by his silence, as if they were old friends strolling in the park. In fact, she had only been introduced to Smith briefly.

"I don't quite know where to begin," he said.

"Let me help," Sarah offered.

"All right."

"Short version. A few hundred years ago my ancestor, Andrew Slayte, met and befriended a Korean from the village of Sinanju. This was Master Go."

Smith stopped walking.

"News to you, I see," she said. She strolled on. "Here are the parts you might be familiar with. In the last years of the nineteenth century, another ancestor of mine creates an advanced automaton named Ironhand, only to have him stolen in France during World War I. Eighty years later Ironhand comes to my house in Providence, Rhode Island, remote controlled by a German who wants me to give up other secrets regarding my ancestor's engineering accomplishments.

"Lucky for me, the current Master of Sinanju—a white American, of all things—has also dropped in to visit, along with his Korean trainer and their cute research assistant. They drive away Ironhand, but the research assistant is wounded in the process. Smitten by the research assistant, I accompany them to a private hospital in New York, which is obviously their base of operations."

Smith stopped again. Her eyes met his, quite sober. "Since no Master of Sinanju would work for anyone less powerful than a king, it's easy to assume they are a part of a powerful organization working under the direction of the top levels of the U.S. government. Since assassination is forbidden under U.S. law, it's no leap of logic to conclude this agency is secret. I could be wrong about some of this—I don't understand the Caucasian Master part of the puzzle, either." She shrugged and rolled on, unstoppable. "Regardless, you, as director of the Sanitarium and Mark's superior, are obviously the one in charge of whatever this splinter government or secret intelligence unit is. Knowing Chiun's tendency to adhere to tradition—although, again, the White Master is in contradiction to that—I know he would only work for a man he considered to possess the authority of a king. You, Dr. Smith, must be one of the most powerful people in the United States, and therefore the world."

Dr. Smith opened his mouth to respond. Sarah never let him.

"Shortly after I arrive at Folcroft and figure all this out, Chiun returns from some endeavor with Remo in a state of catatonia. Chiun's distraught. Remo appears to be beyond his help and certainly beyond the help of conventional medicine. I, however, know how to save him. Uh-oh, I've raised your radar again."

They had strolled to the end of the private hall. This was a secure wing, designed to house Remo, Chiun and other CURE secrets, but Smith felt naked as he was bombarded by this girl's revelation. He was astounded and, frankly, irritated that she knew more than him about some topics.

"Understand that my ancestor Andrew helped his friend, the Sinanju Master Go, recover from a similar infirmity. Master Go was put in a coma by some sort of mystical mesmerist, but it was the same kind of affliction. Go neglected to own up to this in the Sinanju record of history, because Chiun didn't know of it. I used the Andrew Slayte technique to revive Remo."

"You saved Remo?"

Sarah Slate laughed lightly. "I just did what old Andrew did, Dr. Smith. Chiun could have saved Remo. I tried to tell him, but Chiun was too vexed with me at the time to really listen."

"I see."

She became serious. "All that night I sat with Chiun and Remo and felt his loathing. Chiun hated me because I told him I could save Remo. The poor man felt beyond hope of bringing Remo back. I gave him hope, but he believed it had to be false. Therefore, he believed I was unconscionably cruel."

Smith tried to take in all he was learning. He wasn't aware Remo had been so desperately ill, nor that Chiun was in despair of saving him. Remo was comatose for days, but Smith assumed Remo would eventually come around, with Chiun's ministrations....

"Chiun credits you with saving Remo," Smith said. "Thus the token of respect." A token of respect from Chiun was a brilliantly rare thing—if you were not a potential employer, when it smacked of salesmanship.

Sarah Slate, with a pretty child's face, standing there in Mark Howard's baggy sweatpants and shirt, looked like a teenybopper at a slumber party. She'd raise suspicions trying to get a driver's license. And yet she held a place of esteem in the eyes of the Master of Sinanju Emeritus, who esteemed no one….

"Yes, well, here I am," Sarah said with a shrug. "Mark's been trying to protect me from the truth, but I know all the basics, don't I? So what are you going to do about me, Dr. Smith? Neutralize me?"

She was so frank, so sincere he was taken aback, but he shook his head slightly and gave her a sour smile. "Ms. Slate, I can assure you of this—you will never be neutralized." He inclined his head; somehow she knew he was indicating the emblem on her throat. "You are untouchable."

She furrowed her brow. "Because of a little gold charm?"

Oh my God. Smith hadn't considered that little fact before. Chiun hadn't just gifted her, a non-Korean child, with the emblem of Sinanju—he had *gifted her with gold.*

LOOKING WORRIED, Mark Howard appeared in Smith's office.

"Sarah knows all about CURE, doesn't she?" he asked. "She wouldn't tell me what you talked about, but I guessed. Nobody told her anything, I swear. She knew about Chiun the moment she laid eyes on him, and she figured everything else out on her own. She's perceptive."

Smith was chewing antacids. He nodded, agreeing with everything his assistant director said.

"It's not her fault, Dr. Smith. You can't possibly—"

"You're right. I can't."

Mark Howard limped to the ancient sofa against the wall and collapsed into it, relieved.

"I'll be blunt. The reason I can't, specifically, is because of Chiun. He's taken an unusual interest in her. If I were to harm her, his response would be disastrous."

The merciless explanation stiffened Mark's spine. "I understand."

"You don't. You're not coldhearted enough to understand."

"Maybe not." The silence was a potent thing until Mark asked, "Does that make me unfit for CURE?"

Smith answered without hesitation, as if he had already considered this very point. "I would have said yes once."

"That's not an answer."

"It is an answer."

Mark thought about it and he nodded.

"Mark, I will admit to you that Ms. Slate is just one more example of my loss of control. I feel as if this organization is on the verge of flying apart. Remo is rebelling like a hormonal thirteen-year-old, and suddenly makes it known that he has a father and two children who know something of this organization—which is intolerable. Chiun has as good as threatened to have my head if I approach them. Still, I can't sit back and ignore the security threat they represent. There's Ms. Slate, who is dropped in our laps and manages to lay bare the nature of this organization simply because she has happened to read her family journals and make a few erudite conclusions. Complicating all of this, there is my own nagging need to determine what or who or how CURE was used to make all this happen."

Smith ran out of steam, then he perked up when he

saw the raw news feed on his computer screen. In Rio de Janeiro, the people were in the streets.

THE PRESIDENT of Brazil stepped onto the platform, shouting in Portuguese and shaking his fist.

"The Extreme Sports Network has a proved history of cheating, and the United States government condones it," said the bored voice-over of the translator. "This is yet another example of ugly America forcing the world to accede to its dominance. In this we witness the next phase in U.S. unilateralism and it will not be tolerated."

The Brazilian president was beating the podium with his fist, his face shining with sweat, while the English dubbing sounded like the translator was reading from an insurance policy.

"Now, the United States assassinates the Subway Surfing Champion of Brazil. They, expletive, stole the prize from us. We demand, uh, we demand the United States officially recognize Antonio Genoino as the winner of the Pro Train Surf. Brazil demands that the United States compensate the family of Mr. Genoino and compensate the government of Brazil for the loss of our national treasure, in addition to turning over the prize purse to the government of Brazil for the creation of an Antonio Genoino museum."

Smith pursed his lips thoughtfully.

"He's not serious?" Mark Howard asked.

"He'll get the dollars. With U.S. international relations in a political tar pit, I assume we'll pay off the Brazilians in the form of rain-forest-protection subsidies, which means the government can use its own rain-forest funds elsewhere."

"Maybe the Brazilian government did this, then, for the cash?"

Smith nodded. "If the events in California were unique I would consider the possibility, but we've been watching this pattern for months, and most of the events are unrelated to the Brazilians. But there are many nations that share the Brazilian president's disdain. Every nation that sees itself disadvantaged by the U.S. is crying foul. Athletics is big money and high-profile."

He brought up a long list of sporting events on the screen beneath his desktop glass, starting with an African mountain climbing race eighteen months ago. Twin teams of contestants were air-dropped into some of the most unexplored wilderness left on the continent, inhabited by warring tribes who were known to kill outsiders on site. A military contractor got lots of promotion for his new stealth helicopter by handling the rotation of cameramen, who were shooting the teams for Shaft, the new "real man" cable network. The teams were on opposite sides of the mountain, and yet the European team was sabotaged by somebody. Very little physical evidence was retrieved, but the bodies of the dead climbers were returned home. One of them was scalded. The surviving climbers reported a burst of steam just before the fall.

The European survivors made it to the summit two days after the North Americans.

Other events on the list might, or might not, have been the result of sabotage. The extreme-sports trend killed a lot of people, just by its very nature. The games were dangerous, and they had to evolve constantly to keep their viewers interested. They had to be bigger and more deadly all the time. There was also the problem of the underskilled participants, who often went into extreme sports because they couldn't make the cut in traditional professional sports.

Then Extreme Sports Network launched as a spin-off of Shaft Network For Real Men. They funded existing events and developed their own, and their viewership increased with every fatal accident.

"If ESN is not the perpetrator, who benefits?" Smith mused.

"No one else benefits," Mark Howard assured him. "We've been through this. We've looked everywhere."

"What about the consortium angle?" Smith prodded.

"My investigation has come up with nothing," Mark said. "No common theme among the participants. There's no organized-crime connection that I can find, although they're starting to get interested. There's a lot of big wagering happening on the ESN events, but the dollars are going down, not up, because of the suspicious wins. Everybody is getting suspicious."

"Insurance?" Smith persisted.

"No big policies are getting paid off. The contestants are not insurable." Mark looked frustrated. "I still think it could be a nationalist thing. Somebody with a political agenda."

Smith grimaced and tapped his desk screen. "There are too many anomalies for me to buy that as a motive. Whatever the Brazilians and the Europeans will say, the winners are not always from the U.S. The yacht race proved that." Smith tapped the line item for the Around the World All by Yourself sailboat race.

It was the first time Smith acted upon his suspicions

about the events, putting his enforcement arm in the field, or in the sea. Off the coast of the southern tip of South America, in the Drake Passage, the leaders of a solo around-the-world yacht race had met with foul play until Remo put a halt to it. He parachuted onto the boat of the new leader and waited for sabotage to happen. It came in the form of a stealthy ground-effect craft that skimmed over the waves. The craft raced out of the islands around the southern tip of South America and attempted to sink the winning sailboat. Instead, Remo sank it. The attackers died before they provided any clue as to their origin.

The attackers did succeed in taking Remo's boat out of the race, however, and that's where the nationalist agenda pattern was skewed. Remo's boat was the last American contestant of its class in the race. A Hong Kong businessman crossed the finish line first and took home a huge prize purse.

"The boat race was broadcast on ESN, even if it wasn't an event they organized," Mark said. "They got the news coverage, they got the new viewers. They've got strong viewership in Hong Kong as a result."

Smith asked, "Is it your estimation that someone at ESN could be behind this?"

Mark nodded tightly. "I think it could be. They've got big resources. It would take big resources to put together the naval attack team Remo met in the Drake Passage."

The no-expense-spared approach was a hallmark of the saboteurs, as Remo's second encounter proved. Remo joined in with a group of extreme parachute racers. They jumped from an extremely high altitude and whoever used the least total time to touch the ground was the winner. This was military-style HALO jumping taken to its most dangerous limits—by opening their chutes at ever lower altitudes, the jumpers cut their times considerably. They also hit the ground with considerable force, but the attitude was that a pair of broken legs was a small price to pay for a million-dollar prize purse.

But at the championships that Remo participated in, many of the jumpers paid a larger price—the ultimate price. Their chutes melted before they could be deployed. Remo's intervention saved a few lives, but not all.

It took weeks to determine that the chutes had been hit with narrow-beam microwaves from the ground, which reacted with a special woven metallic lining of the chute packs. The chute packs were supposed to have been provided by an ESN sponsor, but the ESN packs were stolen at some point and replaced with sabotaged replicas. Nobody noticed until too late. The cost of the woven alloy fabric and the near perfect replication of the sponsor chute packs must have been considerable.

An American did officially win the skydiving race—ESN's policy was to declare a winner for every network-sponsored event, regardless of "extreme circumstances." ESN presented the prize purse in a ceremony right there in the burn unit of a Portland hospital, where the winner was undergoing extensive skin-grafting to replace his roasted dermis. The media made light of the fact that the champion's medical bills would eventually double the one million dollars he

won—not that he was ever likely to regain consciousness to appreciate the irony.

The award ceremony was longer than coverage of
the HALO jump itself, with viewer share that was just
as high. It seemed ESN could do no wrong. ESN ad
revenues were exceeding projections.

In a brazen ploy to steal the core audience of traditional professional sports, ESN began staging weekly
events on Sunday afternoons against the big, traditional
sporting events. Lately they were starting their contests a half hour after the start of professional football
games, and their ad campaign told viewers to switch to
ESN when they became bored with whatever else they
happened to be watching.

The audience did as it was told. Ad revenues ballooned.

Smith didn't care about the massive financial losses
suffered by some broadcast corporations. In truth, he
cared little about the increasing death toll during ESN
events.

But the stability of the United States of America—
that was his to protect.

More and more people and nations looked at the
U.S. as the world's biggest bully, and anti-American
sentiment was getting an extra boost from these foolish, dangerous games watched by foolish people. Still,
Smith was tempted to believe that these acts were designed to further discredit the U.S.

The truth was, ESN had a vested interest in killing
people. Viewership dropped when people stopped
dying, only to rebound after a fatality. Two fatalities
meant a big jump. The more footage it had to show of

the actual death-causing chain of events, the more viewership it drew in.

ESN played spots with its VP of programming, Herbert Essen, produced to look like a public-service announcement for hunger-relief donations. Instead, they informed ESN viewers that they would not broadcast video of the fatal accidents themselves. This would be disrespectful and a violation of community standards. In addition, ESN had programs in place to provide extra compensation to the families of those killed during ESN-sanctioned events.

This thirty-second spot was paired up with a three-and-a-half-minute commercial for ESN extreme-danger DVDs. It promised to show what ESN could not show on cable—and it delivered. Horrific accidents and on-screen deaths were there in high-definition, wide-screen video and surround-sound stereo. Volume one sold so fast that Volume two was rushed out ahead of schedule. An extreme edition box set, with a third DVD containing ten bonus minutes of life-ending accidents, was under a hundred thousand Christmas trees during the holidays.

There was a hullabaloo when the major TV news channels broke the story of a "massive deception" perpetrated on the American people. None of the profits from the wildly popular DVDs, it was revealed, were actually going to the victims. Because the DVD spots ran side-by-side with the serious promises of the vice president of programming, the public was deceived into believing that the DVDs were the programs that ESN had in place to help the victims' families financially. In fact, the programs were nothing more than a policy of tiny donations made by the network to the victims' families.

"Buyers are outraged," insisted the network news programs, desperate to prop up the traditional professional and college sports programming that subsidized the news. The networks had interviews to prove just how angry the public was.

"They played on our sympathies for the poor victims," one weeping mother said. "I didn't buy those repulsive programs to watch. I bought them as a way of helping the less fortunate."

A federal investigation was launched to determine the extent of the fraud while hordes of angry customers were deluging the irresponsible cable network with refund demands, or so the broadcast news networks said.

"Show me hordes," Herb Essen asked when interviewed on a nonbroadcast cable news network. "Where's the federal investigation? If the federal government was investigating, don't you think I'd know about it?"

The broadcast networks tried to save face. "There's now evidence to prove what forces were at work to derail the federal fraud investigation against the cable network before it even started," one commentator said, then winked at the camera.

"This I love," Herb Essen said when interviewed again on cable news. He and the correspondent were watching a broadcast of the network anchor and chuckling. "Wink!" Essen laughed. He had the moment looping on his television. "Wink! Wink!"

Within twenty-four hours the new American catchphrase was "Wink! Wink!" Comedians, newspapers, all the late-night talk shows used "Wink! Wink!" It even appeared on the network of the commentator who made the original wink.

The ridiculed commentator wanted to sue ESN, but calmer marketing heads prevailed. They convinced the anchor and the entire news department to pretend the whole sorry thing had never happened—but it was months before "Wink! Wink!" fell out of the lexicon of John Q. Public.

Harold W. Smith had never been a TV watcher, but he knew the power of television. He knew the ridiculous reality-television trend and the love of sports were coming together in the Extreme Sports Network and creating a media giant with the power to command big ad dollars. And maybe, with the power to create an international crisis.

6

The woman saw a beautiful soul among the obnoxious rabble—a man of great age and insight, steeped in the vast wisdom of the Orient and dressed in the beautiful, aura-enhancing colors of heaven.

The old Asian was so unlike the others who came here, such as the ugly retiree with the bad toupee and the facelift scars. "Hey, freaky ticket lady," the wig wearer said. "Give me my tickets, would you?"

She dutifully counted out tickets to the man and his ghastly clown of a wife. She disliked these crude and rude people who came to Sedona in pollutant-spewing vehicles. Mostly they were crass retirees from Phoenix, with too much time and money and too little spiritual understanding. Either that, or it was carloads of horny, drunk college boys out of Flagstaff.

This special corner of Arizona used to attract visitors who came to experience the natural auras in the Sedona countryside. They came to bask in the spiritual density radiating from the Sedona people. Back then, this place attracted the Wiccans and the earth-lovers and those who channeled the immortal souls of long dead luminaries, and that combination of rare people helped make Sedona one of the few places on Earth where the New Age of Aquarius was truly dawning.

These rude, lewd sports people didn't get it. They came for the quick thrills. Sedona wasn't a place for quick, vile thrills!

The ticket seller wondered what the wise old Asian man in the silk robe was doing here at the southwestern ENL quarterfinals. Surely he wasn't here as a spectator, was he? She peered around her customers looking for him again; just seeing the resplendent, ancient man gave her *ki* a spiraling boost of goddess energy.

She was surprised when she couldn't find the robed man again. He was no longer waiting to get inside. He had to have changed his mind and left this abominable place, which proved just how wise he truly was.

CHIUN SNIFFED and looked disparagingly around him at the morning crowds milling through the entrance. None of the staff had noticed Chiun and Remo slither through the front gate without a bar-coded ticket.

"I'm here under protest," Remo said. "For the record."

Chiun ignored him, tromping atop the rocky top tier of sandstone bleachers, which were carved out of the desert hillside. At the bottom of the bleachers was a circular stage area, which made the entire place look like an ancient Greek amphitheater until you accounted for the hill behind it. A paved raceway curved and twisted down the hill. From the flapping green flags at the top of the hill to the finish line, where it emptied out diagonally across the stage, the track was more than a mile long.

"I know this is CURE work," Remo said. "I just can't figure out how we got here."

"Is your confusion enjoyable?" Chiun marched them away from the hillside and away from the sandstone bleachers.

"Smitty didn't know where we were going after Albuquerque, right? I never told him and I was the only one who knew. I would have assumed we were headed into Yuma if I were him. See the family and all. So instead we go west across the top of Arizona and so Smitty has a job for us. I mean you. He must have planned this little side trip since before we left."

"He did not."

"So when did he give you the orders to come here?" Remo demanded.

"Two hours ago," Chiun answered.

"Two hours ago we were driving the Sinanju-mobile through the middle of nowhere. You didn't get any phone calls. You don't even have a cell phone."

"The Emperor sent his request in a blog."

"Oh," Remo said. Now he remembered that Chiun had spent some time reading the online journals on his portable plastic iBlogger. Remo was not computer savvy, but it made sense that the thing could receive personalized messages. Blogs were Chiun's newest passion—replacing Spanish-language television soap operas for the time being.

Chiun chose a seat on a small stone ledge, several paces away from the designated audience bleachers.

"Since when do you let Smitty order you around in an e-mail?"

"I do not," Chiun responded. "He has never done so before."

"So what did he do, hack into your eye-booger account? Aren't you afraid he'll see what you're reading?"

"The Emperor knows well enough not to invade my privacy," Chiun said icily.

"Huh."

"What?"

"He did something that's got your tail in a knot, Chiun. What is it?"

"If you must know, he had Ms. Slate transmit the message to me."

"What? Really? That's really strange. What's gotten into him, I wonder? He's got to know he's giving Sarah more insight into CURE. It's like he doesn't care if she knows."

"Betrayal foments anarchy."

"My betrayal you mean. So, if he spills the beans to Sarah and then needs her silenced for CURE's sake, it'll all be because I had the brass cojones to stand up for myself—that what you mean by 'ferment'?"

"Mutiny is mutiny."

"So is self-respect."

Chiun gave him a look that said, "You are an imbecile." Remo had seen the look before, once or twice.

"Hey, maybe you should cut me some slack since I actually went along for the ride, even though I'm no longer following CURE orders and I've got plans of my own."

"What would you desire, a certificate of achievement? A ribbon with your name in gold-colored foil?"

Chiun wasn't even paying attention. His eyes were riveted to the hilltop in the distance as the loudspeaker announced the first round of the day.

Remo looked around. "What's the event? I don't even know what we're all here to see."

"A display of Western idiocy."

"The election's over."

"Athletic idiocy."

"That narrows it down to every professional or college sport played in America. Give me a hint."

"Be silent and watch."

The first race began, simulcast on a pair of fifty-foot video screens.

Remo was caught off guard by what he saw. "Are you effing kidding me?"

"I have ceased to be amazed by anything I see in this land of whites."

"They're naked!" Remo said.

"Yes."

"They're luging!"

"They are naked luging," Chiun agreed. "Most perceptive."

Remo's highly focused vision brought every unpleasant detail into sharp relief. There was a field of five contestants starting from the hilltop and speeding down the long paved track. They were, undoubtedly, naked except for their safety helmets. Two men and three women were on their backs on luge boards, like oversize skateboards, and they picked up speed after the first turn. In the traditional luge pose, they were on their backs rolling feetfirst with their heads lifted to watch where they were going. And they were naked.

Their hands gripped the tiny wheeled luge platforms beneath them, and they leaned their bodies as their speed grew and they swept around the second curve—still naked.

"They're not even attractive," Remo added insistently.

"And yet, see how the rabble appreciates it?"

"Woo-hoo!" shouted a man sitting at the end of the bleachers nearby, squinting through binoculars. "Lookit those woobies wobble!"

"Them cheeks are almost touching ground," another spectator added.

"Hey, number six is really enjoying himself," another said.

"Repulsive," Chiun observed.

"At the very least," Remo agreed.

The crowd began to chant. "Moguls. Moguls. Moguls."

"Why do they summon Moguls?" Chiun asked.

"Those ridges in the racetrack are called moguls," Remo explained. "When you go over them... This is gonna be gruesome."

The five naked racers flew over the moguls, and the ridges created spectacular vibrations in their bodies, eliciting explosive cheers from the crowd. The lugers remained focused on their performance, and seconds later a large, powerful-looking woman with silver hair got the checkered flag.

"Man, that was a great one!" enthused the baby-faced middle-aged man sitting close by. "Hey, you guys, didn't you even bring binoculars?"

"First time," Remo explained, and stopped breathing. The smell of the man's breakfast Budweisers was lethal.

"Come 'ere and look, then!" He was fiddling with a silver, brushed-aluminum box tucked between his legs and mounted with a slim bracket to his binoculars. "One of them new digital high-definition camcorders. Records right on to the DVD, too. I can zoom this sucker in so tight I can count body hairs."

"Sweet," Remo answered.

"Bought it just for ENL. Drive out twice a month from Tempe during the regular season. I have to keep the thing out of sight, though. Them a-holes at ESN don't like the audience making their own video. Cuts into their DVD sales."

Remo looked the other way, which the baby-faced man took as a sign of extreme interest. "I pop these suckers in at parties and it brings the house down!"

"ENL?" Remo asked abruptly. "What's the *E* for?"

Chiun ignored him.

"Hey, you really are a virgin." The baby-faced man chortled. "*E* for Extreme, of course. Extreme Nude Luge."

Remo said to Chiun, "Well, now I know why we're here. Smitty thinks this has something to do with all the killings at the extreme sporting events, like those skydivers who got burned up in Montana."

"The skydivers you allowed to be burned up over Montana," Chiun corrected. "It is little surprise the Emperor is perturbed."

"Hey, watch this," the man with the camcorder said. "They're about to make the result official."

Remo watched. The five naked lugers were now standing around with their support teams, drinking Gatorade. The PA from a small wooden shack squawked to life. "In today's first event, the winner is Mrs. Jean Hebbleman."

The woman who had won, a solidly built giantess in her fifties, began whooping and jumping up and down with excitement—still naked. The man with the camcorder diligently recorded every second of it.

"That's beautiful," he murmured.

A family in the front row waved to Hebbleman. "You're the greatest, Grandma!" shrieked a scruffy third-grader in a SpongeBob SquarePants shirt.

"Yee-uck," Remo declared. "Little uncomfortable with all this, huh, Little Father?"

"It is horrid and vulgar."

"Plain old luge is horrid and vulgar. They put on these tights, then roll downhill watching their packages the whole way. This is much worse."

As the golf carts transported more contestants up to the hilltop starting line, Remo said, "I still haven't figured out what's so extreme about it."

"Simply observe," Chiun said.

The first crash came in the third race. There was just one woman in the field and she was easily the most skillful nude luger among them. Her quick start gave her an immediate lead, but the young man in second place luged aggressively and closed the gap. At the second long curve he bit his lip and leaned carefully, hardly reducing his speed.

"That dope's trying for an inside pass," the baby-faced man blurted, trying not to blink as he maneuvered his thighs to aim his camera. He didn't want to miss a thing.

But he wasn't going to make it. Remo and Chiun saw it even before the kid did.

He started his pass inside, pulled alongside the intense-looking woman in the lead, then the young man's wheels lost their purchase. He skidded sideways for a few feet before flipping into the leader, then they log-rolled off the track and across the rocky hillside. The hill descended underneath them, and their momentum continued all the way down to the bottom. They flopped to a halt, their bloody, naked bodies tangled together.

"Woo-hoo! Now that's extreme, friend!" the man with the camcorder shouted.

"Little Father, would you think less of me if I up-chucked?" Remo asked.

"Not at all. But do it elsewhere."

EACH TIME CHIUN WAS SURE the Western world could sink no lower, a new and more repulsive form of exploitation and entertainment was unveiled. Remo, as white as he was, at least had the good taste to be disgusted with these proceedings. If only he would stop asking when they could leave...

"If you know what Emperor Smith suspects, then you know what we are here to do," Chiun chided.

"I know what *you* are here to do. I don't work there anymore, remember?"

Another headstrong act of rebellion by the Master of Sinanju. Chiun sighed mentally.

"That skydiving thing in Montana was worth millions. I seriously doubt nude luge is big business," Remo added.

"You are seriously mistaken, then," Chiun said. "See how the crowd grows? It is still early in the day and the number of spectators will swell by three times before the climactic races of the day. The ultimate winner will receive great reward."

"Really? How much?"

"Figure it out for yourself. See it as an opportunity to educate yourself."

Remo asked the infantlike man with whom he had apparently formed a deep friendship.

"Today's purse is a hundred grand cash," the man said. "That gets you into the semifinals, then the finals. Whoever wins this year's championship goes home with a cool million bucks, buddy. Plus endorsement contracts like you wouldn't believe."

"A million bucks? For riding a skateboard naked?"

"It's harder than it looks."

"Hey, Little Father, I just got a great idea," Remo said, turning to Chiun, who felt the cold hand of dread on his age-weary and weakening heart.

"My son, do not even say the words."

"You and I both know I could whup these losers."

Remo was wearing the same grin that was worn by the young pranksters who untied fishing nets in Sinanju to vex the adults. This was not like untying nets. Remo was joking, surely. "Please do not pull on my leg."

"I'm serious. I need a job, right? And look what drops right into my lap—an easy cool million. All I have to do is get naked and roll down the hill a few times."

Chiun waved his words away. They were unworthy of a response.

"Okay, then. Let's leave. I'm bored."

"We will stay until the finals in order to unmask the perpetrator of poor sportsmanship."

Remo conferred further with his friend, then barked loudly, "What?" He turned back to Chiun. "He says there's twelve more races before the finals. It goes until dusk. I'm not sitting here until dusk."

"Then go."

"But you're going to stay and keep handling the stakeout?"

"Yes. I am obliged to fulfill our contract as best I can."

"I'm not going to leave you here by yourself."

"Why not?" Chiun demanded.

Remo didn't answer, instead saying, "Extreme Nude Luge it is, then. I'm going to take a walk before the next big race." He walked away.

Chiun was not so blind he could not see that Remo was saying absurd things to get a reaction. Chiun didn't believe for an instant that the headstrong young fool would actually carry through with his threat. Still, he felt a niggle of dread when the next event was announced. The racers gathered near the top of the hill. Chiun examined the naked men and was vastly relieved that none was Remo Williams. All were typical American fat men. Remo had failings—many in fact—but he was not obese.

Chiun's alarm resurged when he spotted Remo flitting around the mountain, disappearing from view where there were apparently stairs along the backside of the hill to the starting gate.

The blaring announcer said the race was the first in

the second round of elimination. Chiun's imagination ran riot, wondering what spectacular grotesque was being added to the race to make it even more appealing to the audience of trashy whites. Soon he realized that "elimination" referred to the paring down of the pool of lugers until just a few contestants remained to compete in the final race that determined the day's champion.

Chiun watched the race closely, although his mind was elsewhere and he found himself involuntarily scanning the amphitheater for his son. But he was sure Remo would never do anything so outlandish and so disgraceful to his honored trainer.

Bodies tumbled off the track on the very first swooping turn of the next race, taking out three contestants. The man in fourth place was declared winner, to the dissatisfaction of the crowd. An ambulance removed the other fools, whom Chiun had no pity for. The ensuing races were less eventful except for the near riot that resulted when one of the favorite athletes lost and was eliminated from further races. This man had the corpulent body and bushy mustache of a walrus. The man maintained himself at a level of obesity that provided optimum movement when he luged the moguls.

"See, that's what's wrong with this sport," the nearby cameraman declared angrily. "There's more to it than just winning or losing. They need to take showmanship into account. Big Wally, now, he's a true performer."

Chiun was the only one present who failed to agree enthusiastically. He had just spotted Remo again, coming out from behind the hill. Moments later he took his seat next to Chiun.

"Glad to see me?"

"I never imagined I would be happy to see you attired in your undergarment shirt and artless trousers, but it is a relief, considering the alternative."

"Brought you something, Little Father." He handed Chiun a red round chunk of plastic.

"Thank you, Remo. I will treasure it always."

"It's a luge wheel."

"How much did the gift shop gouge you for this?"

"Just stop it. Remember that wreck a couple of races ago? This is why it happened. Look inside at the axle. See the flanges that keep the wheel in place?"

Chiun examined it. A small rim of metal—and a bright ring inside of it.

"See this one? From the same luge."

Chiun nodded.

"The first wheel was created with a ridge of metal to hold it in place but weak enough to fail as it was used. The second wheel has much less space for the wheel to shift."

"Right. So when the guy goes into the turn, all of a sudden his wheel shifts over a half inch and he loses control. His luge board flew down the backside of the hill, and I managed to get to it first."

"Let us pay a visit to the winner of the race who benefited from this failure."

"Okay, but let's make it quick. They're gonna get me in as a wild card in the sixth."

PETE CRISP WAS in the infirmary, looking queasy. The nurse gave him a plastic medicine cup full of thick pink liquid, which he downed as Remo and Chiun entered.

"Lucky break for you up there," Remo commented.

"I don't feel lucky at the moment."

"How do you think it happened?"

"Fiber. Way too much fiber."

"Stop right there. I've had enough yech for one day, thank you. I was asking about the crash. Remember, you won the race because of it?"

Pete Crisp looked wary. "Who are you guys?"

Remo turned to Chiun. "Well, who are we?"

With a pert frown Chiun extracted two identification badges from his sleeves. "We are Hsu No Jong Yaun and Mu Nuk Lo'k, special investigators for the Federal Gaming Commission. Answer the question."

"Uh, the crash? I don't know how it happened. Looked to me like Chappy the Fin took the turn too sharp. Once you start a fast skid like that, you might as well just forget it."

"We suspect sabotage," Chiun said, every word an accusation.

"Hey, I didn't sabotage nothin'!" Crisp said indignantly, then gripped his stomach as a wave of pain filled his gut. When he opened his eyes again, he was alone.

7

"He doesn't know about the sabotage of the luge vehicles," Chiun said. "That doesn't mean someone did not sabotage the vehicles in his behalf."

"Glad we have that figured out. Now let's go. Smitty can hire some laboratory to come and check out the equipment."

Chiun didn't deign to answer, but simply returned to their seats to observe the rest of the day's events.

Pete Crisp had his gastrointestinal distress under control enough to make an appearance in the last race of the day. By then, Remo considered himself an unwilling armchair expert at the nude luge, and he saw right away that Crisp didn't have what it took to be a champion. He was graceless and uncoordinated, and he was far more concerned with staying in the race than with winning it. As it turned out, staying in the race was once again all he needed to do in order to win. The two leaders suffered wheel-bearing failures in such rapid succession it looked like a single crack-up. Crisp swerved around the crash and luged to victory.

Crisp was clearly not the favorite, but the race was still considered a huge success from an entertainment perspective. The two women who crashed were young and tough, and after disentangling from each other they began a dusty catfight that nobody was in a hurry to break up. As they were identical twins, it was impossible to tell them apart after they lost the helmets.

"Our business is with the winner," Chiun stated firmly over the appreciative roar of the crowd.

"Your business, not mine," Remo reminded him. "Besides, we already know that poor schmuck is clueless. They must have some way of remote controlling which luge boards break down during the race so he wins."

They moved in for the award ceremony, which was quick and informal. Crisp posed with the race officials and gave a brief interview to the Extreme Sports Network. He thanked his mother and Extreme Nuggets breakfast cereal, which provided him the extreme nutrition he needed for excellent performance.

"Can we go now?" Remo asked. "The racing is over."

"Then why are the people not departing?" Chiun asked.

A twenty-two-foot screen was alight with the opening credits of *Mogul Mania,* featuring the greatest moments in nude luge in extreme slow motion. Chiun blanched as a well-endowed woman flopped outrageously on the screen, one frame per endless second.

"On second thought, let's stay," Remo said. "Hey, look, you buy popcorn at that stand and they let you put on your own butterlike topping. Much as you want."

Chiun ignored the comment and led the way out. "Remo, I hope you never follow through with your outlandish threats."

"Hope is good for the spirit."

"Promise me you never will do something as foolish as luge without clothing."

"I guess so."

Chiun's eyebrows were heavy. "That was not convincing."

The door of a nearby ticket booth flew open. The woman standing there had frizzy, dishwater hair that looked as if it hadn't been cut in years or washed in weeks. Her tunic was a flannel sheet with poorly sewn sleeves and seams, and its bright tie-dye colors had faded to dirty splotches.

Her lower lip quivered. "Oh, thank Goddess, it's you! I thought I would never see you again!"

She strode barefoot to Chiun with her arms out, only to come up empty-handed. The wise, ancient Asian man had vanished like a spirit—which, surely, he had to have been.

8

The prime minister of Jamaica held a press conference in time for the morning news. The verdant gardens were in Kingston, where the sky was blue and cloudless, the Caribbean Sea was turquoise, and the prime minister's face went from dark brown to scarlet.

"The Americans always win de games. Jamaicans, dey just die trying," the prime minister proclaimed. "Yesterday, our special girl Beetrice Goldings, she was cheated out of another hundred t'ousand dollars by the crooks and the thieves of the Extreme Sports Network. Dis is poor sportsmanship."

Mark Howard was getting ready for work in the suite he now shared with Sarah Slate at Folcroft Sanitarium. He should have moved out weeks ago, but moving out posed its own problems. Where would Sarah go? Home, to the Slate mansion in Providence?

He didn't want her to go home.

Right now, something was bothering him, and it wasn't Sarah Slate. It was the prime minister of Jamaica. Howard knotted his tie too long and undid it, tying it again, and he tried to figure out where the PM's head was at.

"Today I am calling on all athletes from Jamaica to no longer compete in competition organized by the Extreme Sports Network of the United States," the PM stated. "We won't compete until the Americans make dere games fair to all de world!"

The prime minister of Jamaica was a dignified, impeccably neat black man who was known to be restrained and friendly. Today he was angry and passionate.

Sarah came out of the shower in a bulky bathrobe, brushing her hair. "What's the matter?"

"He's sure mad."

"He has a right to be, doesn't he?"

"I don't know," Mark Howard replied, but he didn't know if that was even the point.

"I'm extending a request, too, to my counterparts in Grea' Britain, to also pull ut of all events sponsored by this network of cheaters and a nation of bullies!"

The PM stalked away from the cameras.

"Pretty strong," Mark said.

"He's just jumping on the bandwagon," Sarah said.

"I suppose he is," Mark admitted.

"AMERICANS DO NOT always win in our events!" exhorted the president of Extreme Sports Network to the cue-ball, old-school talk-show host. They were sitting around a circular table, and the highly credible interviewer had his shirtsleeves rolled up his arms and his glasses coming down the bridge of his nose.

"That's not what the rest of the world thinks," he said.

"Look, I have a pie chart to prove it," the president of ESN said.

The ESN president felt like a moron with his poster board, but this interview was arranged at the last minute, and he didn't have time to get his PowerPoint slides transferred into whatever format the TV show needed. Still, the pie chart was eighteen inches in diameter and quite colorful. The sixty-six-percent share in pale yellow represented wins by U.S. competitors or teams. Bright purple, red, blue, green and orange were wins by non-U.S. competitors.

"The winners are still mostly Americans," accused the interviewer, who had so much journalistic integrity his eyeballs were newsprint yellow.

"Give or take five percent, that's about the same percentage of U.S. participants in any and all our events since we launched the network," the ESN president shot back.

"Quite persuasive. But they don't tell the whole story. What about the discrepancies in dollar winnings?" On the monitor, a freeze-frame of the poster board was displayed side-by-side with a professional-looking PowerPoint slide of a similar pie chart. "This is also a chart of wins from the same events, this time illustrating dollar winnings. The yellow is U.S. competitors and that's eighty-seven percent. The smaller slices are other countries."

The ESN president gulped. The interviewer's chart looked much more professional and persuasive.

"Looks to me like you're letting the Americans win the high-profile, big-prize contests, then throwing some bones to the other countries on the smaller games."

The ESN bigwig was sweating profusely. To his horror, the cameraman got a close-up of the beads of perspiration on his upper lip. "I'm not aware of these results so I can't speak to them."

"Since ESN began programming its biggest media events opposite the more traditional sports such as football, there have been no non-American winners."

"That's not true."

"Our chart proves that it is." The ESN president's sweaty mouth was now split-screened with a big red pie chart that showed that one hundred percent of the winners were American.

"I'm going to have to investigate this myself," the ESN president stammered. "I don't see how this can be factual."

The journalistic nodded smugly. "I guess it's up to the world to decide."

9

Remo was feeling like a big fat heel. Chiun was ticked at him for keeping secrets. When Remo asked Chiun not to come along today it only exacerbated the sour mood that had come upon him late the previous night as they roamed Revelry Hills vainly searching for a campground. Chiun reluctantly allowed the search to expand to a few other select Southern California zip codes, and finally agreed to take the first RV lot they could find. Remo could have said "I told you so," but wisely refrained.

"We shall simply park at the All-Mart," Chiun sniffed, as if this were a perfectly acceptable alternative. "There is never a lack of such places."

Ever since he got the RV idea into his head, Chiun had been talking about the wonders of chain stores that allowed RVs to overnight in the parking lots. Since there were countless stores like All-Marts across the country, in every town and city, Chiun insisted they would never be without a place to park the new, mobile Castle Sinanju. The problem was that Chiun had probably never been to an All-Mart. Remo didn't think the old Master knew what he was getting himself into.

They found an All-Mart in West Hollywood, and even the parking lot smelled bad. They parked there, regardless, and Remo thought that Chiun was beginning to see the impracticality of the Sinanju-mobile.

He found the address he wanted in Burbank and stuck on a fake mustache in the elevator. He hated it. It felt stupid, and he just knew it made him look stupid, no matter what the Romanian image consultant had claimed. The fifth floor was dominated by a perfectly made-up and manicured receptionist. Several office suites were in orbit around her.

Time to be charming, Remo thought unhappily.

"Hi. Romeo Dodd. I'm hear to see, uh… Let me check my planner." He pulled out the crumpled FedEx receipt and examined the smeared characters in a circle along one margin. "Dasheway? You have a guy named that?"

The receptionist, whose nameplate said was named Dayla Darrin, didn't show a hint of emotion. Maybe her face paint was too thick. "You do not have an appointment."

"How do you know? You have his appointment book memorized?"

"I am personally acquainted with everyone on his appointment schedule today," she droned. "I'm sorry to say I am not acquainted with you, sir."

"You don't sound sorry," Remo answered. "Anyway, I don't have an appointment. I'm here to pitch him a TV-show idea."

"All proposals must be submitted by mail."

"Don't have time for that."

"I'm sorry, sir."

Remo sighed. His new career wasn't getting off to a roaring start. "You're a load of laughs, Dayla." He strolled back to the elevator and pushed the button as he folded his receipt into his pocket and removed a tool, brought along for just such an emergency. It was a paper clip, which he held between thumb and finger at his side. Then he flicked it.

The paper clip flashed through the office. Dayla never saw it coming, never saw the little bent wire snag itself into her hair. All Dayla ever knew was that her hair was flying off. Her mouth dropped open and her eyes rolled upward and she grabbed at her shaved scalp as the wig plopped to the floor behind her.

Remo glided in as Dayla hit the deck, scrambling to get her hair back in place. She never saw him sneak past.

"Hi? Got a minute?" Remo asked, stepping into the office labeled Olaf Dasheway.

"Who are you?" Dasheway was a sallow man in his upper fifties. His suit was expensive, but there was no disguising the sloppy signs of chronic stress.

"Romeo Dodd. I've got an idea for a TV show."

"How did you get in here?"

"Chill, Dasheway. I'm here to save your ass."

Olaf Dasheway had been in show business for years and had sat through thousands of pitches for TV shows. He ended up producing maybe ten or twelve of those. Some of them made him a lot of money.

Then he stopped listening to other people's ideas. His ideas were always just as good. He knew TV. He knew what the world wanted out of its TV. Or, at least, he used to. The world had turned against him.

"Listen, buddy, I need your ideas like my wife needs another pair of black shoes. Out." Dasheway pointed the way.

"Listen, your company is about to go under. All your series tanked this season, and you've got nothing in the works with any chance of being big. You need something big."

Dasheway didn't need one more moron telling him what he already knew. "Get out."

Dasheway's intruder nodded thoughtfully. "Okay, I'll go, but before I go I want to tell you about my special talent."

Oh, great, Dasheway thought, expecting the guy to expose his privates. The guy didn't do that, just told Dasheway about his special talent.

"Fine," Dasheway said. "I'm thrilled for you. Now leave."

"You wouldn't tell me to leave if you believed I really have this special talent," Remo added, opening the office door. "Maybe you should watch."

Dasheway was intrigued. The guy was awfully calm for a lunatic. Most nutcases wouldn't have left so agreeably. He went to the hall, watching the intruder.

The intruder stopped by the receptionist's desk. "Hi," Dasheway heard him say. The guy started chatting.

Dasheway laughed to himself. Chatting up Dayla Darrin was a waste of time. Half the celebrities who came into this place—TV stars, big-name producers and even a billion-dollar film director—had tried to make time with Dayla Darrin. Nobody succeeded.

Dayla made a strange sound and got to her feet. The

sound was a giggle. Dayla never giggled. She was holding her purse.

"I need the rest of the day off!" she said breathlessly as she rushed back to Dasheway.

"But—"

"Then I quit. Bye."

She went back to the stranger. He tried to take her hand. She practically straddled him all the way to the elevator.

"Wait!" Dasheway called, and thank God he reached them before they were gone.

10

Olaf Dasheway was trying to regain his composure. "I'm not saying I believe you. You and Dayla could have set up that little show for my benefit. I have to see evidence."

"Fine." The intruder, Romeo Dodd, was in the back of the limo looking unimpressed. He was definitely hard to read. Dasheway thought he looked normal enough at first glance. His shoes were definitely expensive. Maybe stolen. His Chinos and mauve T-shirt were as bland as white bread. Nothing out of the ordinary there.

Then, you start noticing oddities. What was the deal with those huge wrists? Did he overwork them obsessively? Guessing his age was next to impossible. Old enough to drink legally and too young to retire—that was about as close as Dasheway could pin it.

The guy's eyes didn't seem to fit in the picture. They gave Dasheway the willies. They were cruel eyes, but not romantically cruel movie-star eyes. Just plain cruel.

There was definitely a lot that was odd about this person, and Olaf Dasheway was daring to hope the man really could do what he said he could do....

"You understand that I need to test you." Dasheway was trying to go belligerent on the dark-haired man, but Romeo Dodd was unflappable.

"Fine."

"I pick the victim. I mean target."

"Okay."

Dasheway picked a target that he knew would be almost impossible. They entered the Baron Souprema Cafeteria with only a minor fuss. The cafeteria required jackets for lunch dining.

"I'm not going to buy you lunch, friend, until after I see you perform," Dasheway informed the man.

"Fine. Hey, this really is a cafeteria."

"Trendiest place in L.A.," Dasheway explained with a shrug. The Baron Souprema Cafeteria was the epitome in West Coast chic. It combined cafeteria self-serve lines and Formica booths with high-priced showpiece dining. "There she is," he said to Remo. "See the blonde?"

"Which blonde?"

Dasheway made a face.

"Give me a break. There's twenty-five blondes in the booths alone. You'll have to be more specific."

"Hey, look closely. Recognize anybody?"

"To be honest, they all look vaguely familiar. They from the same modeling agency?"

Dasheway sighed long and loud. "Get off it. First booth. Blond hair. Big butt. Tell me you at least recognize the butt." Dasheway had to hand it to the guy. He was a pretty good actor. He had to be acting, right? "It's Roberta Lorez. Otherwise known as Quimby Lorez. Otherwise known as…?"

Remo snapped his fingers. "Blo-Lo! Yeah, I've heard of her."

"You've heard of her? That smart-ass lard-ass makes twenty-nine million a movie. And sometimes her movies don't even make that much."

"Didn't she make a movie called *Juggly?*"

"*Joggly.* Listen, millions of guys around the world would love to score with Blo-Lo. I want to see you do it."

Remo shrugged. "Okay. Here I go."

Dasheway was ready to bolt. If the scene turned ugly, he did not want to be associated with this guy Romeo. But what if the guy actually did it?

Dasheway held his breath as Romeo said hello to Roberta Lorez. She gave him a nasty look, but the look, if he was seeing things right, melted.

A moment later she ushered him into the booth. Dasheway's amazement and delight ballooned as she giggled and leaned over the table in a classic cleavage exhibition. Dasheway strolled toward the booth, trying to listen in.

"You know why they call me Blo-Lo, don't you?" he heard Roberta Lorez ask. She was panting like a sprinter.

"No." Romeo was looking uncomfortable.

"I'll show you!" she gasped delightedly and skootched under the booth.

"Ms. Blo, you've got me all wrong. I just wanted to come over and tell you how much I enjoyed you in that one movie you did with Jack Nicholson." Romeo Dodd was deftly slithering around on the booth, avoiding the hands that were snatching at his trousers from beneath the table.

"I never did a movie with Jack Nicholson," said the voice from below.

"I meant Peter Falk."

Romeo called to the producer, "You satisfied?"

"Not even close!" exclaimed the table.

"Let's get out of here, buddy," Dasheway said. "We've got a program to produce."

THE WHOLE INCIDENT gave Remo a serious case of the willies, but Olaf Dasheway was in an even more serious state. In fact, Remo might have thought him dead if he couldn't hear the producer's hammering heart. Dasheway was sitting stock-still in the back of the limo, a frozen smile on his gaunt face.

"So, you think we'll get ratings?"

Dasheway blinked. His eyes were shining with some sort of unpleasant pleasure. "Ratings? My God, son, we got ratings already. This is going to be the biggest reality show ever. Hell, it's going to be the biggest show ever. Ever!"

"Ever. Got ya."

"We have to get the ball rolling!" Dasheway grabbed the phone from his pocket and jabbed it. "I want Philstock." He said to Remo, "Philstock's my best director." He spoke into the phone. "Philstock, how fast can we have a reality show in the can? We'll shoot it here in L.A. No special locations. No big studio introductions. I want fast."

Dasheway grinned and thumbed on the speaker. "I guess we could have something in the can in a week, not counting casting."

"Casting's arranged."

"But unsigned," Remo reminded Dasheway.

11

The young man had **an attitude** problem. Quite frankly, he carried it around **with him** as if he had a chip on his shoulder.

But that was just **a part of his** personality. Take it or leave it. Truth was, he **wasn't** nearly as ornery as he used to be. Ask anyone.

The young man's life had undergone a radical change some years ago. When he was just barely a man, he suffered an emotional trauma and somehow ended up where he never expected. But the Arizona desert agreed with him. Mostly, the people of the Sun On Jo reservation agreed with him.

Well, they didn't exactly agree with him. Usually they disagreed. They thought he was a loudmouth. Or an obnoxious troublemaker. Or just a jerk. But they all had an affection for him, anyway. You couldn't help but like him.

His name was Winner, and he was the most likable jerk white man in this entire tribe of redskins.

Of course, his skin wasn't white and the skin of his people wasn't red and, for that matter, Winner had never known a black man who was black. But he had known a Latino girl, years ago, with exquisite, dark skin. She had called him Weener and he had loved her, for a few days. Then she was dead.

Nobody called him Weener now. *Nobody.*

Nobody messed around with the things Winner cared about. Like his sister. He didn't exactly go out of his way to be protective, but everybody knew you had better not give Winner's sister any grief or he might give you a lot of it. There had been some trouble in Flagstaff a few years back....

Another thing you didn't mess around with was Winner's people. His people were now the Sun On Jo, a small and mostly forgotten tribe of Native Americans on a reservation in Arizona, some ways outside of Yuma. He hadn't been born here, he wasn't raised here, but he belonged here. He was at home here. Every Sun On Jo was a part of his family. And you had better not effing mess with Winner's family.

"I'm going hunting," Winner said, reaching his head and one arm through the screen door of the nicest home in Sun On Jo village. The nicest home wasn't all that nice by standards outside the reservation, but it was a comfortable home for the odd family that dwelt there.

"Don't have your gun," said the older man who was reading a paper on a kitchen chair at a tiny table by the front window.

"I'll use this."

"That's my beer."

"Thanks."

Sunny Joe Roam wondered what this was all about. "Huh," he said. "I know what it's all about already." But he went to see anyway.

WINNER RAN THROUGH the dusty village and into the desert, circling a sheep pen, avoiding the sharp, tough plants that made up the desert flora as he went up the rocks a short way outside the town. He moved as fast and effortlessly over the desert as a dust devil, but he raised almost no dust of his own. Although he was fast, he was skilled, too. He had been trained by the military. He had been retrained, informally, by his grandfather, Sunny Joe. But a lot of his skills just sort of came to him.

But he wasn't the fastest one in the village.

"What's going on?" said a voice just a few paces behind him when he was halfway up the hundred-foot pile of rocks.

"Dammit, Freya," he said, coming to a stop. "Let me do this alone."

"Do what alone?" She was sitting on a shelf stone behind him, her flowing hair brilliant in the sun. She might as well have been sitting on the bench in front of the Sunny Joe Roam house for all the exertion she showed. Winner was breathing hard and sweating hard.

"Go back. I'll do this."

"Do what, Win?"

"It's another Peeping Tom, if you must know."

She was puzzled. She was so naïve. When Winner looked at her he saw more beauty and innocence than any grown woman had a right to have. Thank God she was stuck out here on the res, where the world couldn't grind her up.

Once, Winner had helplessly watched the world grind up a beautiful young woman, and her face haunted him to this day.

"Frey, I'm asking you to go back. Now."

"Why so serious, Win?"

Winner pursed his mouth and felt the cold hand of ruin on his shoulder. How could he convince her—?

"God, okay," she said, her eyes clouding, as if the cold had touched her, too. "I'll go right away, Win."

She stepped down the precarious rock tumble as if she were going down the slope of a driveway.

Winner turned and climbed with fierce intensity, his hand clawing at the rock, his urgency multiplied, heedless of when the rock scraped his flesh. He had just been reminded what he was protecting.

He wasn't a guy who went out looking for trouble. Not anymore. But if you brought trouble to him, he would give you serious grief. And if you brought trouble to his people, his family, his *sister*, then, buddy, you were declaring war.

And war was something Winner Smith knew how to do.

He crouched, panting in a niche in the rock just ten feet from the summit. He strained his ears and heard the hiss of the Peeping Tom. It was closing in fast. It was going to be a near thing.

Winner reached up, reached out and dug his fingers into a crack in the rock well above his head. It was no wider than a knife blade, and the broken edges cut like a knife, too. The blood made his fingers slippery, and he forced them to lock on to the rock as he swung his body out into open space and dangled, 150 feet over the desert. His body heaved and he yanked himself up again, finding a handhold where there was no handhold, and swung his leg over a hump in the stone. Then he was up, at the top, his lungs crying for breath.

He heard the Peeping Tom, just a few feet away. He squinted through the rocks.

It was the same device.

THE PHONE RANG twenty-seven times before it was picked up. "Hi and thanks for calling Sinanju Assassins. We'll be accepting new clients in the near future, so please leave your name, rank and estimated liquid assets. Please note that payment is accepted only in the form of gold, and we're not talking Gold Cards, here, bucko."

"Remo—"

"Please note also that the House of Sinanju accepts only kings, prime ministers and other leaders-slash-usurpers with nation-bossing status. All others need not apply."

"Remo!"

"Lastly, if you, the caller, happens to be William Jefferson Clinton—buzz off. This is your final warning."

After a moment, Smith said, "Are you finished?"

"Oh, it's you. Hi, Smitty."

"You knew it was me and your soliloquy was for my benefit."

"My who? Don't answer. Here's Chiun."

"I don't want Chiun." Smith knew he'd made a big mistake the moment the words were out of his mouth. The Masters of Sinanju had extraordinary hearing—easily listening in on any phone conversation in the room.

Remo came back on the line. "That wasn't very nice. If you're trying to get rid of both of us, why bother calling? We've already been picked on by the West Hollywood All-Mart manager today. Told us the Sinanju-mobile was too big for their parking lot. He changed his tune eventually, didn't he, Little Father?"

"Tell Master Chiun I was not being insulting or disrespectful," Smith said, knowing his words were being heard by the old Master Emeritus even as he spoke. "Tell him that the purpose of my call was to try to talk some sense into you, Remo."

"Huh. Not a very successful call by any estimate," Remo told him.

Then Smith heard a *click* as Remo hung up. Smith immediately dialed again into the RV telephone.

"Hi and thanks for calling Sinanju Assassins—"

"Remo, I obviously will get no intelligent response from you, so please give me over to Chiun, who has the decorum and wisdom to answer his Emperor's questions."

"Pretty slick," Remo conceded. Smith thought so, as well, when Chiun barked for the phone. The compliment was just right.

"Good morning, Emperor. I trust you spent a restful evening?"

"It was fine, Master Chiun," Smith said. "I hope your night was restful."

"Considering the tiresome journey and the boorish companionship, it was comfortable enough."

"Both of you are laying it on a little thick, don't you think?" Remo demanded in the background.

"Can you tell me anything about what happened yesterday?" Smith asked.

"Ah. My foolish son insisted on driving across the deserts of California and the Valley of So-Called Death. "

Smith sighed. "I meant at the luge contest."

"A hideous spectacle. It is designed to make the most of the physical unattractiveness of the contestants. They place deformities in the surface of the pavement to vibrate the flabby flesh of the participants!"

"So I understand," Smith said patiently.

"This is then displayed on giant electronic screens to the whoops of the imbeciles in the crowd. When the contest is finished, these are replayed on the same giant screens along with previously filmed contests. If that is not sufficient for the cretins in attendance, the souvenir stands sell vile collections of filmed video contests. Remo purchased one for you."

"Yes," Smith said, struggling to keep the inexorably slow pace Chiun set. "The package was delivered this morning. The delivery fees were charged to CURE."

"He thanks you," Chiun said off the phone.

"Tell Remo it was not necessary to send it by special courier. The cost was enormous."

"Truly, I never estimated how febrile the white mind could become, and yet that vile display was evidence enough," Chiun said in wonderment. "I was repulsed, of course, but fascinated that so many people would flock to such entertainments. Are you certain you wish to rule such a backward people?"

How could Smith answer a question like that? "I take it you found no evidence of foul play?"

"Yes, there were flaws in the craftsmanship of the luges," Chiun said. "It was easy enough to detect."

Smith almost took the phone away from his ear and looked at it. "Master Chiun, I wish you would have reported this immediately."

"None of these luges are built to the standards of the Olympic counterparts, who are foolish enough when competing in their uniforms. But there were some devices that had been purposely engineered to fail."

"I wish you would have sent me one of those devices."

"This we did do, Emperor."

"It wasn't in the package with the DVD," Smith insisted.

"Remo deemed the item was heavy and might be shipped more economically via a standard service."

Smith gripped the phone. Remo's way of goading him. He couldn't allow himself to be goaded.

"May I have the shipping number?"

There was a moment of muffled conversation, after which Chiun informed him delightedly that the tracking number started with the digit 1, and included at least two 7s.

Exasperated, Smith got around to his second important topic. "Chiun, do you have any idea yet what Remo is up to?"

"Vacation!" Remo shouted in the background.

"I have uncovered a clue as to his plans, Emperor," Chiun whispered. "He intends to tour the homes of the stars. I will keep you updated."

Smith heard the phone disconnect, and he unhappily began searching the databases of packages being shipped from the Sedona area of Arizona to Folcroft Sanitarium, and soon found the package of evidence sent by Remo. MARK HOWARD LIMPED into the area outside Dr. Smith's office. "Mrs. Mikulka, are you okay?"

"Yes, Mark," the elderly secretary said with a wan smile. "I just had a little shock this morning."

"Oh?"

"Dr. Smith," she said conspiratorially, "received a very unusual package. It was labeled for general delivery, so I opened it for him. I must say…" She seemed unable to finish.

Mark entered Smith's office, walking slowly. "What's the matter?"

"Remo spent $536 to have this delivered to me by special courier. The evidence? He sent it second-day, economy class."

"What's the DVD?" Mark asked. He looked at the montage of vivid images on the cover and raised his eyebrows. "Ah. Nude luge. One of the Extreme Sports Network's fine productions. I never realized there would be so much blood."

"I think he shocked a year of life out of Mrs. Mikulka," Smith muttered.

12

"You're not going to listen to me, so I'm not going to tell you not to come," Remo explained.

"You're right, Remo, I would not listen. This is disrespectful behavior on your part."

They stepped from the massive, glimmering RV into a cordoned-off corner of the All-Mart parking lot. The manager of the All-Mart gave Chiun a cheery wave that was not returned, then he went back to his team of workers working vigorously on the asphalt with scrub brushes.

"What behavior is that? Keeping secrets?"

"Exactly?"

"I learned it from you."

"Your conspiracy dishonors me, who has given you everything."

They entered a cab and Remo read an address off his crumpled FedEx receipt, which he stuffed back into the pocket of his Chinos. After a silent cab ride, they stepped onto a sidewalk in Hollywood. If Chiun wanted to tag along, Remo was going to take him sight-seeing.

"Little Father, I'm allowed to have some life. I never agreed to being owned—by you or by Smitty. Another point—I'm supposed to be Reigning Master. I'm supposed to be the one calling the shots."

"So the time has come to expose my back to the clumsy knife of the new and swollen-headed Master."

"Come on, Chiun, that's not the way it is. I'm not new. I've had the title for a couple of years now. You can't say I've been throwing my weight around."

Chiun glared at him.

"Maybe a little. But I'm entitled, aren't I?"

"Entitled to betrayal?"

"Entitled to actually use some of the authority I'm supposed to have? Entitled to being ticked off at being treated like CURE's stupid grunt?"

Chiun looked away. "This is a filthy city."

"You say that about every city."

"Every city in this land is filthy."

"Compared to Sinanju? At least we're not wading in mud and smelling the fish rotting."

"SMITH," Winner declared.

Smith orchestrated the lies. Smith lived in a world of clandestine operations. He lived in a shadow world.

Once, Winner dwelled in the shadow world himself, but he was a soldier then. A doer. Smith—the Smith who was responsible for the device—was never a doer. He was a watcher, a thinker, a voyeur who issued orders. Somebody, who didn't even know who Smith was, followed the orders. They deployed the device—and it wasn't the first such device.

Winner watched this one through the gap in the rock. This one was better than the first one. Some sort of an airship based on a weather-balloon design. It was a translucent blue that should have camouflaged it against the clear skies of Arizona. There was a small electronic pod dangling beneath, with steel claws for gripping.

It wasn't all that sophisticated, really. Near silent compressed-air canisters jetted it along on a plotted course to whatever target could be reached with the prevailing air currents. The electronics inside would be expensive and the plastic shell would be some sort of military-grade armor.

The first device was air-dropped in the middle of the night onto a rocky hillock well outside of the village. The desert-colored electronic device had righted itself and started listening to the goings-on in the Sun On Jo village.

It didn't listen long. Smith underestimated Winner and the entire village. Never mind that they used stealth aircraft to deploy the device; they woke everybody up. Winner sprinted in a big circle, came up behind the device and stepped on it.

This new device, he noticed, had video pickups all around it. No sneaking up on this one. That didn't matter. Winner wasn't even going to let it get into position.

He grabbed a rock, tossed it lightly in his hand to get a feel for its weight, then leaned around the hilltop and delivered the rock at the dangling plastic device.

It sensed him instantly and began to program evasive maneuvers, releasing compressed gas from its jets as the rock slammed into the plastic shell. The ceramic-reinforced carbon-fiber shell fell into the desert in little pieces.

The thing was designed for a direct hit, and the electronics inside were exposed but still intact. The airship was making a valiant attempt at escape.

Winner tossed the beer can next. The can hit the device and burst open. The device did the same thing that any cheap boom box would do with beer spilled into its guts—it stopped working forever.

SMITH SAW it happen, as well as could be expected. The eavesdropping pod's video pickups weren't the best, but they caught a ten-frame-a-second video of something colorful that homed in on the pod and drenched it in liquid. The final image, just prior to the impact, had a corner of the label in focus.

"O'Doules," Smith deciphered. He tapped out the name. The response told Smith that it was an internationally marketed brand of nonalcoholic brew.

Ironic that a half-million-dollar Department of Homeland Security long-range eavesdropping device had just been ruined with nonalcoholic beer. Smith couldn't even have the man responsible arrested for possessing alcohol on a dry reservation.

The image flickered and the command window showed the failure of the systems. Just before the signal itself stopped coming from the airship there was a dramatic drop in the altitude indicator. The DOHS device went down. Smith didn't delude himself into thinking that there would be anything to salvage.

The head of CURE was so frugal he was known to reuse adhesive tape, yet he had wasted a million dollars in U.S. spy technology in under twenty-four hours.

He got to his feet, opened the door to his office and sat again, preoccupied to the point he failed to notice the young man who was standing in the doorway expectantly.

"Dr. Smith? Can I come back in?"

"Sorry. I've finished."

Mark Howard limped to the oddly situated second desk. He had been ordered specifically not to ask or seek information about Smith's activities. That worried Mark. Dr. Smith didn't keep things from his assistant. Smith trusted Howard; the simple and irrefutable reality was that if Smith didn't trust Mark, Mark would be gone. Probably for all eternity.

So what was Smith keeping from Mark now? And why?

Two options presented themselves. One had to do with the current open wound in CURE security—Remo's family and the tribe at the Sun On Jo reservation in Arizona. Smith would want to know exactly what the Sun On Jo knew. He would protect Mark from these investigative activities because they could have fatal repercussions. Remo wouldn't be happy....

But Smith had to know. In some ways, Mark was surprised that Smith had kept CURE going with all the loose ends in the once airtight security wall.

That led his thoughts inexorably to the second target of Smith's secret activities. Sarah Slate. She knew about the Masters of Sinanju, and that knowledge led her to deduce the nature of CURE, and that made her a grave risk.

Mark hoped Smith would agree to his plan to mitigate that risk.

But Mark loved Sarah Slate, and Smith knew it, and if he was planning on taking unpleasant measures, he would certainly not have involved Mark.

It made him feel sick for a moment, but he didn't believe that was happening. Sarah had become precious to, of all people, Chiun. Harming Sarah would invite Chiun's wrath.

Chiun killed hotel bellboys who interrupted his TV shows. God only knew what would happen if he became truly enraged. He pictured Chiun exacting his revenge on Smith—for starters. Next he would likely move on to the White House. The President and his staff would be wiped out in minutes. Where would the old Master go from there? Whoever he saw as most closely connected to the President. Not Congress. Probably the military. The Joint Heads of Staff, maybe, annihilated.

Mark was probably exaggerating the scenario in his head, but the truth was that a wrathful Chiun just might take such extreme measures. Smith understood that. Smith wouldn't risk the stability of the nation over Sarah Slate.

Somehow, that made Mark feel much better.

13

Winner Smith ignored his sister when he came back into the small village, and as usual that lasted for maybe two or three minutes.

"I'm not leaving your side until I know what's going on," she explained simply as they entered the home of Sunny Joe Roam, their biological grandfather. Sunny Joe looked up from the week-old *Yuma Observer.*

"I'm going to my room," Winner stated, but a door couldn't be closed fast enough to keep out Freya. There was shouting.

"I'm getting my own house," Winner stated as he came out again.

Sunny Joe shrugged. "If you think it will help."

Freya gave him a confident smile. "It won't help, Win."

"I'm getting my own house in Ulan Bator."

"It won't help, boy," Sunny Joe said.

Winner knew that it was the truth, but the truth made him even more frustrated. He started walking. Out the door, out of the village again, into the desert.

"This won't help, either," Freya said, keeping up without trouble and as unfazed as if they were taking an afternoon stroll. Both of them were at home in the desert of Arizona.

"That pisses me off."

Freya looked at him sidelong. And she smiled. She was beautiful. Even Winner knew she was beautiful. Their blood ties precluded him from feeling the same way about her as other men felt....

"You know what ticks me off even more? Say some day you do get hooked up with some guy, what then? I'm still screwed. Because no matter how good he is, I still have to keep an eye on you. And you're still going to be insinuating yourself."

"Maybe I'll marry a man from Ulan Bator."

Winner laughed harshly. "It won't help, Freya," he said, mocking his own helplessness. "Somehow, you'll still be a pest. I'm not sure how you'll do it, but you'll find a way."

Freya considered it. "Who was it that sent the thing to spy on us?"

Winner didn't answer that.

"It was people working for Daddy or against Daddy," she continued. "Tell me that much at least."

"For," Winner admitted.

"Smith. The unhealthy old man who talks to Daddy on the phone. Is he the boss or is Junior the boss?"

Dammit. She basically knew everything, didn't she?

"Junior?" Winner laughed. "He's just some gofer. Smith sent him out here because Remo wouldn't return his phone calls. Hey, maybe you ought to marry Junior. Did you see the way he lost his marbles when he spotted you?"

"No," Freya said, but her face pinkened.

"Liar." Not too long before, Remo had been spending time in the reservation when various efforts were made to communicate with him. Mysterious phone calls began coming in to the reservation from callers who refused to identify themselves. Not that Winner Smith didn't know the voice of Harold W. Smith.

Remo didn't want to talk to Smith, and his continued refusal to communicate had finally required Smith to send his assistant out to the reservation to fetch their father. The man was the infamous Junior—known to the Sunny Joe Roam household as the Smith sidekick whenever Remo called the office.

Junior, whose name turned out to be Mark, had taken the scenic route from Yuma to the reservation. No stranger to the desert was capable of following the unmarked and unimproved system of roads that led to the reservation without wandering around the vast wasteland for hours at a time. That's what the Sun On Joe people called the scenic route. Mark had gone only four hours out of his way, which wasn't bad, actually.

When he had convinced Remo Williams to depart with him in the middle of the night, Freya had come to the door of Sunny Joe Roam's house to say goodbye. "You could see Junior's IQ go down ten points every second he stood there looking at you."

"Thanks for letting some guy check me out, big brother." She was on the defensive.

"He wasn't even really checking you out," Winner said. "I mean, he couldn't even see you. I think it was love at first sight."

"Get off it."

"I mean it."

They walked in silence for another twenty minutes, the village receding behind them. "Would it make you worry less if I married Junior?" she asked finally, but there was no playfulness in her voice.

"Maybe," Winner admitted.

"Would that stop them from trying to spy on us?"

"I don't know. I don't know what they're after."

"Whatever they're after, Win, I can deal with it."

Winner swallowed. He wasn't thirsty, but there was something painful in his throat. "Maybe not."

Freya said, "Sure, I can."

"Freya, maybe not. You don't know what these men can do. There's nothing more ruthless than intelligence assholes with power and too much self-importance. Whatever you've been through and no matter how good you are, you don't know these people."

Freya rolled her eyes. "Where've I heard that before."

Winner stopped and took her hand, and the young woman with the golden hair couldn't remember him ever doing anything like that before. He looked afraid.

"Remo knows and I know. You trust the world more than you should, and that might get you in trouble. That's a good reason to protect you from Remo's boss. All I'm asking is that you be a little more careful and let me be your big brother."

When they started walking again, Freya looked at the horizon and picked up the pace. Winner squinted and finally saw the tiny splotches of darkness swimming out of the heat waves a few miles ahead. The desert sped beneath their feet until they reached a small band of dying immigrants.

There were twenty of them, who had gotten this far into United States despite the enhanced security systems designed to keep illegal aliens from making the dangerous crossing. There were always people desperate and foolish enough to make the attempts. There were always men heartless enough to take their money and lead the way. It wasn't unusual for the band of aliens to be abandoned halfway through the march by their guides, who would leave them to die or find their own way.

Freya trickled water onto the broken lips of the men and women. She never came into the desert without a canteen and a mobile phone. They stayed with the band of aliens until help was due to arrive. A small train of ambulance SUVs raised a dust cloud in the slanting shadows of the late-afternoon sun, never noticing the pair that strolled casually away from the scene.

"You're going to get a reputation," Winner told Freya. "The golden-haired American Indian angel who comes out of the desert to save the dying people."

"There are worse things," Freya said.

"Let's go find the guys who left them here," Winner said. "INS'll never track them down."

"And do what, arrest them? No, thanks."

"So we don't arrest them."

Winner felt something as hard as polished wood clamp onto his elbow. Freya held his arm and shook her head tightly, and for the first time in years Winner saw the old haunted glimmer in her eyes.

"No. Don't even say it."

She released him, and Winner nodded, mesmerized

by the small and flickering light that he had thought was long gone, like a spark of alien life living inside the once-troubled soul of Freya of Lakluun.

14

Chiun was on his mat in the middle of a circular meditation chamber, which was raised a step above the rest of the Airstream's remodeled interior. The rattan blinds were slanted on the 180-degree picture windows behind him. The smog-filtered sunlight cast a filmy backlight on the ancient Master, making his yellowing tufts of hair look dingy.

"You thought to elude me, Remo Williams, Master of Backstabbing and all the Betraying Arts?"

"Hey, you told me to wait outside while you went into the gift shop. I stood there for an hour then went in to look for you."

"You were gone when I returned. I suppose it was inevitable that I be discarded. It is the way of Americans, is it not? Once an item is no longer new, once it shows a hint of age, into the trash pile it is tossed. The whole Western world has become a disposable culture. Use a thing, then put it in the waste bin. But I had thought you would have at least had the decency to tell me to my face, Remo Williams."

"Tell you what?"

"That you were casting me off, of course. Even the

foul natives of the North of America have the decency to face their grandfathers when they abandon them on the iceberg."

"You left me and I came straight back to the Sinanju-mobile. You were obviously way ahead of me."

"Remo, I have been way ahead of you always, since the moment of our first, infamous meeting. Therefore I know full well the depths of your perfidy."

"Whatever." Remo sighed and lowered on scissored legs onto the second mat. Chiun had generously un-rolled it for Remo in their meditation chamber. Remo shoved a hand in his pocket and wriggled out his mangled FedEx bill, along with a shiny ballpoint pen.

"From whom did you pilfer that trinket?" Chiun demanded.

"Gift. Supposed to be worth a lot."

Chiun snatched the pen from Remo's hand. "It is gold."

"I can tell gold when I see it. That was the first question on the written exam at the Rite of Attainment, wasn't it?"

"What quality of gold?" Chiun quizzed.

"Fourteen carat. I know it's not pure, but it's meant to actually be used and that's what I'd like to do with it now. Use it." Remo held out his hand.

"It is French!"

"Like it or not, they make expensive pens in France. Can I please have it?"

Chiun glowered at the inscription on the pen and threw it with the force of a crossbow. Anyone other than Remo would have been lobotomized, but he caught it before it impaled his forehead and used it to pore over the notes on the back of his FedEx receipt. He kept the paper held up so Chiun could not see it.

"Will you tell me now the nature of your prostitution to the Hollywood filth peddlers?"

"Maybe I'm having my biography produced for the big screen."

"The emblem on the pen belongs not to a film producer, but to a famously disreputable television trashmonger. This would be the appropriate media for the telling of the life of the pale piece of a pig's ear that calls himself Master of Sinanju—even as he turns his back on the Master's duties to which he is obligated."

Remo got the drift of the conversation. "Did Smitty call with more busywork?"

"You care not," Chiun sniffed. "Suffice it to say, I am taking my leave again shortly to attempt to discharge the duties you refuse to perform."

"After all the progress you've made getting our parking lot shipshape, now you're leaving?"

"I am not leaving the city. I shall simply drag my weary bones to a local venue to witness another display of American tastelessness. If your new patrons at the studio wish to provide you with females, I will not be here to dampen the mood for your rutting."

"Sorry to hear that."

Chiun scowled fiercely. "Perhaps I should use your cheap trinket to ink myself with this location. In this way, you can be notified by the authorities if I should meet with foul play."

"If you meet with foul play, the foul players are going to be the ones needing help."

"I shall add the message, 'Do not resuscitate.' If I am

fortunate enough to be struck down, death would be a blessing compared to this daily shame and dishonor."

Remo sighed loudly. "How about I just go with you, Little Father?"

Chiun stood up in a smooth motion. "The cab is waiting."

15

Anga Meridorsku was as tough as they came, but at the moment she didn't feel so tough. She felt as if she had a bowling ball wedged in her intestines.

But the show had to go on, so she left her private dressing room in her stocking feet.

"Anga, thank God! We've only got fifteen minutes to suit up!" Her manager ushered her nervously into the box, giving her a whispered command. "Don't let them see you sick—show your stuff."

Anga was a pro and she was desperate. Her career was on the brink, and her options were limited. What happened today could make her or break her.

"And here's Angry Anga Meridorsku," sang the announcer, a suntanned man in a dark suit. He stood in the middle of the polished ice in the glow of a spotlight. The crowd cheered and hooted and booed Anga, but she ignored them as the Waifs began prepping her.

"I guess Angry Anga wanted to make an entrance. Better late than never, Anga."

More cheers and boos from the audience in response to the signs overhead: Applause and Boo. As the announcer moved on to insult the other skaters, Anga allowed her digestive turmoil to show in her face. The cameras would be filming her every second, but she was supposed to be angry after all.

Her prep crew was doing their thing—carefully padding her legs, slowly wrapping her ankles in flesh-colored elastic. Her prep crew consisted of four small women, ex-cheerleaders and part-time porn stars, chosen for their small size to accentuate Anga's powerful proportions. They were unnecessarily touchy-feely as they helped Anga don her gear. They thrust out their bottoms with unnecessary frequency as they knotted her leather sports bra and tied Anga's ice skates. The Waifs were just a part of the show.

Anga was the reason the Waifs were here, and if Anga screwed it up today, she and the Waifs would all be out of a job. Gad, with this knot in her gut she felt she could barely skate, let alone compete.

It was going to be brutal out there today. Anga opened her mouth, and one of the Waifs put the flag between her teeth.

When the bell rang, the doors of each staging box jumped open like the starting gates at a horse race. Hands on Anga's powerful, leather-clad butt cheeks, the Waifs propelled her onto the ice. Eleven other competitors were ejected from their own boxes.

"And now, ladies, skate like hell!" the announcer thundered.

The announcer was yanked skyward out of the rink on bungee cords and the competitors collided brutally together where he had been standing. The competition was simple: the last skater with a flag still in her teeth was the winner.

The reality was more complicated. Anga muscled through the opening crash of bodies and lunged at the nearest competitor, who dodged, ducked and turned on Anga with a lithe grab. Anga jerked her head away, grabbed the woman's arm and yanked her off her feet. It was that platinum South Carolina priss. She'd actually been a legitimate skater once—an Olympic contender. She tested positive once too often, and now she could only skate in the Extreme Skating League. Anga snatched the dangling pink nylon out of her teeth so fast it cut her lip.

"This ain't the Olympics, is it, pretty priss?" Anga shouted, shoving the flag into her cleavage. The crowd roared with approval.

The music was something classical. The audience loved it when they used the classical symphony crap just like at the traditional figure skating events. Anga skated fast at her next victim, who turned on her to meet the onslaught—and then the tremor struck.

The ice rink vibrated with sudden thunder. The ice heaved and buckled. The crowd cheered wildly. Anga's opponent waved her arms for balance even as Anga slammed into her and grabbed the nylon flag from her mouth. The woman's body flopped onto the ice and spun away, and Anga had the flag in her hand.

"Who's next?" she shouted through the flag in her teeth. The crowd cheered and stomped their feet. Anga felt stupid saying it, but her agent said it was her signature.

The truth was she felt less confident than she sounded. It was hard to kick ass when you were this constipated. But kick ass was what she had better do.

The first tremor died down, but there would be others, coming at computer-randomized intervals. The field of competitors was already down from twelve to three, and now it was time for a gang bang. Any time two or more competitors teamed up temporarily to take on another competitor it was a gang bang. Today, Anga was the target.

Anga didn't handle gang bangs as well as she should. That's why her star was slipping. That's why she'd failed to win a match in more than five weeks. She had to prove her worth, right here, right now. All at once she knew it was her moment of truth.

She skated right at the two attackers and double feinted, fooling the woman on the left completely. Anga shouldered into her just as the next tremor shook the ice. The crowd went nuts. The ice cracked underneath their feet, and Anga went down hard on top of her opponent.

The woman's knee pounded into her gut, and Anga felt a cannonball of pain, but she channeled it into action. She slammed the heel of her palm into the woman's chin, then snatched at the flag. Teeth chips came out with it.

The crowd saw it all on the big screen and erupted happily. Anga glimpsed her last opponent skating at her hard, coming in for the kill, and Anga did a logroll. She pushed herself to her feet with a muffled shout and saw her attacker bearing down on her. Anga dropped low again and her attacker tripped over her, crashing heavily to the ice. Anga skated powerfully after her, but the next tremor hit at that moment. It was a big one. The ice shaker was up to its highest setting. Huge portions of the ice rink shattered to powder or buckled like broken sidewalks. Anga put on the brakes, but not before a crack in the ice snagged one of her skate blades and sent her crashing down.

Somehow her opponent had used the opportunity to get back to her feet. The green-flag bitch was coming right at her, and Anga's heavy abdomen felt ready to explode. She propped herself up on her arms and tried to stand but her leg gave way and she was totally helpless.

But then, just as disaster seemed unavoidable, the tide turned again. The green-flag skater made a shocked face, and Anga saw the woman's skate blades sink into the ice as if they were red-hot. She didn't have time to think about why.

The woman's skate locked up in the ice, and she flopped onto her face. Anga leaped off the ice like a frog and grabbed the dangling green flag. The woman grabbed the flag herself and attempted to wriggle away, but Anga shoved herself into the air and down again—a classic body slam. The green-flag woman opened her mouth reflexively, her breath left her with an ugly sound and Anga had the green flag.

She had won. The green-flag woman was hacking and gasping, and the woman with the shattered teeth was crawling off the ice with a trail of blood behind her. The crowd was ecstatic.

Anga barely noticed it. Her gut was gonna erupt any second. As she skated to her box, she saw her manager waving frantically. It was the hand signal indicating she should do the line.

Anga stopped on the ice. Her sickness looked like disdain and toughness to the crowd and to the cameras. She sneered at everyone and everything around her.

Only she knew it was to keep her from being violently ill right then and there. She stared at the nearest camera and bellowed, "Who's next?"

The crowd loved it.

"I GUESS you're a star," the man in the dressing room said. Under other circumstances Anga might have been interested.

"I don't care who you are or what you're doing here, just don't stand between me and the john."

"Not so fast," the man with the dark eyes said, stepping between her and the door to the washroom. "We wanted to ask you about the meet."

"We?" Then, for the first time, Anga noticed the small Asian man against the wall in a robe of some kind. The old Asian regarded her as he might regard something spoiled in the refrigerator.

"How did you manage to win out there?" the younger one asked.

"I won because I'm the best," Anga snapped.

"No, that's not it."

"Get out!"

"There were ice-skating blades getting hot all over the place. A little here, a little there, just to throw off the balance or slow somebody. Then at the end there, that last lady got the full treatment. The ice melted right out from under her and tripped her up. How did that happen?"

"You're lying," Anga snapped.

"So you don't know anything about it?"

"It didn't happen," she insisted.

Anga was in too much gastrointestinal distress to lie

effectively. She really didn't know about the sabotage on the ice. Remo allowed her to push past him and beeline for the lavatory. He and Chiun slipped out in a hurry and made their way to the Anga Meridorsku team equipment locker, where the Waifs were storing away equipment for the next day's event.

The four of them were cast from the same mold, all tiny and wiry, and on the verge of being attractive when not snarling, which was seldom.

"Congratulations," Remo said by way of greeting. "How'd you trip up the competition?"

The smallest Waif tossed a metal box into a steel storage cabinet. The sound was loud and grating and Remo smiled, ingratiating. She took up a position in front of them, arms folded, snarl growing more intense. "What did you say?" she demanded.

"Just wondering how you did the little trick with the hot skates. I have to hand it to you—it worked great. The lady from the Irish team went in up to her knees. She never knew what hit her."

"You saying we cheated, pretty boy?"

Remo was wearing his happy face. People who snarled, he knew, became very agitated around smiling happy people. "And you did it well," he added generously. He held one flat hand over Chiun's head, then moved it over the Waif's head. "Hey, Chiun, she's actually shorter than you."

"I'm big enough," the Waif challenged with a ring of invitation. She tucked a lock of dark hair behind her ear and cocked her hip. "We didn't cheat, pretty boy. Anga won fair and square."

"That's right," the others answered in chorus. They

had taken up battle ranks behind their leader. "We don't like people who accuse us of cheating," a willowy blonde added.

"You know what we do to people who tick us off?" added an Egyptian girl with stick arms.

"Hey, I guess I was wrong," Remo said, convinced of their sincerity. "Sorry for the inconvenience."

"You're not getting off that easy." A wispy black girl slipped behind them and guarded the door.

"Remo, stop playing," Chiun complained.

"This is your assignment, not mine. You handle it."

"Grandpa can go," the leader announced. "Our beef is with you, pretty boy." She yanked off her halter top with a flourish. The other Waifs followed suit.

Chiun colored crimson and stomped his foot as he barked, "Remo, come!" He turned in a whirl of skirts and swept aside the now topless door guard. She spun into the others and bowled them over.

Remo paused outside the door long enough to grab a photographer from *Extreme Women of Skating* magazine. "You want to triple your circulation next month?" he asked, and pushed the photographer in the direction of the open door. He whooped at the vision of the famous Waifs in a topless tangle.

"That's a cover shot!" the photographer exclaimed. The bursts of his flash punctuated the threats of the Waifs. "That's a centerfold!"

Chiun was boiling. "Such women are hideous, Remo. Tell me you would never stoop to rutting such a creature."

"I thought the dark-haired one was kind of cute, in a praying-mantis kind of way," Remo observed.

"But coarse, and not at all feminine."

"On the other hand, they're nothing like the big-boobed bimbos that you're always complaining about, Chiun."

"They have their own faults."

"You haven't approved of any woman I ever showed an interest in. So I guess I should let you pick my women. Which means I would end up with some mud-wallowing Korean teenager with good teeth and hips as big as a tool shed."

The photographer sprinted past them and waved his camera. "I owe you big-time, buddy!" he shouted, and slammed the exit door as the Waifs, in hastily donned jerseys, scampered after him and screeched for his blood.

"They do look like they were made out of wire and kindling," Remo admitted. "I promise, no waifs."

Chiun shook his head sadly. "That still leaves much room for error."

"You want me to say 'no wives,' right?"

"Of course you should take a wife—one that is appropriate. The sooner you do so, the sooner you will sire a suitable trainee, and then I may finally retire."

"You want to retire like I want to sire a litter with the dog-faced women you call 'appropriate.'"

"Bigotry is ugly, Remo," Chiun sniffed.

"I'm not a bigot. I like lots of Korean women. But the Sinanju purebreds you want me to shack up with? Pee-yew."

Chiun sighed. "Then I must resign myself to more years of toil and labor. Oh, when will my aching bones be allowed to rest? Must I wait for the comfort of the grave?"

"Speaking of pee-yew, you know what's kind of familiar about this whole thing?" Remo stopped, looking back at the stadium.

"I know of many things, but I'm certain you have an idea that is quite unique."

"Digestive disorders," Remo declared.

"Very unique indeed."

"No, think about it. The winner of the Nude Luge had all kinds of noisy things going on in his lower guts. And the skater winner couldn't wait to get to the crapper."

"I do not wish to discuss this," Chiun snapped.

"But it's weird, isn't it, that both of them had the same problem? What if they were taking some sort of performance-enhancing drug that happened to have intestinal side effects?"

"We would have sensed it," Chiun argued. "Now the subject is closed."

"Maybe we would have sensed it, maybe not. But there's another reason that doesn't make sense—both of them won because of obvious sabotage. So why go to the extra trouble of drugging up the competitors?"

"Yes. Why? And why are we still discussing it? Next you will want to have a long conversation about their nasal secretions."

"You have to admit it's a weird coincidence, Chiun," Remo said.

"Weird enough to fascinate a mind which has matured little since his days of puberty and carpenter worship."

Remo shut up, but he was thinking about his problem all the way back to the RV.

Where the telephone message light was blinking.

16

Mrs. Mikulka took the call as she was straightening her immaculate desk before leaving. She left earlier these days.

"Hi Mrs. M. It's Romeo."

"Yes?"

"You know, dark hair, snappy dresser, hangs around with the old Asian fella?"

"Oh, hello, Romeo, how are you?" Mrs. Mikulka sounded sunnier than she felt. She knew Romeo, of course. He had been around forever, although she was never sure exactly why, and Dr. Smith never offered an explanation. Mrs. Mikulka had finally decided that the old Chinese gentleman might even be the owner of Folcroft Sanitarium and the young man was his servant. How else could they gain unrestricted access, even to Dr. Smith's office?

"I'll put you through to Dr. Smith right away, Romeo."

"No, thanks. I'd like to leave him a message. Would you take him a note, please?"

"But he's in his office."

"Can't explain, Mrs. M. Be a dear."

"Certainly, if that's what you would like. Go ahead." She held a pen over her generic Folcroft Sanitarium memo pad—Dr. Smith didn't believe in spending a premium for personalized stationery.

"Here goes. 'Dr. S—no more blimps.'" A moment later he added, "Still with me, Mrs. M?"

"Yes, Romeo. Did I hear you correctly? You said—"

"You heard me correctly Mrs. M. It's sort of a business code."

Mrs. Mikulka doubted that. This call was most unusual. "Do you wish to add a closing salutation? 'Regards' or 'Sincerely'?"

"Hmm. Yes." He gave her the closing salutation he wanted her to use. "That's more business code," the young man explained. "Thanks, Mrs. M!"

Mrs. Mikulka had never heard such gibberish in her life, but she was only the messenger. She knocked on the doctor's office door and entered. Dr. Smith looked surprised to see her.

He took the note and became visibly agitated.

"I'm sorry I did not know his last name," Mrs. Mikulka said. "I seem to have forgotten it. But how many Romeos would you know? Also, he said you would know the code word at the bottom. She pointed one wrinkly finger at the closing acronym "USOB."

"Yes, thank you, Mrs. Mikulka. I understand it perfectly."

Mrs. Mikulka bade the doctor and Mark Howard good-night and left. Mark waited expectantly for Smith to explain himself.

"I'm keeping this to myself, Mark," Smith said. "Please don't ask questions."

Mark Howard didn't ask him, although Harold Smith was sure the young man knew what was going on. Mark would have guessed that Smith was doing some sort of intelligence gathering on the Sun On Jo reservation. The reference to a blimp in the message would have assuaged any doubts. What better to perform close-proximity surveillance in the predictable climate of the Arizona desert?

Smith also knew that Mark knew why he was being kept in the dark about it. It was because of the possible consequences of such surveillance. Remo Williams or even Master Chiun might take this violation of the reservation's privacy very personally—and Smith did not want them to have any other target for the wrath other than himself.

But Smith had to know what the Sun On Jo knew.

Still, the threat from Remo was blatant enough. He was promising to make Smith's worst nightmare a reality—exposing CURE. Mrs. Mikulka was just a first step.

Would Remo really do it? After all, Smith wasn't really interfering with the Sun On Jo people, simply monitoring them. While the CURE contract with the Masters did have a family immunity clause, nothing in the contract stipulated he would not perform surveillance on any and all blood relatives of the aforementioned Masters of Sinanju.

Not that it mattered. Remo would be extremely angry if Smith persisted. Even sweet old Mrs. Mikulka could have figured out the meaning of "USOB" if she thought about it.

Smith couldn't *not* persist. The Sun On Jo knew something; he had to know what they knew.

Maybe, just maybe, they knew even more than Smith about some things....

17

Colonel Simonec did the unthinkable. He called Washington.

"Better have a hell of a good reason for getting me out of bed," General Elsey said.

"I just need a confirmation on this order, General," he explained. "It's another request for a USSA."

"So?"

"General, we've had two requests for Unmanned Stealth Surveillance Airships. Both times we had control of the airships absconded by other authority, and both times the equipment was lost. Now there's another request, only this time they want the Big Ear."

"I see," the general in Washington said. The Big Ear was the best USSA in the surveillance arsenal at the Department of Homeland Security Technology Development station on the military base in Yuma.

"The orders come through the correct channels?" the general demanded.

"Of course, sir," Colonel Simonec said. "General Smith signed them. He's got priority override clearance."

"But?"

"General, I'm throwing away the biggest piece of equipment I've got. It's as good as lost if I follow these orders, and quite frankly, I don't have anything else in the garage that's worth spit. Just a bunch of those partially functional recovered prototypes."

The general in Washington sighed. "Let me see what this is all about, Alf."

Colonel Simonec hung up and waited. He didn't wait long.

"Colonel Simonec, this is General Elsey." Suddenly the general in Washington had gone totally military on him.

"Yes, General Elsey?"

"You will follow your orders as specified."

"But, General Elsey, I won't have any equipment left," Simonec whined.

"Follow your orders," General Elsey repeated firmly.

Simonec hung up and grumbled. "Follow orders. Follow orders. Cut your own neck, Simonec. Might as well cut my own nuts off, too. I'll be sitting here with nothing."

He returned to the operations room, where the small overnight rotation was waiting expectantly.

"We gotta give them the Big Ear," Simonec complained.

His operations team groaned. "We'll be defunct. We'll be sitting here with our thumbs up our butts."

"You think I don't know that? I'm gonna take the heat for it, too, so you grunts are getting off easy. Now give them the Big Ear. Maybe this time it will actually come back to us."

Colonel Simonec bristled at the laughter from his

underlings. Maybe he'd take up disciplinary actions to fill the long hours ahead of him.

THE NEW DOHS HANGAR at Yuma operated behind a privacy fence almost twenty feet high, which was a joke. You had to be deaf and blind not to see the airships that launched from there night after night.

Tonight, the black blob that floated gracefully from the hangar was the biggest black blob of them all. It moved faster than the others. It was absolutely silent. Nobody on the night watch failed to witness the black stain blot out the sky. Officially, of course, nobody saw anything.

DAWN IN ARIZONA WAS breathtaking. The Sun On Jo reservation, a hundred miles south of everywhere, was surrounded by desert that a white man would have called desolate. Sunny Joe Roam was not a white man, and when he looked at the land awakening to the sun he saw nothing but beauty.

Until he saw the wreckage.

It was larger than the other wrecks, and spread widely in an almost perfect circle.

"Winner. Boy."

Sunny Joe's grandson was helping to rebuild a hogan wall that had collapsed. They just didn't build hogans like they used to, Sunny Joe thought. Then he recalled that he helped build that wall the first time, when he was around about fifteen.

"Coming," Winner said, but Winner didn't come for some ten minutes. That's how long it took for them to settle the next log into place. Sunny Joe didn't grow impatient. Reservation time didn't pass the way white-man time passed, and the reservation was a better place because of it. But Sunny Joe was wondering why Winner didn't have his own reasons for hurrying himself up there. After all, he had to know what Sunny Joe wanted him for. Didn't he?

"Son of a bitch," Winner said when he came to Sunny Joe's side and spotted the distant wreckage.

"I thought you brought it down, boy. I was going to chew you a new one." Sunny Joe knew Winner well enough. Winner wasn't a liar. He acted however he pleased to act and always took responsibility for it.

"This is bad news, Sunny Joe," Winner said. "Smith's ignoring Remo's warning."

"He must think we got something important up our sleeves, but what in the world could it be?" Sunny Joe asked as they strolled swiftly to the crash site.

"Whatever it is, it's important enough to waste bigger and better spy drones on. I didn't hear this one. Didn't even hear it hit the ground."

They stood in the circle of destruction. The curved, blackened plate that rested on the earth at the center of the circle looked intact, but every other component was in fragments.

"That's why," Winner said. "It didn't crash hard. No crater. It touched down then burned itself to pieces. I guess the Sun On Jo engineers will never figure out its military secrets now."

"Guess not," Sunny Joe agreed seriously. "So why did it come down? Was it one of them throwaways?"

"No. Just the opposite, I think," Winner said as he picked through the slivers of chips and circuit boards.

Sunny Joe Roam didn't touch the stuff. It wouldn't tell him anything. What he knew about technology was limited to stunt-man devices used during his years as a Hollywood daredevil. What he would have liked to know right about now was why the thing crashed, if Winner didn't crash it. Of course, he thought with a wry grimace, who else could have crashed it besides Winner and himself?

Something gold glinted in the morning sun. The two men waited for Freya to reach them, and only Winner shifted his stance impatiently.

"My ears were burning," Freya announced.

"We were just about to start talking about you," Sunny Joe confirmed. "What'd you do here, little daughter?"

She pulled a long folded strip of leather from the back pocket of her jeans and allowed it to fall open. It was a sling.

"I hit it with a rock," she explained.

"Freya, I asked you to stay away from those things," Winner said. "You don't know what this man is capable of. He's a murderer. He'll order your execution with a phone call, just like he orders these things sent out to spy on us."

"I can protect myself."

"Not against this man. If he thinks you're a threat, who knows what he'll do?"

When they reached the village again, the work on the hogan was at a halt and the meager population of the village was gathering. They knew about the latest spy device. They didn't understand it, and that made them afraid.

Sunny Joe Roam didn't like having fear brought to his people.

When Sunny Joe had come back to the reservation years ago he found his people on the verge of extinction. A disease had killed off many of them, and there were no children. Any old man, especially an old Sunny Joe, needed to hear the laughter of children—it was the sound of life. When the plague was eradicated, Sunny Joe encouraged his people to bring new life into the reservation. There were new wives, many of them wooed on the Navajo reservation up north, and now there was the sound of children.

Sunny Joe Roam never wanted to feel the fear and the hopelessness that had sickened the air of the reservation once, not too long ago. He would not allow it.

"Sunny Joe, why's this being done to us?" one of his old friends asked.

"You hold your tongue for a little while, Horse Mouth. I'm going to see about something I can do."

"Sunny Joe," Horse Mouth said more quietly, "does somebody mean us harm?"

Sunny Joe couldn't answer that question, and everybody just got more scared.

THE BLUE PHONE RANG. Smith took it, expecting Chiun.

It wasn't Chiun.

"Hello, Dr. Harold W. Smith of Folcroft Sanitarium in Rye, New York, who is also the head honcho of a supersecret government agency called CURE."

Smith felt his heart leap into his throat. "Remo, what are you doing?"

"Yes, it is me, Remo Williams, a former New Jersey

policeman who was framed for a murder he did not commit, then drafted into the organization called CURE. What I am doing is trying out my new cell phone. It seems to be working pretty well."

"Where are you?"

"Where am I, Dr. Harold Winston Smith of Rye, New York? I am in Hollywood on the Walk of Fame. I came here to perform some vandalism. It's just one of the ways I'm taking out my anger. Guess who I am angry at, Dr. Harold W. Smith?"

"Are there people around?"

"Lots of people. Here's someone now. What's your name, honey? Travistah? Nice name. Nice outfit. I'm talking to my friend Harold in Rye, New York. He's with CURE. What? Quite a bargain, but no thanks."

Smith wanted to hang up, but was certain that would make things worse, not better. "Travistah left. She wanted me to give her money to keep talking to her, Dr. Harold W. Smith," Remo explained. His voice was modulated to carry far. "So, anyway, I thought I would give you a call and talk about how angry I am. I hope it doesn't bother you if all these people listen in."

"This is ludicrous, Remo," Smith said, for want of something better to say.

"Ludicrous? Naw, I'll tell you what's ludicrous— Alan Hale Sr. gets a star on the walk of fame, but Alan Hale Jr.? Nowhere to be found. They snubbed the Skipper and that's just wrong."

Was this relevant? Smith couldn't recall Alan Hale Jr. In what films was he the leading man? How did it have a bearing on any of this?

"Another thing that's just wrong is you spying on my

family. I thought I made that clear. Or did Mrs. M mix up the message?"

"She delivered the message. I chose to ignore it."

"Hold on." Remo lowered the phone, but Smith could still hear every word perfectly. "Hi, Officer. Sorry for being so loud. I'm talking to a very old man who doesn't listen well. Maybe you've heard of him, Dr. Harold Winston Smith of Rye, New York? He pretends to be the man in charge of Folcroft Sanitarium, but really he's the head of this assassination arm of the U.S. government called CURE. Okay, I'll try to keep it down." Remo came back on the line. "Cop thought I was bonkers. Okay, he's gone now. As I was saying..."

"You don't need to continue this," Smith said.

"Don't sweat it. Nobody believes me. They think I'm some crazy screenwriter. Maybe next time I'll go somewhere they'll believe me. You know, some TV news show or something. Now, did you understand *that* message?"

"Yes," Smith said tightly.

The connection was severed. The automatic tracing system had it pinned down to a newly activated mobile phone that was, indeed, in Hollywood, California. The phone disappeared from the system a moment later, as if it had ceased to exist.

"THANK GOD you showed up!" Olaf Dasheway shouted. "You're late, you know. Three minutes." He brandished his wristwatch.

"I'm on time. Your watch is wrong. Okay, let's do this thing."

The producer glared at him. "You ready to lose the nose wig?"

"Nope."

"Please."

"Nope."

Dasheway sighed. "It's gonna look kind of silly."

"So sell it," Remo said with a shrug. "Tonight at nine—how can a guy this dorky looking get such fabulous babes?"

The producer considered that. "Maybe. You ready to work your magic?"

"Ready," Remo said.

18

The first episode of *The Ladies' Man* was in the can.

Olaf Dasheway called all the networks for the screening.

"I'm gonna work this like nothing you ever saw before," the producer told Remo as show time approached.

"I have to hand it to you," Remo said. "You got a lot of bigwigs to show up, but they look pissed. Not your kind of pissed."

Producer Dasheway insisted they have a bourbon to celebrate, but Remo was sure Dasheway had a bourbon or six every night about this time, whether or not a celebration was called for. Remo had politely declined a drink, but Dasheway poured two tumblers anyway, then drank both. At the moment he was on Remo's third bourbon.

"Good luck," Remo said as Dasheway slammed down the tumbler.

"You're all the luck I need, Romeo," Dasheway gushed as he went to greet his guests.

"What kind of a cheap stunt is this, Dasheway?" a vice president of network programming demanded.

"Not a stunt, an auction. I'm auctioning off my new television show."

"Like we got money for a new TV show," barked a woman with a city map growing out of the corners of her eyes. Other than her eyes, she was gorgeous.

"You'll find a way to bid on this show. It'll save your network."

"In case you haven't read the news, reality shows are a dime a dozen. They're washed up. I don't care if you've got the President of the United States of America, it's not gonna get people watching."

Dasheway nodded confidently. "Development of the *Slick Willy* show is on hiatus. The former President has nothing to do with the current production. This one is different. We shot the pilot this afternoon, so it's not perfect—"

"You're showing us raw footage?" a narrow man with a fat cigar exploded. "You're out of your mind, Dasheway."

"Either that or my show is the best reality show of all time. You want to watch it or not?"

The studio executives were desperate enough to stay and watch.

The bidding war started while the footage was still playing.

19

Saxony was a phenomenon at sixteen, when her first album, "Look What I Did!", topped the charts. Countless high-school kids bought her albums. Thousands of their fathers sneaked looks at the sleazy CD covers. Saxony sold forty million CDs in four years.

But the world was less friendly now that she was getting older. Saxony was struggling to command the world's attention the way she once did. She was only twenty, and yet a new generation was trying to move in on her turf.

'Gettios was just the place for a star who wanted to be seen while acting as if she didn't want to be seen. 'Gettios was known as the premier spot for al fresco dining in L.A., and the restaurant's private patios offered just enough privacy. Saxony could eat without passersby gawking at her while the paparazzi clicked away from the buildings across the street. When she felt like she needed a little extra media coverage, she'd show off a little. Remove her jacket and enjoy her "private" lunch in a frilly tube top. Maybe bring her boyfriend du jour for some heavy petting.

Today there were no shenanigans on the menu, just

boring business matters and the restaurant's signature Tortellini Bolognese. The young diva forgot all about investments and ring noodles in tomato gravy when the stranger slipped into her private patio.

"How the hell did you get in here?" she demanded.

"I wanted to have lunch with you, Saxony," said the stranger, a dark-haired man who leaned over the table, getting close to her. Saxony saw a pair of shockingly cruel eyes that somehow pressed all her buttons.

Her secretary saw a goof in good shoes, bad clothes and a really bad mustache. The intruder had thick wrists and a trim physique. Definitely paparazzi or a stalker.

"Brutus!" the secretary shouted. She was a professional-looking woman in her thirties. Her job was to be the business face for Saxony Corporation.

Brutus jerked the lattice door open, saw the stranger and leaped like a pouncing jaguar. Somehow the stranger moved himself at the last second, and Brutus hit the edge of the marble tabletop with his abdomen.

"Ouch. Sorry. Didn't mean to cause a ruckus," said the stranger, his eyes never leaving the face of the world's biggest female pop star. Saxony, as if hypnotized, never took her eyes off him, either. "I guess I'm not welcome. I'll go now. Nice to meet you."

"Stop," Saxony ordered Brutus, who was getting out his brass knuckles. "Stay, please," she begged the stranger.

"I've disturbed your business lunch," the stranger said.

"No, not at all," she said softly, then cranked her head at her secretary and chief bodyguard. "Get out. Both of you."

There was a ruckus. Saxony was less polite when she asked a second time, but she became sultry as soon as she was alone with the stranger.

"Who are you?" she demanded.

"I'm Romeo."

"God, you sure are."

"I'd like us to get to know each other," Romeo said.

"Yeah. Okay." She lip-locked him right then and there, wrapping her smooth tan arms around his neck. The mashing lasted a full minute.

"God!" She sighed.

"Hey, by the way, you're not jailbait, are you?" Romeo asked.

"Hell no." She dragged her face forcefully against his.

The camera zoomed in tight on their mashing mouths. Romeo was apparently most concerned about keeping his mustache from migrating too far from under his nose.

"Romeo," Saxony breathed, "I want everything you've got."

"Ah, well, I just came to meet you. I don't want to coerce you into doing anything you don't want to do."

Saxony was amused. "I don't know what to make of you, Romeo. You look like a dork and you kind of act like one, but you have these killer eyes. I think you hypnotized me or something."

"No, I can't hypnotize people. I'm just a guy, you know? See?" Romeo closed his eyes. "Now, maybe this will mean you don't like me so much anymore."

"Open them," Saxony whispered.

Romeo opened them and found his killer eyes were on the same level as the highly insured, never-before-publicly-seen bare breasts of superstar Saxony.

"Hey, this is a public place!" Romeo protested, and looked up—directly into the camera that was taping them from the building across the street. "There's probably somebody filming us right now."

"Those jerks are always there. I don't care anymore. Let them see everything."

Twenty minutes later, Romeo said, "It's been really nice getting to know you."

"What?" Saxony had divested herself of all her clothing. The camera didn't miss a thing when she jumped to her feet. "We didn't make love yet."

"Sorry, I can't."

"But why?"

"You move a little too fast for me," Romeo said. "Gotta go."

"No, wait!" She ran after him, across the public dining patio, begging him to stay. "Please make love to me!" But Romeo had vanished into the street.

IT WAS HISTORIC. As the lights came on, the executives of every major studio got to their feet for a standing ovation. Producer Dasheway beamed.

Remo Williams watched it all from behind the one-way glass in the back of the viewing theater. The video operator was slightly in awe.

"You, man, are the man."

"I feel pretty sleazy," Remo confided.

"So why didn't you do her, man?"

Remo shrugged. "She's a kid."

"A *kid?* Have you seen her videos? She might as well be a porn star. You really should have done her, dude."

Remo watched the discussion in the theater grow

more exited. "As it is, I feel like the biggest male whore since Richard Gere," he said as he left.

The video operator was laughing in pure disbelief.

20

The news was out by morning. The new reality TV show *The Ladies' Man* had been purchased by a consortium of networks for an initial run of thirteen episodes at a cost of a quarter billion dollars.

The entertainment newspapers went berserk. What could possibly be worth that much money? How could they possibly get the first episode on the air by next Friday, the scheduled premiere? Why would the networks share a TV show—did they think viewers would want to watch the same program three times, with just two minutes of unique footage on each network?

It was so big it knocked into second place what would normally have been huge entertainment news. International pop diva Saxony had been seen naked chasing a man through an L.A. restaurant, begging loudly for sex. There were a hundred witnesses. Saxony herself had confirmed the behavior in her public plea for her paramour to contact her. More than a hundred thousand calls had come in to Saxony's business offices, all claiming to be the man Saxony was trying to locate.

Remo felt someone kick him in the shoulder a little before 6:00 a.m.

"What did you do that for?" he asked.

Chiun was glowering at him in the orange sunlight coming into the RV. "What agitates you, Remo?"

"Little Koreans."

"In your sleep you were disturbed. You were active as a dog who dreams of eating chickens. Were you dreaming of fowl flesh?"

"No. Can I go back to sleep now?"

"You have done something." Chiun walked slowly toward the glass patio window, bathed in the brilliant gold of dawn, then he turned swiftly, hiding in the shadow. "You have sullied yourself."

"I didn't sully."

"You rutted, did you not? You lay with another American horror, then washed yourself until her stink was undetectable."

"Didn't do that."

"Then what did you do? How have you disturbed your own conscience, Remo? This is puzzling because you have few scruples. I think this irresponsible new undertaking of yours is unsavory somehow, even to a man such as yourself."

"I'm going back to sleep."

"You will tell me what this great mystery is, Remo Williams! Maybe it is not too late to save you from yourself."

"Yeah. It's too late. Good night."

"You will not tell me?"

"You'll figure it out soon enough."

"How soon?" Chiun demanded.

Remo sighed deeply. "Probably any damn minute."

Remo closed his eyes and ignored Chiun's

complaining, then almost found the peace of sleep when he heard the TV come on in the RV's media center.

Chiun was channel surfing listlessly, but soon enough he found what he wasn't looking for.

"This is the show you have been waiting for. Coming next Friday, *The Ladies' Man.*"

The channel surfing stopped.

"His name is Romeo, and the woman can't keep their hands off him! You won't believe which of the world's biggest stars will fall under the spell of *The Ladies' Man!*"

Chiun filled the Airstream with a shriek, and Remo Williams knew he wasn't going to get any more sleep. Not today. Maybe not ever.

21

Sherman MacGregor hated Romeo the ladies' man.

"He's hogging the publicity," he growled. "The average Joe's got only so much attention to devote to world events, and he's taking all of it."

Sherm MacGregor's mother shrugged and said nothing.

"I know it's just one day, but all day. That's all I've heard all day is Romeo this and Romeo that. On the plus side, the public is tuning in to see just the advertisements for Romeo the ladies' man, so our spots are getting a hell of a lot of extra viewership."

His mother wasn't buying it.

"Yeah, okay, so nobody cares about us with all *The Ladies' Man* excitement. How could I know this would happen? I never even heard of this jerk until I turned on *Good Day U.S.A.* this morning. So get off my back."

MacGregor turned away from the life-size portrait and used a tiny rake to make patterns in a little sandbox. It was some Japanese thingamajig that was supposed to make him feel more calm.

"I don't want to be calm. I want things to happen!"

There was nobody there to respond to this, so he summoned his receptionist.

"What's up, Mac?"

"I want a report from Sydney."

"Sidney in human resources?"

"Sydney, Australia," MacGregor snapped.

"Sure, Mac."

Steph Mincer was his receptionist from way, way back. Back in the old days he had encouraged people to call him Mac. Back then he was a different kind of man and MacGregor Biscuit Company was a different kind of dry-goods operation.

In the 1980s, MacBisCo was a smooth-running business that produced and sold economical foodstuffs in supermarkets across the United States, Canada and Mexico. They made pancake mixes and microwave popcorn. They manufactured butter-flavored crackers and were a leading supplier of par-baked dinner rolls. And they made breakfast cereal by the truckload.

Oat rings and marshmallow pieces and peanut butter balls and fruity-flavored little chips, they made them all. Half the supermarkets in America sold their own brand of value-priced cereals from MacBisCo.

Meet General Generic, proclaimed a trade magazine in 1997, with him on the cover as their man of the year. "Who else could make such a success without having a single branded product on the market?"

"Yawn," said his wife as she packed her bags. "Trouble is, you are General Generic, Mac. There's nothing exciting about you. Not your looks, not your opinions and for sure not your personality."

She told the divorce court that MacGregor was such

a monotonous personality that living with him amounted to emotional cruelty. The courts agreed to the tune of $2.9 million annually.

"She's right, you know," his mother told him on her deathbed. "All you ever cared about was money. You never did anything new with this company."

"Except make it profitable," MacGregor protested. "When Dad died it was almost insolvent."

"Very mundane, Sherm, to insult my dead husband as I'm about to die myself."

"Mother, you don't mean that."

"Oh, Adam," said his mother to herself, "why weren't you my son instead?"

Adam. Adam Fence. Cousin Adam ran the competing cereal company up the road.

Fence Flour Company and MacGregor Biscuit Company were launched by two half brothers in 1887. Battle Creek, Michigan, soon became the breakfast-cereal capital of the world, and new companies came and went.

In the 1890s Fence Flour Company became the biggest of them all on the success of a special new variety of corn flakes that took the country by storm. Celebrities like Mark Twain and President William McKinley were enthusiastic eaters of Fence Patented Premium Corn Flakes with Sorghum.

But Fence had stolen the formula for this brilliant innovation from his half brother, Gerald MacGregor. A patent-infringement suit achieved nothing for the MacGregor Biscuit Company, and a family feud lasted decades. It took World War II to bring about a hesitant reconciliation.

MacBisCo never quite made a name for itself, but was known as the place to go for cheap knockoffs of popular foods. It depended on periodic infusions of cash from the Fence family to keep it from closing its doors. Then Sherm took over and turned MacBisCo into a thriving business.

Somehow, he never felt appreciated. The Fences were the real stars in the family, even to the Mac-Gregors. The Fences had the looks, the huge corporation and the hundred-room mansion. MacGregor's family home had only twenty-six rooms.

Sherm MacGregor was irritated by it all. Then frustrated. Then angry. He carried around his anger for a lot of years until his mother laid on the last straw.

"Adam Fence?" he hissed. "The guy practically bought his MBA. He goes to the office two days a week. His lawyers run the company. He's a pampered poodle. I'm the real deal."

"Adam is a success," his mother said. "He acts like one. He doesn't sit in his office and push around papers. He travels the world."

"He has three butlers."

"He acts like a gentleman."

"He's a well-trained pretty boy."

"He makes things happen, Sherm."

"I can make things happen," Sherm said. He showed her.

They buried his mother without ever knowing that Sherm had finally made something happen. He used a pillow to make it happen. There were no signs of murder.

"How's that, Mother?" he asked the coffin. "It's just

the start. I'm gonna do what you said. Things are happening now."

He started planning what was going to happen. Yeah, it was just more paper-pushing, but a guy had to be careful. You couldn't just make big things happen. You had to plan for them.

MacBisCo was gonna get real big. Extremely, outrageously big.

Any day now.

"Where's Sydney?" he demanded, stomping into the reception area.

"Right here, General." A human weasel came scampering. "Didn't know you were looking for me."

"I told you never to call me General. And I'm not looking for you. I want Sydney, Australia! What is going on in Sydney, Australia?"

Sidney from HR shuffled his feet. "I have no idea, Gen—"

The silence was icy. "Get out of my sight. You're fired."

"But I've been here thirty years."

"Out!"

The HR weasel scampered off. MacGregor found his receptionist glaring harshly at him.

"How long have you been here?" he asked Steph with a sneer.

"Long enough to think that I knew who I was working for. You used to be a nice guy. What happened to you, Mac?"

"I am Mr. MacGregor to you. Get me Sydney or I'll get someone who can."

She thrust the phone receiver at him.

"Talk to me," he said into it. "How's it going?"

"Everything is coming together. We have all arrangements made. Our man is ready to compete."

"What about the party preparations?"

"All the decorations are in place. We'll have some big surprises ready."

"What about our man? He fit enough?"

"He's fit, everything's ready. I always come through, don't I?"

"Yeah. Thank God I've got one competent man on my staff."

MacGregor slammed the phone. "Now, there's a man who knows how to get things accomplished," he remarked, slamming the door to his office.

THE FOREMAN WAS in Australia, if not actually in Sydney. The Sydney office was just an encrypted relay to his mobile phone. You couldn't be too careful. The foreman was a wanted man in more than thirty nations, and he was infamous for *never* getting caught.

A good foreman hired the right crew to do what needed done. The foreman knew all the right people, whatever the job.

His most important subcontractor in recent months was the Russian kid with the doctorate in bioelectronic engineering. The kid knew a thing or two about mixing chemicals and microwaves to create thermal dynamics. You could do a lot of funny things with advanced thermal dynamics.

"Is that enough? It's a big outback."

The Russian kid lifted the handles of the wheelbarrow. It was full of heavy rubber sacks oozing blood. Testing the weight, he nodded. "It is enough. I go now."

"Okay. Good luck."

Petyr marched his cart to the dock, alone in the dark. Good luck, the foreman told him. The foreman was an American who talked too much. Petyr didn't need luck, nor did he believe in luck. It was meaningless to say good luck.

"G'day, Pete."

Petyr's guide was outback trash—rotting teeth and powerful body odor. Like every other Australian, he said "G'day" whenever you met him. It was strictly for the tourists. The Australians were an ingratiating bunch. Petyr dumped his soggy load into the rowboat.

This guide had one attribute that made him useful: he knew this armpit of the outback very well. He knew where to find the crocs.

"What kind of experiment is this, anyway?" the guide asked as he rowed them deep into the swamp. Petyr ignored him.

"There's a croc," the guide announced finally.

Petyr donned a rubber glove and opened a rubber bag of ripe kangaroo meat. The chemical marinade had not slowed the decay. Not that the crocodiles cared. Petyr tossed the chunk into the water and the croc snapped it up.

"Nothin's happening to the croc, mate," the guide pointed out a minute later.

"Nothing is supposed to happen," Petyr answered. "Go."

The guide rowed him up and down the swampy channels. Finally he couldn't contain himself any longer. "Well, you must be expecting something to happen, right? I mean, why give the crocs a treat for no reason."

"There's a reason."

"Don't have nothin' to do with the big footrace, does it?"

"No," Petyr lied.

"That's funny. Never had anybody interested in Jaiboru Junction ever before. Now in the same week we got the footrace comin' here and we got you boys doing experiments on our crocs."

Petyr pretended to ignore the guide's comments, but he was listening closely. The guide was getting suspicious. He was apparently not quite as half-witted as he acted.

"I will tell you a secret if you can keep silent."

"Sure. No worries, mate," the guide said.

Petyr could tell the guy was playing up the Aussie-talk. "See, the promoters are afraid someone might be hurt when the race is here at Jaiboru. I am giving the crocs a little something to make them more gentle."

"Gentle crocs, huh? 'At's a good one, mate."

"That is why I must not give any of them more than one dose. I don't want them to become too sedated."

"I hope not. Them crocs is our best tourist attraction. Not that we ever had tourists before now."

The guide seemed pleased to know the secret, and he was pleased at the bonus Petyr offered to help him keep the secret.

"I think we got about every croc this side of the ridge. You gonna dump your leftovers someplace safe, I hope?"

"Where?" Petyr asked. "Where would be a safe place where no crocs could get an extra serving?"

"I know just the place." The guide took him to the shore and pointed up. "That ugly rock. Dump the leftovers up there and the birds'll eat it. Nobody'll care if a few of them buzzards keel over."

Petyr agreed. He jogged up the footpath to the rocky top and emptied his bag. The scavenger birds were already circling.

"That stink travels fast." The guide chuckled.

Petyr took out a book and began to read as the guide set about rowing them back.

They were miles from Jaiboru and the dawn was still a half hour away. Now was the time to erase the problem of the nosy guide. When they had gone but a hundred yards, Petyr stretched and grabbed a bottle of water.

"Like one?" He held it up.

"No, thanks," the guide said from the rear of the rowboat.

Petyr took out the small air gun. The dart was loaded with enough serum to knock out a big croc. It would have more permanent results on a scrawny Aussie. Petyr turned in his seat and triggered the gun. The yellow feathers glanced off the guide's arm, but they left a scarlet rip in the flesh. That was all Petyr saw before the guide splashed into the swamp water.

"Why'd ya do it, mate?" the guide demanded.

Petyr inserted a second dart and fired. This time the guide ducked under the water and the dart missed him entirely, but the crocs wouldn't miss him. A big one was already closing in fast.

The guide slurred drunkenly when he surfaced, but he couldn't scream. He got enough of a dose so he had to fight to stay conscious, but he'd have been better off letting blackness take him. Then he wouldn't have been aware of the croc clamping his body in its great jaws and taking him under.

Petyr took the oars and stroked leisurely back to town, enjoying the outback daybreak.

22

Smith was always gray. Today he was a corpse. A corpse that munched antacids like peanuts.

"He can't be serious." Mark Howard gave a little disbelieving laugh.

"Looks serious to me."

"It's a canny concept, actually," Mark said, and Smith looked morose. "Think about it, Dr. Smith. Unattainable celebrity women losing control and getting naked on TV for some guy off the street. And he'll do it every week. It's got everything the public wants."

"It's got our enforcement arm putting himself on television," Smith said miserably. "You're right. It was a canny move. He socked CURE right in the stomach."

CHIUN SAT in his seat and fastened his belt, then fixed his gaze on Remo Williams. Remo ignored him for what seemed like hours.

"Go on," Remo said finally. "You've got a lot to say. Let's hear it."

"I do not know where to begin."

"You usually start with a little name-calling, then move into blaming me for whatever, then tie it up with how your life is made awful by your association with me."

"This is a joke to you, Remo? You find all of it amusing?"

"I'm smiling to mask the pain."

"You jest to hide your shame."

"Shouldn't you be watching the wing? It looks wobbly."

"Master Yeou Gang, the Fool, he also was full of self-loathing for the vile thing he had done. Like you, he prostituted himself. He traded on his talents for gold."

"What did he do that was so awful? Kill somebody?"

"Hush and heed. Yeou Gang was a simpleton. He learned what he must know to be Master, and he memorized the history and lessons of Sinanju, but never could he truly understand the meaning of these lessons. Yeou Gang and his mentor, Master Ghu Ung, traveled to the lands along the Nile. Reluctantly did they go, for the monarchy was in a strange state. And yet, Master Ghu Ung knew that unsettled empires often yield the most opportunity for an assassin. In Kemet, King Merenre was dead, and the child, Pepi II, was pharaoh. His mother was regent, Ankhenespepi II, who was the widow of two kings, Pepi and Merenre. Although she was not pharaoh, she was a skilled ruler and the power of the throne was with her. She was short-sighted, for in the end her determination to rule as a pharaoh and claim the immortality of a pharaoh unsettled the people, poisoning their convictions in their gods. Her son ruled long enough to see Kemet break apart under this stress, and for generations afterward it was ununified. Still, that is not the point of the story. Why do your eyes glaze?"

"Just trying to keep them all straight in my head. What is the point?"

Chiun glared. "I am only just beginning to tell it. Allow me to relate the story at the proper pace. Our history is not like some fast and furious television entertainment that must move every eight heartbeats from one thrill to the next."

"Sorry."

"Master Ghu Ung appraised the situation, as did Master Yeou Gang. Yeou Gang was determined to seek employment with the boy king Pepi II. As pharaoh, Yeou Gang reasoned, Pepi II controlled the treasuries of Kemet."

"Sounds reasonable to—"

"Yeou Gang was a fool. It was obvious to all save Pepi II that he was just a symbolic king at that time. The regent was the true ruler of Kemet. Master Ghu Ung and young Master Yeou Gang introduced themselves in the court, where they were well received, of course. Ghu Ung deemed it wise to exercise patience, so as to better learn the subtleties of the power sharing and to see what events the arrival of Sinanju Masters might cause to happen. Yeou Gang was eager to peddle their services and earn his first profits as Reigning Master. When the boy king began subtle overtures to the Masters, Ghu Ung stalled him."

Remo nodded. "Playing hard to get. Drives up the price. Smart move."

"A foolish mistake. The boy king lost interest, for he was only playing the game of ruling the nation. He knew not the seriousness of his role. The woman regent, Ankhenespepi, hired them for much gold, although less than perhaps the boy king might have paid if negotiations were skillfully done.

"Ghu Ung did not recognize the libidinous nature of the regent, nor the adolescent cravings of his protégé, who was not yet in his sixth decade and quite immature. Thus, Ghu Ung blindly agreed to take service with the regent. For Ankhenespepi, the masters were of great service, ridding the court of those who sought an opportunity to remove her and take her place, knowing that this boy king was malleable."

Chiun looked at Remo meaningfully.

"I'm waiting for the punch line," Remo said.

"You see how this service was right and correct."

"And good and kind. They acted like most proper Masters. But...?"

"Ankhenespepi came to young Master Yeou Gang and begged of him the favors of the flesh. Yeou Gang gifted her with these favors, but Ankhenespepi was not sated. On the contrary, she beseeched Yeou Gang to remain in Kemet as her consort. Yeou Gang declined.

"Ankhenespepi asked if he was not attracted to her. Yeou Gang replied that he was. She asked Yeou Gang if he had met more beautiful women in his travels.

"Yeou Gang knew the lessons of protocol taught to him by Ghu Ung, but he did not understand these lessons. He knew he must flatter the great rulers who hire the Masters, but he did not have the intellect to know when to hold his tongue. He assured the regent that she was by far the most beautiful woman he had ever encountered.

"The regent pressed Yeou Gang further. She asked the young Master if there were women in Sinanju more skilled at lovemaking than she. Again, Yeou Gang told Ankhenespepi what he thought she wanted to hear, assuring her that she was unparalleled at lovemaking."

"Was she?" Remo asked.

"It does not matter," Chiun replied.

"Yeah, it matters. You're condemning Yeou Gang for what he said, but maybe he was telling her the truth."

"What he said was foolish, regardless of what he believed, because in so saying it he gave Ankhenespepi a tool of coercion against which he could not argue. She made him say the words, then weighted him down with his own words until they became his conviction."

"Give the poor guy the benefit of the doubt. Why shouldn't he tell the truth?"

"Have you heard nothing I have said to you, all these many years, about the art of negotiation?" Chiun demanded. "Only a fool tells the truth to his employer. Surely you know this lesson, from recitation if not from practice."

"I know my lessons better than you think."

"That is doubtful, else you would know the folly of interrupting wisdom when it is presented to you like a rare gift."

"Please go on."

Chiun's scowl made it plain he was deciding if he would go on or not. The suspense wasn't killing Remo. Chiun didn't leave stories untold once he started them.

"Whatever he truly thought of Ankhenespepi, she convinced him that he was infatuated with her. She convinced him, too, that she was in need of a lover, as she had no husband. Only a Master of Sinanju would have the skills to carry on an affair with a closely watched royal regent without being suspected. Any other man would eventually make a mistake, be witnessed sneaking to or from his liaison with her. 'Such exposure would be used against me to depose me of my role and clear the way for my son to be saddled with a regent who will be a usurper,' she told the fool Yeou Gang. 'Would you allow your true love to face ignominy and allow an entire nation to face its future under a dictator?' By the time she was through with him, Yeou Gang was under her control.

"But when he told Ghu Ung he planned to stay with Ankhenespepi, the wise old Master knew the truth. Ghu Ung asked, 'It is better to plunge your own people into poverty and starvation than to let this woman be denied a throne for her infidelities?' Yeou Gang heeded this, for he was nothing if not dedicated to the village. This lesson was ingrained in him.

"Yeou Gang went to take his leave of Ankhenespepi, explaining his reasoning, to which the regent had her own justification. She would pay Yeou Gang to stay with her. Sinanju would get its gold, and Yeou Gang would be her savior."

Remo's ire was rising, but he kept it to himself.

"This did come to pass, despite the pleading of the wise Ghu Ung. Yeou Gang was satisfied that this was the best decision, and was too stubborn to be swayed. Why are you fidgeting? Do you need to go to the bathroom?"

"Just getting my boxers in a bunch over your lesson."

"Ah. You understand its meaning?"

"Not at all. What's Yeou Gang the Gigolo got to do with me?"

"You are repeating his mistakes," Chiun said reasonably. "Yeou Gang's prostitution could not be kept secret. Within his lifetime, he was known as the Trollop of Sinanju and by other names less tasteful. This damaged the reputation of the Sinanju assassins for years to come. Of course, the gossip about Yeou Gang took decades to spread to all the courts of the world. You will accomplish such ruination by Friday evening, primetime."

"So what happened to Yeou Gang?" Remo asked.

"He left Ankhenespepi when she couldn't continue embezzling gold sufficient to pay his fee and could no longer convince him that he was in love with her. And Yeou Gang was nothing if not determined to be a good Master to his people. He returned to Sinanju and Ghu Ung retired there, although he feared what might become of the new Master without guidance.

"It was only then, as Yeou Gang sought new employment, that he began to hear the name-calling. Yeou Gang eventually understood this difficult lesson, if he understood nothing else in his life. His actions had repercussions that were long-lasting and uncontrollable. The image of the Sinanju Masters was tainted around the world. Yeou Gang knew years of shame, and the befouled reputation was not soon forgotten."

"But even the Masters would rather not have the story down in writing," Remo added.

Chiun did not disagree.

"Miss, how long until we land in Sydney?" Remo asked a passing flight attendant.

"Depends on how soon we take off," she replied, roaming his body with her eyes. "Need help passing the time?"

"Do not seek a dalliance with him unless you wish to have yourself put on film and televised across America," Chiun warned.

The flight attendant bit her lower lip thoughtfully. "Okay."

"It was a rhetorical statement. Be gone, hussy."

"You don't let that old man tell you what to do, do you?" she asked Remo.

"Sweetheart, you wouldn't believe it if I told you."

"Come up front with me," she urged.

"Sorry. Maybe another flight." When the plane finally raced down the runway and started the long journey to Australia, he said, "I'm not like Yeou Gang."

"He was pure-blood Korean."

"I'm not like Yeou Gang in other ways. This TV show is kind of sleazy, sure, but it's not the same as performing stud service for the wanna-be queen of the Nile."

"Yes, it is like that."

"But there's no sex. The Chinos don't come off."

"You slobbered your lips against those of a famous diva, whose identity even now tantalizes the nation. They show this on the television. They also show her without her garments."

"She got herself naked. We mashed lips, but I never groped her goodies. That took a little self-control, you know."

"This makes it acceptable behavior?" Chiun demanded.

"Hey, even I know it's a sleazy thing to do," Remo admitted.

"So why do it?" Chiun demanded.

"Because I can."

"That is not a reason."

"Maybe someday it'll make sense."

Chiun looked away from the wing for a moment. "So. There is a hidden agenda. Remo the dramatist has more feats of tomfoolery up his undershirt sleeves."

"Maybe I do."

"You will tell me of your plans."

"No, I won't."

"You will, lest you carry out more idiotic schemes that reflect upon me. I will not go into my retirement with the reputation of Sinanju sullied."

"Go to hell, Chiun."

Chiun didn't respond. In fact, he was silent the rest of the flight. Remo tried to enjoy the silence, but he knew he was going to pay for it one way or another.

He always did.

HAROLD W. SMITH meditated on his computer screen, hidden beneath his glass desktop. Everything that he had ordered was now in place. He had but to issue one more command to use it.

He might be stepping over the line. What he did now could turn his rebellious enforcement arm into a vengeful rogue assassin. Was it worth the risk?

The problem was, Smith didn't know what he was even trying to learn, but he was convinced the Sun On Jo could hold a part of the answer to the question that plagued him.

He had to know. He had analyzed the elements of the problem time and again, logically and dispassionately, and every conclusion was the same: he had to know who had pulled CURE's strings.

Somehow, years ago, CURE was used to bring Chiun and Remo together. Only recently was Smith made aware of the fact that Remo Williams was himself a descendent of a Sinanju Master—the master who journeyed to North America before Columbus and founded the small tribe called Sun On Jo. The odds of CURE bringing these two incredibly unique persons on an intercept course out of sheer chance were immense. Smith had even tried to calculate these odds, allowing for ridiculous assumptions to weigh the chances.

They were still incalculably large. Someone or something must have made it happen. Whatever made it happen also made the Sun On Jo happen.

Smith had always prided himself on CURE's independence. Even the commander in chief of the United States could not give orders to CURE, save the one order to dismantle the agency completely.

To discover now that the very core of CURE had been engineered in some way to be what it now was— this was deeply disturbing. What other machinations had been made? How else had Smith been manipulated? What was CURE being used for?

He had to know. The answer had to be important. Smith could not allow himself to be a pawn in a king's crown.

Smitty issued his commands, then sat and waited.

COLONEL SIMONEC WAS almost relieved when the command came through and ended the unbearable suspense of waiting.

Unexpectedly, he had taken delivery of two new airships today. He didn't dare hope that he would get to keep them. Surely the faceless general would send him another incontrovertible order to throw these two new beauties away just as he had wasted the other airships.

"We're sending up EBE 1," Simonec announced to his ground crew chief.

"Aw, come on, Colonel. We just got her today! Can't we have her even one day before they scrap her?"

"That's an order, mister!"

"Yes, Colonel."

But he knew how his close-knit crew felt about it. The EBE had arrived like a gift from heaven. None of them even knew there was such a thing as the Extremely Big Ear, and now two of them were sitting in their hangar.

The unmanned airship displaced little more than its predecessors, but the construction was different. The gas bag was some sort of extraflimsy Mylar that somehow collapsed itself into hundreds of tiny chambers. They couldn't puncture the skin with a power saw.

"You shoot this, and it would probably absorb the round. If the round tears through it, it'll damage maybe five or ten percent of the chambers and the thing will still fly," one of the operators explained.

But the real art was in the electronics.

"It's a laser," the operator told the colonel.

"My toaster has a laser in it. So what?"

"We think it reads vibrations in gases in the 95-to-100 degrees Farenheit range. You know, like bouncing a laser off a glass to pick up the vibrations caused by the sound inside the room? If this does that using air, and only on the air that is coming out of the mouths of people, then think what the range would be. It could eavesdrop from fifty miles away. If you're not in line of sight, it uses a wide-spectrum thermal sensor to identify targets that are vibrating with the spectrum of human speech, then points the effing laser at that thing."

The colonel shrugged. "But will it work?"

"The bitch of it is, we might never know."

They launched the EBE 1 and watched her disappear into the Arizona desert. Sure enough, their remote control was overridden within minutes.

"Distend finger, insert in nostril," an operator said despondently. "And wait for the thing to never come back."

But it did come back. A message came in thirty hours later that signaled the return of EBE 1 control to Yuma.

"I'll be damned," the operator said, and he called up the ground crew. The EBE didn't need a team to haul her in on tethers. She had no tethers. She simply touched down on a flat-topped, cushioned cart and two ground crewmen wheeled her immediately into the windowless hangar.

Simonec hustled in, unable to believe his luck. One less blot on his unofficial record—the bureaucracy didn't like officers who lost expensive equipment, even when they were officially not responsible for the equipment. Even if the equipment did not officially exist.

"Man, I'd love to know what she's been doing all this time," he said as a crewman plugged her in for diagnostics. He jogged up the stairs to the top level, where the control room was situated under a dome of glass panels that gave it an unobstructed view, to guide difficult landings visually.

"What's she got?"

The crew chief grimaced. "She's clean. And I mean clean. Even the GPS trail was erased."

Simonec knew he ought to be satisfied, under the circumstances, to have his equipment returned at all. Still…

"That pisses me off."

"Yeah," the crew chief said thoughtfully.

"Who do they think they are?"

"Those DOHS heads think they run the whole government now," the crew chief said. "There's something big brewing on our turf, so why not tell us about it?"

"Yeah? How come?" Simonec demanded indignantly, reminding himself to start using better military protocol.

"Hell, my watch can record a GPS trail," the crew chief said. "Next time we should just clip it onto the EBE and see where it goes, heh heh heh."

"Yeah." Simonec chuckled, too, just as insincerely. "It's a nice watch."

"It's not regulation. Sorry, sir," the crew chief said. "It's a calculator, too."

"Really? Must have been expensive."

"Naw! Look." He held up his wrist and displayed the watch face, with the words LearnForFun printed in a circle. "Got it from the LearnForFun network when I upgraded my cable package. It's cool, but not valuable."

"Wouldn't kill you to lose it."

"Naw."

"Hmm."

"Yeah."

The colonel nodded, then said. "Yeah."

"Yeah?" the crew chief asked meaningfully.

"Yeah," the colonel said, eyes darting.

The crew chief grinned mischievously. "Yeah!"

THERE WASN'T TIME to reconsider the unspoken conspiracy. An order came through before the postflight maintenance on the EBE 1 was complete. The next mission was to launch just after sunset.

The EBE 1 was ready, and she launched on time.

"All systems functional," the crew chief told the colonel. "She's working fine, although she's registering some sluggishness in the controls. Like maybe she's a few ounces heavy or something."

"Enough for anybody to notice?"

"Naw."

The system notified them that control of the EBE 1 was being assumed by a user with top-level security access. This had become routine.

"I sure hope they won't notice," Simonec said.

"Yeah," the crew chief added.

HAROLD W. SMITH FROWNED at the control window and brought up the specs on the EBE 1. The airship wasn't handling with the same agility as she had the day before. As she maneuvered to her destination coordinates, he skimmed the specifications and engineering test notes. Humidity, the test result indicated, could cause sluggish response from the unit, as was common with any lighter-than-air ship. But the problem wasn't humidity, not in the southern Arizona deserts.

There were other engineering notes. Temperature fluctuations were blamed on tiny helium leaks. A bug in the system might cause the unit to reset the baseline helium fill depending on the buoyancy at system start-up. Inside the air-conditioned hangar, perhaps, there had been a leak and reset.

Smith accepted that. What choice did he have? There wasn't anything he could do to investigate it further without sacrificing mission security. Why waste time and energy worrying about something that wasn't apparently of consequence and over which he had no control?

That made him stop and think.

What if the entire mission were such an exercise in futility?

What if this problem wasn't a problem at all? What if he could never solve the mystery—then what would he do?

Harold W. Smith chastised himself for digressing. The mission wasn't just about the mystery of who pulled CURE's strings; it was about how much the Sun On Jo knew about CURE. Once he was satisfied as to the extent of their knowledge, he could decide what to do. His first instinct would typically have been to initiate the shutdown of CURE and the annihilation of the Sun On Jo. Heartless, but necessary.

But Smith had learned then of the blood ties Remo—and Chiun—had to the Sun On Jo. He was contractually obligated to harm none of them. But what made the assassination of the Sun On Jo truly impractical was the inevitable response from Remo and Chiun. Remo would want revenge, and his revenge would come in the form of realizing Smith's worst nightmare. He would expose CURE. He would expose Smith. He would probably expose the culpability of every President from the past thirty years. The scandal would be immense and just might be too much for the United States to withstand.

Smith couldn't walk away from this. He couldn't allow CURE to continue with this enormous question mark hanging over it.

His espionage wasn't intrusive and went unnoticed with the latest EBE unit. So far as Smith knew.

He took the airship to its station. Like the station of the previous nights, it was about five miles from the actual village. Smith turned on the listening mechanism and the various sensors, and began recording everything.

THIS TIME the EBE was gone only eight hours before it signaled its return to the Yuma base and landed without incident. The crew chief surreptitiously snatched off his watch, which had been clasped to a small frame strut.

After the airship was moved inside and the EBE was undergoing her postflight maintenance, the crew chief and the colonel met in private.

"Nothing on her drive again?" Simonec asked carefully, reluctant to steer the conversation immediately into the subject of their transgression.

"Nothing on her, as always." The crew chief was reluctant to go on.

"Well?"

"Well what?"

"Where'd she go, dammit?"

The crew chief's eyes became very shifty, and it seemed an effort for him not to look around the tiny operation room for any third parties. "It's an Indian reservation."

"Indians? Navajo?"

"Naw."

"Hopi? Payute?"

"One of the little tribes. Sun On Jo. Never heard of them, but they have their own federally recognized reservation not too far from Yuma."

Simonec considered this. "Where else?"

"Nowhere else. It parked outside the one and only town on the Sun On Jo res and never moved until it was time to come home. You know, I half suspected the EBE was being used for some sort of big sting on the illegals coming in from Mexico."

Simonec nodded. "Me, too. But then why just focus on the Indians? Maybe we're looking at something bigger after all."

"Maybe the Sun On Jo are a part of the White Buffalo societies. You know, redskin freedom fighters. You think the DOHS has got a line on some real terrorism brewing?"

"I think I'd like to know *what* is brewing," Simonec said. "But I guess our hands are tied." He looked right into the crew chief's eye as he said it.

"More or less. We got another mission already on the books for tonight with the EBE, Colonel."

"Be nice to know if they have any other targets in mind," the colonel said, just for the sake of saying it.

"Yeah," the crew chief said, not meaning anything by it.

"Yeah."

SMITH TOOK the EBE by the reins that night and tested her out. She was still sluggish, just like the day before. He didn't worry about it. She was just a prototype, after all. She wasn't even supposed to be in the field yet.

Still, the EBE was doing a superlative job. Smith had recorded hours of conversations by every Sun On Jo in the village. The tribe as a whole was restless, probably made uneasy by the crash of the other spy ships, but there was no indication that they were aware of a third ship spying on them. Still, Smith had the sense that the people were disturbed by something unnamable.

He had hoped to overhear the people talking about their history, their theology or their legends, and he was especially looking forward to hearing Remo's family discuss him. Even a passing reference might have provided Smith meaningful insight into their understanding of Remo and his work.

Nothing. Although restless, they kept their feelings to themselves. Many of the adults were sleepless that night of the EBE watch, but they didn't while away the hours conversing about it. Smith jumped restlessly from one audio feed to another, searching for anything of value.

In frustration, he sent the EBE home before dawn, having learned nothing.

23

"The natives are restless," Mark Howard mentioned when they heard another scream from far, far away, somewhere inside Folcroft Sanitarium.

"The man sounds like he is in pain," Sarah Slate said in concern.

"He's dreaming. That's Mr. Fyster. Old man from a rich family, various emotional problems. He's been here for years, as quiet and contented as you'd imagine. All of a sudden last night he started having nightmares that woke him up six or seven times. He wasn't the only one. Lots of agitated patients."

They were strolling the grounds slowly, hand in hand, enjoying the night air. Sarah looked over her shoulder. "Moon's not full."

"Sometimes it happens this way—at least that's what the doctors tell me. Especially in a place like this, without a lot of disturbing and loud patients that you might find in another mental health facility. I guess one of them starts screaming and sets off the others."

They walked for a few minutes, then Sarah said, "That doesn't sound right."

Howard was grimacing. His leg was hurting slightly,

but he had a quota to fill. His wheelchair awaited them fifty feet up the brick path.

"What else could it be?"

"You tell me, Mark," Sarah said thoughtfully.

Mark settled into his wheelchair. "What do you mean?"

"Something is disturbing you?" she said, but she wasn't really asking. "You've got something on your mind."

"No. That's not it. Just something—out there."

"In the trees? In the ocean?"

"Not really." Was she teasing him?

"In the night?"

"In the world."

She was pushing him now, along the brick path. "Are you talking about all the bad blood on the news?"

"What are you getting at?"

"I don't know."

"I'm sorry. I snapped at you. I've never done that before."

"So why did you?"

Sarah Slate, Mark decided, would make an excellent psychotherapist. "When I start feeling like I'm trying to tell myself something, and I can't figure it out—I get frustrated. I guess I get grumpy. I didn't realize until just now that I was feeling that way."

"Mark," Sarah said, "are we still talking about international tensions, or the patients of Folcroft?"

"I don't know."

Mr. Fyster screamed again. As muted and distant as it was, the sound cut through the peace of the evening and the steady hush of the Long Island tide.

A small bunch of bushes near the path rustled in response to the scream.

"What's in there?" Sarah asked.

"Probably a raccoon."

She steered Mark down the path, and they both kept their eyes on the bushes. It was quiet now. Maybe the raccoon had fled in the shadows.

When there was another scream, as quiet as the squeak of the wheelchair axle, the bushes shrieked and seemed to be torn apart. Something big took to the air and soared into the nearby trees, shrieking briefly.

"What was that?" Mark asked in disbelief. " Did you get a look at it?"

"Not a good one," Sarah said. "It was big."

"Must have been an owl. They get pretty sizable."

"Mark," Sarah said, "I think it talked."

LOIS LARSON WAS so old that the birth year on her official documents included a question mark. "I was born on a farm way back up the hills," she said. "Never had a birth certificate until I was in my twenties. I never saw a doctor until I was in my thirties."

She still didn't take kindly to doctors. She stayed in this place because it was very nice, and she didn't want to burden her family. Lois occasionally became confused. Being ninety-six—or ninety-seven—years old, a woman was bound to get a little confused now and again. Lois didn't take kindly to being confused, either, and tended to get angry and boisterous. They called her "Incredible Hulk" Larson. Lois didn't quite understand the joke but, being all of ninety-eight—or ninety-nine—pounds, she was delighted to be nicknamed "Incredible Hulk."

She was, right now, doing what some of her friends called "hulking out."

"Come and get me, you overgrown chicken!" She shuffled a few more paces down the path, her tennis racket in both hands. "I've had about enough of you."

The bushes were quiet. The nearby trees showed no signs of life. Lois kept moving. "I'll find you. You know I will. You ain't gonna be stirring up no more trouble."

She stopped again. Another copse of trees. Her challenge went unanswered.

"How about we head back inside, Lois?" asked Larry, her nurse. Larry was a heck of a piece of a nurse, Lois had to admit.

"No. I have me a crow to catch."

"We've been out here for an hour," Larry complained, allowing himself to approach one step too close.

"You better not try nothin'!" Lois Larson declared vehemently. "You know what I'll do?"

Larry knew well enough. He could still hear the crunch of Lois's tennis racket against the forehead of Nurse Rubin. Nurse Rubin should have known better than to mess with Incredible Hulk Larson when she was hulking out.

Lois Larson was a sweet old lady most of the time. Tough, yeah, but she didn't hurt people unless people got unreasonable with her. Like right now, she was hunting for the crow that was "skeering" the patients and nothing was going to stop her. So you just let her go hunting—with a big nurse keeping an eye on her. This was the kind of personalized accommodation that the public mental health facilities simply did not offer.

An hour was about the limit to Lois's stamina. She reached an outdoor veranda near her room and sat down heavily on a green metal rocking chair, lips pursed in frustration.

"That bird probably took one look at you and flew south for good," Larry said comfortingly as he took another rocker. "You do that to me sometimes, Lois."

"You's just trying to make me feel better," she said, unable to hide her pleasure.

"Hello?" said a voice inches from her shoulder.

"Son of a gun!" Lois tottered out of her chair and swung around in a full-body blow. The bird flopped into the air with a surprised sound that ended with the crack of the tennis racket against its foot.

"I got you, you monster!" Lois shuffled after the bird, which somersaulted out of the air and landed hard on the lawn. It picked itself up on one foot and craned its head to see Lois Larson coming at it in a green rage.

"Why?" it asked, then threw itself bodily off the ground, clawed at the air and barely managed to get out of the reach of the slow-moving nonagenarian.

"I don't like birds that eat my friends, that's why!"

"Why? Why?" the bird cried. It nearly collapsed on the earth again, but it found extra height with a few painful strokes that took it into the treetops a hundred feet away.

"Aw, nuts," Lois gasped, then collapsed from sheer exhaustion.

SARAH SLATE HAD heard the talk. She didn't know what to believe, but she knew she had to help that bird. Mrs. Larson claimed to have broken its foot with her tennis racket—and one of the nurses witnessed it. As for Lois Larson's claim that the bird was a man-eating carnivore—that was a little hard to swallow.

"All it talks about is chewing," Lois told her. "It comes to folks' windows in the night like asking for permission. I heard it myself."

"Really," Sarah asked her. "What did it say?"

"I told you, girl! It said 'chewing.' 'Chewing?' it says. 'Chewing? Chewing?'"

Sarah wasn't about to argue with Lois Larson. Still, just because it said "Chewing?" was it necessarily a flesh-eater?

"It didn't say 'chewing,'" corrected another longtime Folcroft patient. "It stood outside my window for ten minutes so I heard what it said most clearly." The man skootched close to her and said, "*Chewin.* Not '*chewing*' but '*chewin.*'"

"Oh, God." Sarah Slate was so surprised she didn't notice the old man's hand on her knee. "Thanks, Mr. Hampton."

She was gone before he could ask her to dinner.

"DON'T GO OUT THERE!" cried a gaggle of ancient patients in the sunroom. "It'll try to eat you!"

All those worried old women had their own set of serious problems, and now they were too scared to take a step outside because of some misplaced fears.

"Don't worry, ladies," Sarah said. "I'm going to take care of this problem once and for all."

"Oh, really?" asked a white-haired woman in her fifties. Her wide eyes told Sarah she was very afraid, very often, and yet she effortlessly placed her confidence in a strange woman who looked too young for the high-school prom.

"You work here?" asked another woman, less trusting.

"Pretty soon everything will be back to normal," Sarah declared loudly so that everyone in the sunroom could hear her. The patients looked at her with doubt or hope. She smiled and met their eyes, each and every one of them, then left the building.

She crossed the grounds fast and felt as if she were walking a tightrope. She poked out a number on her mobile phone.

"They're in a meeting. They're not to be disturbed. I'm so sorry, Sarah," Mrs. Mikulka said. "Where are you, dear?"

"On the grounds. Trying to solve this bird problem. Have you heard what the patients are saying?"

"Oh, yes, they're quite upset and staying indoors."

"Mrs. Mikulka, there's a bunch of sad-looking people down here, and I think I can make them feel a little better. Would you help me out? I need somebody with your authority."

"Oh, goodness. Oh, my. What do you have in mind, dear?"

THE SECURITY CHIEF joined her fifteen minutes later. "I wanted to hear about this for myself," he said.

"Wait here," Sarah said. "I'll call when I'm ready." She snatched the medical kit and the body bag from his hands and tromped away into the trees until she could barely see the man.

"Hello? Here I am. I'm looking for you? Can you hear me? I'm here to help you."

One of Sarah's charms was a melodious voice, which she lifted into the trees. She had worked miracles with that voice, more than once. She would do so again.

"I can help you find Chiun," she said. "Come to me. I'll help you. I will help you find Chiun."

Already she heard the rustle of large wings overhead, and when she turned her gaze up she saw the creature on a branch an arm's reach above her head. It asked, sadly, "Chiun?"

"I know Chiun. I'll help you find Chiun. I'll help you feel better. Come to me. Come to me."

The great creature with the dangling foot allowed itself to be embraced. It was heaving with the exertion of standing on one foot and slumped into her arms. Sarah stroked its great head and tried to explain to it what would happen next. "Don't be afraid," Sarah cooed. "Don't be afraid."

The bird cocked its head. It truly seemed to be reassured by her words. It didn't object when it was laid on the ground and zippered up inside the body bag.

Sarah held it close to her chest again and called for the security chief.

"You got it?" he asked.

"Yes."

"So you want me to, you know?" He held up the shotgun.

"Yes, please."

"Crazy-assed scheme, but maybe it'll work."

"Okay," Sarah said through the small opening she left in the zipper. "Don't be afraid. Here it comes."

The bird wasn't afraid. When the shotgun blasted, it didn't even flinch.

WHEN THE BRAVE young woman and the grim head of security emerged from the trees, they were greeted by a crowd of patients and staff standing at the widows inside the sunroom. They had heard the shotgun.

Sarah Slate, purposeful but unsmiling, raised the plastic body bag. The patients buzzed. A few clapped. A few of them wandered outside, feeling their freedom again.

Sarah avoided them all, making her way to the private wing of the sanitarium with her grim prize.

HAROLD W. SMITH and his assistant entered the room feeling uncomfortable. The track-hung walls between the suites had been opened, and now Mark's and Sarah's rooms were a single home shared by them. The coziness of her small decorating touches and the intimacy of their relationship made Smith uncomfortable.

At their arrival the big bird winged off a chair back to Sarah Slate, who was sitting on a small couch. She coddled it in her arms and it burrowed into her chest as she stroked its domed head.

Smith sat and watched her soothe the creature tenderly. The bird looked as if it needed nursing. It was gaunt, its purplish feathers ragged, and its left foot in a swath of bandages.

"Can I hear it?" Smith asked after the bird calmed down.

"Tell Dr. Smith," Sarah suggested.

The bird glared at Smith, then at Howard.

"Give her a minute," Sarah said. "She's a little spooked. Be forewarned—she's fond of dirty limericks."

"Why do you think it was saying his name?" Mark

asked, deliberately avoiding the name himself. They had agreed not to prompt the bird.

"Even the patients heard it. I heard it myself. She enunciates well," Sarah explained.

"But will she say it now?" Smith asked.

"What? Chiun?" the bird asked.

Smith stared at it.

"Ask pretty," the bird said.

"That did sound like his name—" Smith started.

"Ask pretty!"

"Say the name again. Please," Smith said.

"What, Chiun?"

"Yes. Thank you."

"You're welcome."

"Obvious she's well-trained," Howard observed. "But is she really saying 'Chiun'? Not 'Chewing'? Not 'Chin'? Not something else?"

"Not 'chewing' *not* 'chin' *not* something else," the bird ranted. "Chiun! Chiun! Chiun!"

"It's mimicry talents are amazing," Dr. Smith admitted. "Chiun could have a pet, one we don't know about. But how did she find her way here?"

"She's a hyacinth macaw, right?" Mark asked. "I've never heard of them having especially good senses of loyalty or tracking, especially if she has never been to Folcroft before."

"Right," Dr. Smith agreed. "The instinct to return to a former home is one thing. Tracking a human being to a strange location is entirely different and much less explicable."

"I assume you've never known Chiun to have a giant parrot in his suite?" Sarah asked.

"No."

Mark slowly knelt by the coffee table where the bird had been perched among the remainders of a bag of trail mix. He reached out his hand. The parrot hopped onto the table and cocked its head. Mark touched the top of its head, just above its huge and woeful-looking black beak. He stroked it gently.

The bird hopped on one foot to the edge of the table and cocked its head over the side, looking at the brace that still constricted Mark's wounded foot. Then it looked at Mark, cocked its head under his fingertips and waggled its own bandaged foot.

"Birds of feather!" It laughed uproariously.

"Oh, my God." Sarah pressed her fingertips to her lips.

Mark Howard took his hand away. "That doesn't sound like mimicry."

Dr. Smith shook his head, but said nothing. It had not sounded like mimicry to him, either. It sounded like creative word play. That took intelligence.

Parrots were supposed to be very smart, but no animal was that smart.

He carefully reached his hand out, as well.

"Eek! Get thee behind me, Satan!" the bird shrieked at him, and Smith froze. The bird stared hard at him, then threw back its head in gales of abrasive laughter.

Smith grew red faced.

"It's a joke!" The bird was suddenly on Smith's lap, rubbing its head against his chest. "Get over it!"

"Yes. I will. I will get over it."

"Sheesh." The parrot raised its wings for a moment. They were incredibly large and majestic inside the walls of the hospital suite. With one flap it was back into Sarah Slate's lap. "Sheesh," the bird commented again.

"We'll contact Chiun," Dr. Smith said, ostensibly to Sarah, but he was watching the bird. "He's in Australia with—"

"Remo?" the bird asked.

"Yes," Smith answered the parrot in a level voice.

"I guess that clears up my doubts about her really saying 'Chiun,'" Mark stated.

"Australia?" the bird asked. "Remo? Chiun? Australia?"

"Yes. They are in Australia."

The bird settled into Sarah's lap, cocking its head to either side, hunching down as if worried. They waited for it. They were all expecting another revelation when it spoke next.

"There once was a young man named Enis," the bird said miserably. "Who was blessed with an oversize—"

24

"My cousin Fellows Fence has accused me of propagating a slogan. Let's see, according to the paperwork filed today in federal court, the slogan is Oaties Is for P*ssies. I went to court today with my legal counsel to assure the court that I did not develop the slogan Oaties Is for P*ssies. I did not publish the slogan Oaties Is for P*ssies. I never authorized any representative or public-relations firm or advertising agency to publicize the slogan Oaties Is for P*ssies. Today, in court, Fellows Fence was unable to provide any evidence of my involvement in the dissemination of the slogan Oaties Is for P*ssies. Nevertheless, I have assured the court that I will vigorously search out my organization for evidence that some rogue employee might be responsible for publicizing the phrase Oaties Is for P*ssies. For that reason, I am forming the MacBisCo Oaties Is for P*ssies Task Force, reporting directly to me. If it came out of my company, I'll find the person responsible for the slogan Oaties Is for P*ssies!"

FELLOWS FENCE STARED at the front page in horror.

Oaties Is for P*ssies.

His big brother, Adam Fence, looked ready to kill somebody. And it wouldn't be the first time.

"I'll sue him into extinction," Fellows said weakly.

"Sue him for what? Cooperating?" Adam demanded. "He's reading right off the complaint you filed, Fellows. You were supposed to make this go away, not turn it into a media frenzy. Look at this!" Adam jabbed at a remote control and a wall-mounted screen came to life. That son of a bitch MacGregor was giving a press conference. "Oaties is for *bleep*ies." If he said it once, he said it ten times.

"Legal's already come back to me on this, Fellows. It's clean. There's no complaint here. We're screwed."

"It's legal's fault," Fellows said. "I cleared this with them. They said we had a case."

Adam jumped to his feet and pounded his fists on his desk. "What the hell are you thinking! They know the law and that's it. They're *lawyers*—nobody expects them to have common sense. But *you* are supposed to have common sense."

Fellows fought to keep his lower lip from quivering. "You blame me for this?"

"Of course I blame you. You did it."

"It's my assistant's fault. Jeremy. He's supposed to run interference."

"It's your fault. Shoulder the responsibility for once."

Fellows saw a slide show in his head, desperately seeking the person responsible for this disaster. It had to be someone else. It couldn't be him. In desperation, he tried to turn the tables. "You should have seen this coming. You should be taking the responsibility for this, Adam."

Adam smirked. "You're right. I bear the ultimate responsibility for all legal actions taken by this company. Which is why the company bylaws state specifically that the president shall be given adequate opportunity to review all legal actions taken by Fence Flour Company prior to them being taken. But you went to court without even giving me a heads-up. You know how serious that is, Fellows? It's a fireable offense!"

Fellows became extremely flushed.

"You better not faint. You faint in my office one more time and you'll wake up in the mail room. As an assistant."

"You're not going to fire me?" Fellows stammered.

"I'm giving you one last chance to save face. One."

"I'll do it."

"It might be too much for a guy named Fellows," Adam said sardonically.

"I'll make it happen. Just tell me what to do."

Adam scowled and sat heavily in his chair. He told Fellows what he wanted done.

"Please, no," Fellows whimpered. "Anything but that!"

FELLOWS FENCE WAS on the morning shuttle flight from Battle Creek to Chicago, and minutes later was on a United flight to Los Angeles. By the time he gathered his wits, with the help of a steady flow of white zinfandel, he was three hours out over the Pacific Ocean.

"I can't believe we're caving in. We're not followers," he ranted. "We're leaders. We made the breakfast-cereal industry into what it is today."

"Overpriced junk?" asked the amused plastic-pellets salesman next to him.

"Extreme Nuggets is junk," Fellows declared. "It binds you up. It's way too much of a good thing. Now I have to imitate Extreme Nuggets."

It was one of the famous Adam Fence handwritten business strategies. He came up with them at the breakfast table. These were legendary documents. They were studied in the MBA program at the University of Michigan in Kalamazoo.

This one had all the earmarks of a classic Adam Fence manifesto. It was bold, it was blatant, it used no careful business-speak.

"Extreme Nuggets is high-profile competition and they're cutting into our sales. We will beat them at their own game by launching Extreme Oaties in less than thirty business days." One bullet point instructed the cereal development laboratory to formulate the new cereal by the end of the week. Another bullet point called for the creation of dummy sales materials to be in the hands of sales reps in two weeks. The most important factor in the launch would be the celebrity promotions, as the final bullet point detailed.

"Oaties is famous for using champion athletes on its boxes, and we'll achieve dominance in this aspect of the extreme-cereals category, too. The vice president of marketing is charged with the responsibility of personally signing the best-known extreme athletes. This will be accomplished within two weeks."

Fellows Fence felt his spirits droop every time he read the part about the "vice president of marketing." Not a name but a title. Adam's way of letting everybody know when somebody's position was tenuous.

"He'd fire his own brother," Fellows moaned.

"I never knew the breakfast-cereal business was so ruthless."

"Oh, yeah. It'll chew you up. It'll spit you out." Fellows wiped away a tear and silently asked himself if he was man enough to endure such viciousness.

25

Jaiboru Junction, Northern Territory, Australia, was in the middle of nowhere—never mind that it was easy to find on the map, off the highway from Darwin to Alice Springs. The truth was that there was a single pitted dirt trail from the highway to the small outback town.

The name was a bold-faced lie. There was no junction in Jaiboru. It was on the way to nowhere. Wauchope was hours away, and Elliott and Tennant Creek were unreachable most of the year without an aircraft.

Situated on a dank stretch of real estate alongside the arid unpleasantness of the Tanami Desert, it offered visitors both the horrible dry and awful wetland outback experiences. That was just what the Extreme Sports Network was looking for when it planned its first Extreme Outback Crocodile Habitat Marathon.

The plan was for a triathlon, originally. The scout producer had to explain to the locals that a triathlon involved biking, running and swimming.

"You can't have people swimming in these waters, mate." The mayor of Jaiboru Junction chortled. "They'll be et."

"They'll be what?"

"Et. Et by crocs. Water's teeming with them."

The producer considered that. "It would be acceptable if some of them were eaten by crocs," he said hesitantly. In fact, it would be great if some of the contestants were eaten by crocs. He was already thinking about how to set up underwater cameras to film the feeding.

"No way, mate. You don't understand. The water is teeming with crocs! They'd *all of 'em* be. et."

The producer considered that, then decided that, for the sake of the program, there had to be some survivors to finish the race.

JAIBORU JUNCTION had been visited by a thousand people in its eighty-year history as a white settlement in the outback, and it quadrupled that number in just the first afternoon of the Extreme Outback Crocodile Habitat Marathon.

"Where's the hotel?" asked the latest stupid American to stop by the new roadside tourism-and-information tent.

"Ain't no hotel, mate," Quimby Summy said with a brown-toothed grin and dollar signs in his eyeballs. "Seems the promoters forgot to arrange to 'ave one built."

The American didn't panic. Most Americans would panic. "And the nearest hotel is…?"

"Two hundred and twelve klicks out that way," Quimby Summy said, happy to be of service.

"So where's everybody staying?"

"Summy's Tent City. My ma and I thought there might be a need, see? We got tents, cots, blankets, mosquito nettin', all the comforts."

The American seemed bored with this. "Not that I'd rent one, but what'll a tent run you in the outback these days?"

"Two tents," piped up the small, elderly Asian man standing nearby.

"Two tents. Lessee, now. We got a grading price structure. You got your bronze package, your silver package and your gold package."

"We shall accept nothing less than gold package," the Asian man stated without hesitation.

"What do you get with the gold package?" The American sighed.

"Not so much what you get as where you're put. Gold package is the farthest from the latrines, see. Not convenient, but upwind."

"Fine. Two golds. How much?"

"One thousand. Each," Quimby Summy said with the smile of a man who could name whatever price he wanted—and get it.

"That had better be pesos you're talking," the man growled.

"Dollars. American. Only place in the territory free of King Brown snakes. Money back guaranteed."

Remo shrugged and handed over his CURE credit card, booking two gold packages for two days in advance. They found that the tents were reasonably clean, and that was end of their list of benefits.

"Why did you allow the man to take advantage of you? You should have negotiated," Chiun intoned. "It would have been easy enough to convince him to give us a better rate."

"Don't worry about it. Smitty's paying."

"Still, you allowed yourself to be taken advantage of. Everything you do in recent days proves you are unfit to move about in the world."

"But I am fit to be Reigning Master of Sinanju? So any nincompoop with a few slick moves can be Master?"

"I hadn't thought so. Look. No phone. No power. How shall I recharge my iBlogger?"

Remo went back to the information-and-tourism tent. "Need a TV, electrical power and a phone."

Quimby Summy grinned wide. "That's extry."

"Whatever. Just put it on the card. The guarantee goes for the extras, too, I hope?"

"Sure," Summy said. "Sure, it does."

Quimby appeared at their tents with a wire tow wagon carrying a battered television. The TV was so old it was from the era when color was a novelty, and the rainbow word Color was emblazoned on the cabinet.

"You guys must have a hell of an expense account," said their neighbor, a cameraman with a Canadian sports channel. "We're sleeping four to a tent, and we still gotta pay some of it out of our own pocket."

"Why bother?" Remo asked.

The Canadian looked terrified. "King Brown snakes, that's why. This valley is the only place free of them for miles."

Remo knew a rat when he smelled one. He explained the shenanigans at the campground to Chiun as they drove into the desert to witness the start of the Extreme Outback Crocodile Habitat Marathon.

"I saw another commercial for your vile television

program," Chiun interrupted. "Your shameless prostitution will be broadcast throughout Australia."

"What's that have to do with anything?"

"We were discussing vile serpents. What better example than your profane abuse of your Sinanju training?"

"Didn't we agree not to discuss the TV show on this trip?"

Chiun fluttered his hand. "You brought it up, Yeou Gang."

"I did not, and stop calling me that."

"I can't call you anything else." Chiun shrugged.

"If you can't say something nice, don't say anything."

Chiun huffed. "Great words of wisdom, which you doubtless learned from the virgin acolytes of the tiresome carpenter. It would give me great pleasure if just once I heard my own wisdom issue from my own pupil."

"Get bent."

"I do not recall teaching you that use of language," Chiun said. "More nun mouthings, I assume."

Remo didn't respond.

"Fine, I shall cease speaking," Chiun concluded loftily.

They drove in silence down the endless highway until Chiun snatched the wheel and gave it a tug. The rental car careened off the road on two wheels.

"What was that for?" Remo demanded, jerking the wheel back and adjusting his body weight to bring the car crashing back onto all four wheels.

"I did not wish to offend your sensibilities with my speech." Chiun shrugged. "This is the way."

"You could have pointed," Remo said. "And I never invited the silent treatment anyway. That was your idea."

"The platitudes from the convent?" Chiun reminded him.

"You're just itching for a fight, aren't you?"

"Chafing under the smothering blanket of shame, do you mean?"

"Can it. Where we going?"

"Bring the car into the shade behind the big rock that is shaped like your head."

"I don't see any—"

"Forgive me. Now I see that all the rocks are shaped like your head. That one." Chiun pointed and Remo headed for the chunk of ugly sandstone, chewing on his tongue. The rock bore only a small resemblance to his head.

26

"Whoa, here they come. Have you ever seen anything like it? This is fantastic! These blokes are really breaking a sweat out here t'day, where the temperature is better'n a hundred degrees. To make matters worse, the sand is reflecting the heat right back up at the runners, and they're literally running inside an oven!" The boyish man in the khaki shorts, shirt and hat was crouching and bouncing, waving his hands as if his enthusiasm were about to burst him open. The video cameraman maneuvered to keep him in the picture.

"Who's he? Looks familiar." Remo and Chiun were waiting in the shade of their special rock a stone's throw from the video crew.

"Why would I know the answer to such a question?" Chiun was watching the line of approaching runners, who were crippled wraiths in the heat shimmering up from the ground. "He is a snake wrangler from the television."

"Yeah, now I remember," Remo said. "I knew you'd know. You know everything, Little Father."

"You could not be more disingenuous, my son. Disingenuous means insincere."

"I know what disingenuous means."

"*Rot* behind me, *rot* here, is where the competitors will leave the desert proper and enter a section of grasslands that's *teeming* with outback predators." The snake wrangler wouldn't have been more excited. "There's some nasty buggers in 'ere. These blokes are gonna have to be lot on their feet to get through without bein' bit, clawed or gored!"

Just six miles into the twenty-one-mile race, the runners were limp with fatigue. The first third of the Extreme Outback Crocodile Habitat Marathon was designed to sap their strength before pitting them against the real dangers.

"What people won't do for a few bucks," Remo commented.

"The prize purse is a million U.S. dollars," Chiun pointed out.

"Really? Again?"

Chiun glared at him.

"I could win this game easy," Remo pointed out.

"You could be a star quarterback. Does this mean you should do so?"

Remo nodded. "You're right, Chiun. I'm making lots more as a television phenomenon."

"Fah!"

The pack of runners began jogging into the grasslands.

"Look at these guys. They're almost dead on their feet already!" the snake wrangler exclaimed. "There's gonna be some seriously slowed reflexes, and this is the exact wrong time for it. Crikey, we're gonna see some *rilly* major bloodshed t'day!" The young-looking man in the khakis made a slicing motion across his throat, and the taping stopped. "C'mon, blokes!" The snake wrangler bolted into the grasslands and his production team jogged after him: a cameraman, a sound engineer, and a harried-looking blond woman in khakis with dark rings around her eyes.

"We supposed to stop the rilly major bloodshed?" Remo asked.

"I care not for these fools. We will merely watch for signs of cheating and report the perpetrator to the Emperor."

Remo followed Chiun through a gap between the rocks. They were positioned along the racecourse. The knee-high grasses were dotted with gnarled trees and shrubs, and all over it the meandering trail was marked with orange flags. Along the path came the runners.

As the rules stipulated, they wore standard summer marathon attire—shorts, sleeveless T-shirts, socks and shoes. This was designed to leave them unprotected from any hazard. Even sunblock was forbidden, and several of the runners were growing pink. The only nonstandard equipment was their headgear—lipstick-sized cameras and microphones. The famous ESN extreme cams fed their signals back to the ESN production base in Jaiboro Junction.

Remo could see their eyes darting nervously about the grasses, watching for dangerous creatures.

"These competitors have no idea what they're in for!" It was the snake wrangler, who was recording voice-overs as he cut across the grass to intercept the race trail. "This is one of the first real danger zones. Look at this!" He swooped down and snatched a writhing serpent off the ground. "Isn't she byoot-uh-full!"

The cameraman skidded to a halt and wrestled his camera to his eye to tape the angry snake.

"Hon, look at this lovely little girl!"

"Keep it away from me," the blond woman warned, backing away in a hurry. The woman began brushing at her clothes.

"She's a King Brown snake, and she's about the most attractive snake in this part of the world, but also a vicious biter! A real femme fatale!"

The snake, with dramatic acumen, chose that instant to bury its fangs in the shiny apple cheek of the snake wrangler.

"Oh, gaw!" He pinched the base of the snake's skull, forcing it to release. "She's given me a kiss, she has, hain't you, you pretty little sheila? Luckily, I've been bitten by the King Brown about two or three hundred times, thanks to spending my boyhood in the outback with my dear ol' dad. This has made me almost totally immune to the venom, but gaw, you do not want to try this at home!"

The snake wrangler cut the take. "Give me a minute to get this out of my system, mates." His eyes rolled into his skull and he collapsed on his back, convulsing. His wife didn't appear to notice as she batted and slapped her own garments.

"You didn't tape that, did you?" The snake wrangler was on his feet again in seconds, and he still held the hapless serpent.

"Course, not, Steve," the cameraman said. "Here they come."

The snake wrangler twirled his finger to get the camera rolling. "I can withstand a smooch from this darling girl, but the marathon runners don't have the same resistance. Let's see how they fare in the first major danger zone on the route!"

"I can't tell if this is better or worse than Extreme Nude Luge," Remo commented from their vantage point behind a nearby bush.

"Nothing could be worse than Extreme Nude Luge, save for *The Ladies' Man*," Chiun assured him.

The first-place runner spotted the production crew and ascertained correctly that he was closing in on a point where something dramatic might happen. He went into a series of skips and hops as he found the orange flags leading him over a warren of King Brown birthing nests. The fangs snapped at his shins and never quite connected, but the second-place runner wasn't so lucky. King Browns latched on to both his calves. The runner screeched and collapsed, thrashing.

"Wow, look at that! There's a bunch of beautiful young ladies who're showing this bloke a thing or two! They're lovely and sleek and really mad about having their nurseries disturbed, and who can blame 'em?" the snake wrangler asked the camera. "I sure can't."

"Neither can I," Chiun added.

"Yeah, me either," Remo said. "Little Father, does it make me a bad person for not caring about the morons in the marathon?"

"No. But plenty of other things make you a bad person. Would you like me to name them?"

"No, thank you."

"It will be no trouble, but sadly it must wait," Chiun

said. "I will accompany the leaders. You monitor the stragglers."

"Say please." But Remo was talking to himself. Chiun was already slipping through the grasses, his kimono a brilliant shimmer in the sun, although he remained unseen by everyone else. The front-runners had moved past the nest of vipers, who were as a group attacking the fallen runner.

"Gaw, lookit all of those pretty babies. I guess that bloke's been bitten at least thirty or forty times now!" The snake wrangler was so excited he was nearly doing jumping jacks. "And see that, how they keep bitin' 'im! They're just addin' insult tah inj'ry now. Every one of them sexy serpents has injected all her precious venom already. My wife knows what can happen when you suffer that kind of attack, rot there, Patty?"

The camera cut and the sound engineer slammed a hypodermic into the shoulder of the trembling blonde. She breathed deep, felt the rush, got her nerve, patted her hair and stepped in front of the camera, smiling.

"That's right, Steve. When I was an outback nurse we saw more than one case where a hiker fell into a King Brown snake nest and there's nothing to be done." She smiled pleasantly. "One bite is nonlethal. Two bites is usually treatable if we get to the victim in time. But in a situation like this, it's not even worth opening the first-aid kit."

Her husband bobbed appreciatively. "Gaw, yaw!"

"His entire circulatory system is swelling shut," she said, waving at the runner, who was moving his arms and legs in slow motion. "Kind of like having a heart attack and stroke all at once. Even if he did survive, his arms and legs would all have to be amputated before they became gangrenous. If he's lucky, he'll pass out in a minute."

"Gaw, what's lucky about that?"

"Saves him from suffering while he suffocates when his windpipe collapses. There he goes now."

"Poor bugger!" The snake wrangler waved playfully at the gasping runner, who was reaching out one hand plaintively, begging for release from his misery. "Just a lovely little miracle what those slim little beauties can do, isn't it?"

Remo heard the whisper of scales on grass and spotted one of the snakes nearby. It wasn't a part of the attack, so it still had plenty of venom. He was tempted to send the snake flying down the cameraman's bush slacks, but knew that it wouldn't shut up the snake wrangler. Besides, the stragglers were now passing over the viper nest, and Remo had his chores to do. He slipped through the grass, pacing them.

They were a sorry-looking bunch, all ropy muscle and jittery faces. Maybe they were only now realizing how much danger they were in.

In last place was a hollow-eyed, scrawny man who was suffering gastrointestinal distress. Remo kept an eye on him, but the runner was clearly terrified and preoccupied with watching the trail. He didn't come across like a man about to perpetrate a big cheat.

None of them did. They followed the curves and loops of the trail until they caught up with the snake wrangler again. Remo slipped ahead, moving like a flash of sunlight across the grasslands. He, for one, had no fear of the dangers creeping and crawling in the grass. His major concern was for the remote-controlled cameras that were set up along the trail by the Extreme Sports Network. So far, they were aimed tight on the path and easy enough to avoid.

"Here's a fresh bunch of beautiful beasties who won't be too happy when a bunch of big ugly feet come pounding on top of them!" the snake wrangler gushed. "Look at this! Isn't she a lovely specimen of the white-tailed spider!" His hand was nearly hidden by a big furry spider. "I love you, sweetheart!" He kissed her golf-ball-sized bottom.

His wife, off camera, shuddered and rubbed her arms as if freezing, face becoming ghastly pale.

"Now, these perfect little pretties…"

At that moment the spider vaulted off his palm and zeroed in on the snake wrangler's wife, who took a deep breath in preparation for a scream. The spider's aim was precise. It entered the gaping mouth headfirst, but was too big to fit completely inside.

"Gaw!" the snake wrangler exclaimed as his wife clawed her face and expelled the spider. The snake wrangler scooped it up before it hit the ground, examining it as his wife became noisily sick.

"I never saw one of these sheilas fly before," the snake wrangler said. "Aw, babe, you killed her!"

The wife was gagging and snatching spider hairs off her tongue, but she stopped long enough to screech at him.

"Poor little girl," the snake wrangler said sadly—to the dead spider, not his wife.

"I saw you fling a pebble at the spider," Chiun accused as he stepped out of the brush at Remo's elbow, not ten paces from the production team. "Such pranks are not helpful."

"I wasn't pulling a prank. I was trying to make him shut his bug yap."

"You only encouraged him."

The snake wrangler was bobbing in front of the camera and waving his arms wildly. "I don't know what we just saw, but it was stupendous and amazing! In all my years I never saw one of these luscious little girls jump like that! And to think we got it on tape!"

Chiun gave Remo a smug roll of the eyes. Remo answered by scooping up a handful of tiny pebbles. He flicked them in rapid succession at the flock of white-tailed spiders. The rocks smashed into the spiders and propelled them through the air. As if attacking, the creatures homed in on the cameraman, the sound engineer, the wife and the snake wrangler himself. The crew fled in terror, the wife collapsed and the snake wrangler broke down in tears.

"All of them are dead! Oh, my sweet beauties!" He didn't even notice the marathon runners as they hopped and skipped through the undergrowth, now devoid of spiders.

Chiun slipped away, leaving Remo with a skewering look. Remo took up the pace again with his stragglers.

"Gotta do something for fun around here," he said to himself.

The grasslands spilled down a slight hill into heavier low trees and shrubs. Remo could see the leaders far ahead. Chiun was out there somewhere. Eventually the trail's twists and turns straightened, and the runners in the front were dashing across it, trying to make up time. There was no danger evident.

But Remo smelled sickness in the air. Animal sickness. Mammal sickness.

The runners in the front pack never hesitated when they saw the kangaroos. After all, they were kangaroos. Only Remo sensed danger.

"You kidding me?" he asked nobody.

The kangaroos began to bounce heavily in the direction of the runners, who noticed their foaming mouths for the first time. There were cries of alarm as the kangaroos closed in.

"What's happening down there?" one of the nearby stragglers asked breathlessly. "Oh, my God, they're attacking."

More animals closed in from the sides, attracted by the noise, bursting into the open as the group of stragglers put on the brakes—and the vision of more kangaroos coming up from the rear started them going again.

"More of them!" one straggler gasped.

"They're rabid!" another shouted.

Remo didn't know if it was rabies or the black marsupial plague or what, but he didn't want to have anything to do with it. A large beast, demented by disease, spotted him and came in his direction. Remo stepped high at the last moment, sailing easily into the upper branches of a small tree. The kangaroo swerved to a delirious stop, trying to find its prey.

"What would you do with me if you got me, anyway?" Remo asked it.

The creature leaped and slapped at him, but found Remo was out of its reach. Remo watched, fascinated, as more sick beasts fell on the marathon runners, pounding them, kicking them powerfully, but mostly just delivering body slams. Luckily the creatures were dizzy and weakened by sickness and began collapsing from their efforts. The beast under Remo's tree fell on its stomach and breathed one last time, blowing foam for yards.

The runners, all but two of them, picked themselves up and continued the marathon.

Remo had spotted the cameras when they entered the valley. They had filmed every glorious second of the exercise. He had a feeling the producers of the show would fail to inform the audience that the kangaroos had been deliberately infected just for today's special event, but Remo knew it had not occurred by chance.

"This is sick," he said, as he paced along with the stragglers. TV was sick. Now he was a part of the whole sick television industry.

Well, not really, he told himself. Right?

There was a whine of a Jeep engine coming to intersect the marathon runners' trail, and the snake wrangler stepped out before the vehicle even came to a halt. His cameraman stumbled out and started taping. Even a thousand yards back, Remo could hear him gushing about the next phase of the marathon.

The race was entering its most dangerous phase: the crocodile habitat.

CHIUN WAS UNSEEN. If he had been visible, he would have looked like a very odd spirit who seemed to float above the ground and drift with an unfelt, swift air current.

He found these proceedings unpleasant and ghastly, and he wished to be done with them as soon as possible. He was also much preoccupied by the behavior of his adopted son.

Remo was often a headstrong oaf. He had been so from the very beginning, and his head strength and oafishness waxed and waned with the passage of the years. But what was he up to now? Was this television foolishness really what it seemed to be?

Chiun knew Remo was making a cry for attention, however wrongheaded his methods. But was he sincerely planning to carry on with this unthinkable, shameful display? Chiun had thought so until today.

Chiun found an observation point along the shore of a thick stew of water. In the middle of the swamp was a narrow shelf of land decorated with orange flags. The ridiculous runners emerged and loped down the trail, eyes peeled for the famous meat eaters. Chiun knew enough of crocodiles. A crocodile would not attack a group of humans.

And yet a crocodile did. The vicious beast with a dark crust lunged from the water, bolted across the bridge and twisted its head to clamp down on the nearest leg it could find before propelling itself into the opposite waterway.

More crocodiles gathered under the surface of the water. Chiun was curious. Crocodiles didn't attack in large groups unless they were starving. And yet, with a burst of noise and water, the animals loped out of the lake and chased down the runners. There was chaos. Crocodiles plunged into the water with their victims and returned seconds later for another. Soon not a single runner in the lead pack remained. Some of them doubtless still lived, but were likely being tucked away into crocodile meat lockers for a later meal.

This was all interesting and atypical. Chiun made a note to describe the behavior to Emperor Smith the Insane. He would assure the Emperor that the crocodiles in question were quite plump enough.

Remo claimed he was repulsed by this television silliness, but he was without chagrin. Even Remo was not so inane—they were observing the wallowing of the hogs and yet Remo did not see himself as lolling in the same mud?

One of the crocodiles discovered Chiun and homed in on his shadowy place on the shore. It was the big one who had made the first kill. The giant brute slithered below the water, as silent as a ripple on a pond, until he rocketed to the earthen bank and closed his mighty jaws on the gaunt and ancient ankle of a weak and helpless old man.

But the great rows of teeth clacked unexpectedly together. No bony ankle. The giant croc didn't have time to be surprised before something else happened that was even further beyond the grasp of its crocodilian intellect.

The tiny little old man stepped on its snout—and pinned it there.

What did Remo's curious reaction mean? Was the young Master up to something even more devious than Chiun had credited him with? Was there some scheme that Chiun had not even guessed?

Unlikely. Still…

The group of stragglers emerged onto the bridge

that separated the bodies of water and for a moment they kept on their wary way. There was no sign of trouble.

Then their faces slowly registered the understanding that there should have been a sign of something. The leaders had not been *that* far in the lead. The runners should be visible a mile or so ahead on the land bridge.

Then the first straggler came across a pool of blood-soaked earth. The great brute held captive under Chiun's left sandal went through a fit of thrashing at that moment. There was panic and much ludicrous scrambling on the part of the marathon runners. The swarm of crocodiles emerged behind them. Another swarm emerged in front. The runners were trapped.

Again, quite unlike the crocodile behavior Chiun knew. Crocodiles and Remo both behaving oddly. What makes a crocodile act like a lunatic? What lessons are there in a crocodile's lunacy?

Far back, another runner emerged from the bush and sprinted across the land bridge in a blood-soaked T-shirt. He was barefoot and his wrists were swollen obscenely, likely a result of the hundreds of ant stings he received after being knocked unconscious by rabid kangaroos. He was Runner Number 10, or so his T-shirt said.

Runner Number 10 was moving pretty well for a dead man. He slipped up on the crocodiles like a shadow and began stepping on their skulls with his bare heels. Crocodile skulls burst open. Eight crocs were dead before they knew it.

Runner Number 10 ran around the other panicking runners, his bare feet flying over rocks and water. Yes, water. For a second he was running on the surface of the swamp....

Then Runner Number 10 stepped around the snapping jaws of the front formation of crocodiles and used his furious fingers on their heads. He poked at them. It would have been comic if not for the sudden red holes appearing in the skulls of the crocs. In seconds, the roar of the monsters was silenced. The crocs were lifeless.

"This is a stupid race and you are all morons," Runner Number 10 announced loudly and clearly for all the hidden ESN cameras to record. "I'd rather die than be a part of it. Goodbye."

Runner Number 10 ran back the way he had come. His body was found in the bushes an hour later, although death had changed his appearance markedly. The wrist swelling was diminished. His hair was bleached by trauma. His last act had been, for some reason, to reverse his shirt so it was on backward.

BY THE TIME Remo rejoined Chiun in the bushes, the confused marathon runners had started running again—less out of dedication to finish the race and more from fear of staying where they were.

"I hope you don't want accolades for your performance," Chiun declared.

"I don't even want a thank-you," Remo snapped and kept moving. Just three miles separated the handful of survivors from the finish line.

"What is your hurry?" Chiun asked.

"There's more in store for these schmucks. I want to see what happens next." Remo took up a position on the watery shore as the land bridge turned into a jumble of rocks alongside a deep pond. Crossing it was a fallen tree trunk, at least a hundred feet long and dotted with orange flags.

"What makes you believe the challenges are not over?" Chiun demanded.

"Let's just watch."

The runners stepped onto the log, slowing to a quick trot. There was no room for passing, and they went single file.

The last runner went slower than the others. He made a show of trying to keep his balance. That was for the sake of the camera. Remo and Chiun saw the lie in his behavior. The runner was scanning the wide tree trunk beneath his feet. He slowed momentarily to step on something, and a nearly invisible mist jetted out of the log a few paces in front of him. The runner entered the mist and pretended to lose his balance, turning a complete circle as he windmilled his arms.

The mist smelled deadly, but the runner was unaffected. After coating himself thoroughly he continued jogging. The mist petered out.

"Bug spray," Remo said, just as the first of the runners stepped off the log and into a swarm of insects that came out of the trees like a wall of tiny pain machines.

"THIS IS a total and complete surprise! I have never seen Australian cicada killer wasps act like this, not ever!" A hundred feet away, the snake wrangler was talking into a camera that he had perched on a rock. He didn't need a cameraman or a sound engineer or his blithering idiot wife. He could produce his own field reports. "These gorgeous big buzzers make a nasty sting, they do. Not too poisonous, but one sting by itself is rilly painful, and these guys are going to be in super agony. I'd be quite surprised if any of 'em gets to the finish line now."

The runners smacked at the wasps, maddening the swarms.

"Those poor chaps are just getting those grand girls all riled up. If they were smart, they'd stay perfectly still, not make a move and just let the wasps come. You might get stung a few times, yeah, but mostly it's nothing but the sweet, soft tickle of their perfect little feet on your skin. Gaw, that bloke's in fer it!"

The last-place runner got his second wind and ran like the wind, leaping off the end of the log. The swarms of stinging bugs seemed to flow off him like water, and he just kept on going. Other runners broke from the swarm and loped after him, still slapping at themselves.

"Funny how the bugs didn't seem to bother that guy too much," Remo said from his vantage point.

"Yes, humorous, which is why I laugh so heartily," Chiun said.

The race was as good as over. The competitors who struggled back up again were staggering from the pain, the dehydration, the exhaustion. One man lost consciousness on his feet. Those who managed to push on were slowed to a stiff-legged gait.

The man who had been in last place pretended to be afflicted, but all that was really bothering him was a few minor wasp stings and his clenched bowels. He even let himself collapse once, but then picked himself up and fought for the lead, crossing the finish line with a lead of just a few paces. A hundred people were in the bleachers at the finish line, and they cheered madly at the dramatic finish, only to be drowned out by the roar of a recorded audience from the loudspeakers.

"Do you hear that? The crowd here is going wild!" The announcer wore an ESN blazer, reporting from a newly constructed announcing booth near the finish line. "What a finish! This has turned out to be the most extreme and deadly event in the history of extreme sports! The official count is not yet in, but we have at least ten fatalities! What a spectacle! We're still trying to make sense of the unbelievable savagery of all the attacks that took place today, but one thing is clear. This was no ordinary marathon. This was competition taken to the extreme!"

Remo and Chiun emerged from the bush, stepping up the steep embankment and onto the junction's waterfront without being noticed.

"Crikey, I can't stand listening to another TV announcer," Remo said.

"He will now interview the winner," Chiun said. "We will observe their interchange."

Remo didn't bother arguing. He knew it was a waste of time.

"He stayed at the back of the pack to conserve energy," Remo said accusingly as he and Chiun watched from the crowd.

"And to avoid the worst of the challenges," Chiun added. "Except for the crocodiles."

"Yeah. He was packed in with the rest of them. Hadn't been for Remo the Good Samaritan he'd be tucked away in a croc locker this minute with all the others." Remo frowned. "What was his plan for getting out of that pickle, I wonder?"

"When we find out, we will also learn what method was used to send the crocodiles into their frenzy to begin with. The snake wiggler is correct in this one thing, Remo—the animals behaved most strangely. Someone has tampered with this swamp."

"No duh, Chiun."

The old Korean turned to Remo, seared him with a look, then ignored him for the rest of the closing rituals of the Extreme Outback Crocodile Habitat Marathon. The "Interview with the Champion," sponsored by Weeder Brand Hydrating Water-Flavored Gel-Packs, was mostly a scripted affair.

"You faced death at every turn. You were suffering from exhaustion, you were poisoned—what kept you going?"

The champion read his answer off the cue cards, then the brave winner of the marathon was ceremonially triaged and wheeled away on a gurney. The camera followed his journey across the waterfront to the official Extreme Outback Crocodile Habitat Marathon Hospital and Morgue, sponsored by Candidas megaperformance footwear.

"If that guy is in cahoots with the network he's hiding it pretty well," Remo said as the crowds dispersed.

Chiun was unhappy. "With someone he is in cahoots."

"Extreme Nuggets cereal company, perhaps?"

"Think before you speak."

"Fine."

Chiun made his way to the hospital, ignoring the network security guard at the entrance. Remo followed the Korean Master through the brightly lighted, air-conditioned tent's main corridor. Chiun flung open four sets of door flaps until he found the room where the champion was being treated by several nurses and a pair of doctors.

"Who are you?" one of the physicians demanded.

"Be gone, charlatan! Go practice your ridiculous quackery on the cadavers. I will speak to this man in private."

"Like hell. Security!"

Chiun put his hands in his sleeves.

"Security!" the doctor bellowed again.

Chiun looked over his shoulder and scowled.

"What?" Remo asked.

"Security!"

"You want me to do something about the loudmouth, is that it?"

Chiun rolled his eyes.

"Security!"

"Fine." Remo pinched the doctor on the upper spine, making him stiffen from head to toe—and stop shouting. Remo caught him when he fell over, paralyzing the second doctor before she could take up the shouting herself. He rolled them both out into the corridor and, with a wave of his hand, offered the nurses the chance to use the exit door under their own power. They scrambled over one another to get out.

"You could at least ask when you want me to do your bidding," Remo said to Chiun. "You could even say please."

"Why? Obviously the task was yours. Certainly you would not expect me to put out the trash?"

"I'm here as a favor to you," Remo pointed out. "I don't even work for your company anymore."

"So you have said many, many times." Chiun stood beside the bed, where the champion was watching them through bleary eyes. "Speak, cretin! Who engineered your victory?"

"What?" The word rolled slowly out of his mouth. Chiun snatched off the IV tube and tossed it onto the floor. "Hey, I need that, man! I'm in pain." The word *pain* dragged on and on.

"No potion in a bottle can protect you from pain such as I can deliver," Chiun announced, and proved his point by grasping the base of the champion's thumb in his own fingers. Chiun gave it a squeeze, and the champion gasped, tried to scream, but seized up like an old car engine with its oil drained out.

The silence endured for fifteen seconds, and by then the champion had flop-sweated what little hydration had been restored to his body. When Chiun released the pressure the champion collapsed on the bed, breathing hard.

"How did you win the race?" Chiun asked haughtily.

"Messages coming on the headset. Somebody was talking to me and telling me what to do. I don't know who it was."

"And yet you followed their advice?" Chiun demanded.

"They told me when to fall back, right before we ran into the snakes. They were on the money that time, so I started listening. They told me to stay in the rear, which I did and I missed most of the attacks."

Chiun's face was impervious. "And this unknown benefactor instructed you to coat yourself with the spray that repels biting flies?"

The champion gulped.

"We watched you activate it. Don't even think of denying it," Remo advised.

"Yes," the champion admitted. "He told me there would be a fresh-cut *X* carved in the tree trunk. I was supposed to step on it, then step into the aerosol spray. I didn't plan to do it! I was set up."

"Who?" Chiun demanded.

"I don't know," the champion replied. "I swear I don't."

"You got a sponsor?" Remo asked.

The champion looked sheepish. "My dad sponsored me. He owns a bowling alley in Pensacola."

"Any promotional deals pending, in case you win?"

The champion was too chagrined to answer. "Nobody thought I had any chance of winning," he admitted.

"Not even Extreme Nuggets?" Remo prodded.

The champion shook his head. "No. But it is my dream to be an Extreme Nuggets champion. I eat them every day. It gives me the extreme nutrition I need—"

"Can it. You must be awfully proud how you came from behind and proved everybody wrong."

For the first time the champion sat up straighter. "Yes, sir, I sure am."

THEY PREPARED to depart, and Remo was instructed to tote five of Chiun's six trunks to the rental car. Chiun took the black lacquered trunk, the one that hissed, and went for a walk. Remo came back to an empty tent, but Chiun arrived minutes later and placed the trunk on the grass. "You may bring this now."

Remo dutifully placed the black box on his shoulder. The chest was still hissing, but far less than it had all morning. Remo did not allow himself to notice. Chiun's chests were Chiun's business.

QUIMBY SUMMY WAS in a beautiful daydream. His life was starting fresh. He had become a wealthy man in just seventy-two hours.

How wealthy? He wasn't exactly sure yet. He spent somewhere around twenty-eight thousand dollars, Australian, to rent a truckload of tents and army cots. Another couple thousand for wages because he sure as shinola wasn't gonna put up all them tents himself. But the latrine shacks, them he did put together all by himself. And that was just about the end-all of his expenses, which came out to about thirty grand, Aussie dollars, maybe twenty-five grand in American dollars. Now, you add to that the rents he'd collected. Fifty bronze packages at eight hundred dollars. Fifty silver packages at nine hundred. A whopping 150 gold packages at one thou apiece. Them cheap packages were just for show, and they made the math get all tough to figure.

Take out some for the credit-card fees, them blood-sucking leeches. Add a lot more for the little extras that were in high demand. Ma's vegemite pitas had sold for five bucks each, and he figured his expenses on them were less than twenty-five cents. And he didn't have to pay his ma a wage. Drinking water was three dollars a bottle compared to ten cents each it cost him. It made him feel like a real businessman to weigh his costs and his income and come up with profits. Made it easy that there wasn't no wastage. He sold out every damn thing by the second day. Toilet paper—now that's where he really cleaned up. He brought in two pallets for a couple hundred bucks and sold them off at two dollars a roll on the first day, five dollars each the second day, and then he auctioned off the eight remaining rolls this morning.

Hell, he couldn't figure it out! It was too damned mathematical. Didn't matter anyway, cause he knew it was more than he'd ever dreamed of.

He gave a hearty welcome to the pair of stupid American tourists who entered the tent that served as the Jaiboru Junction information-and-tourism bureau and the business office of Quimby Summy Enterprises.

"G'day! Nice day."

"I guess," said the morose American, carefully resting a lacquered black chest on the grassy floor of the tent. The small Asian stood next to the chest, expressionless as if he were in his own world. Maybe he was deaf. "I need to talk to you about your guests."

"What about them?" Summy asked, not really caring.

"Who got here before the competition started—anybody?"

Summy shrugged. "Sure. We had people here a week ago. The Extreme Network people, they arranged to board in Susie's attic above the tavern, and the athletes stayed with the families in town. Everybody else stayed right here, with me."

"You seem very proud."

"Provided a valuable service." Summy beamed.

"Tell me about the early arrivals. Who were they?"

Summy stroked his chin. "Mostly sportswriters. The

network let in writers from all over the world. Free advertising for the network, isn't it? Photographers, too, you know, but no video takers."

"Very savvy. Who else?"

"Some tourists came early. One big bunch of Americans got here three days early to scout the track out. Told everybody they were just tourists, but a guy from the network says they're wagerin' consultants. They sell their bettin' advice on any kind of competition. The network don't officially, you know, condone bettin' on their events."

The American seemed interested, and Summy realized too late that he was giving away information that he should have been selling, but what the hell. He was rich. He told the American where to find the wagering consultants.

"By the way," the American asked before he left, "anybody complain about snakes in their tents?"

Summy tilted his greasy head. "What's that?"

"You know, the guarantee?" The American tapped the sign on the tent wall detailing the money-back guarantee of a stay free of venomous snakes. "Anybody ask for their money back?"

Quimby Summy wanted to laugh out loud. "Truth is, there ain't been a King Brown snake spotted in this field in twenty years," he said. "Had us a tanker crack up on the highway and flood the whole field with solvent sludge. Smell in the soil keeps the critters out, and the snakes won't go to a place without critters for eatin'."

"Hmm. My father thought maybe he saw one outside our tents this morning."

Summy got suspicious. Was this guy sniffing around for a refund? But the younger man just said thanks, nodded at the old man and tapped his forehead. Then he said goodbye. The old Asian smiled broadly before he led his son out.

"Both daft as ducks," Summy said, relieved that his excellent mood hadn't been spoiled. He sure would have hated giving up the profits from even two gold packages. Snakes? Here? King Browns, no less? No way, mate.

Something slithered between Quimby Summy's ankles.

A SHADOW DARKENED the tent doorway. Petyr didn't stop stuffing his clothes into his knapsack.

"What?" he asked the stranger.

"Where's the rest of your group? All their tents are empty."

"Gone. Who are you looking for?"

"Not sure." The stranger with the Oriental box was moved aside by a small, incredibly elderly man in a robe of shimmering pale yellow. The old man was a Korean. Petyr knew his Asians, but he didn't know why this one was sniffing around the inside of his tent like a hunting dog.

"What are you doing?" he demanded.

"Why'd you stay after everybody else took off?" the younger man asked him.

"Who are you and what do you want?" Petyr demanded.

The old Korean took Petyr's wrist and squeezed, and then Petyr knew exquisite pain.

He tried screaming. Screams wouldn't come. Paralysis accompanied the agony.

"What's the stink, Little Father?" Remo asked. "This guy keeping roadkill under his cot?"

"He butchered marsupials. They were not fresh. Then tainted the meat, although I recognize not the poison."

Petyr was surprised that they knew what they knew. Had the old man learned this by the smell alone? He didn't care. He was too busy caring about the pain.

The pain went away. "What is the poison and what is its purpose?"

Petyr was a professional and he never gave up his secrets, but all that integrity flew out the window in the hopes of staving off more pain, so he explained about the poison.

The younger man rolled his eyes. "Say again in English, Boris?"

"I am not Boris. I am Petyr. That was in English."

"You catch that, Little Father?"

Chiun frowned. "He shall tell it to the Emperor." Chiun extracted the cell phone from the case on Petyr's belt and tossed it to Remo, who caught it gingerly and examined it like a ticking bomb.

"Open it."

"Won't that break it?"

"I did not mean you should expose the insides! Simply flip up the front panel. You have worked a cell phone before, Remo. I witnessed it myself."

Remo lifted the panel. The phone had a colorful screen that came to life. He carefully depressed the 1 button and held it.

He was amazed when he heard the voice of Dr. Harold W. Smith come on the line.

"This is the personal assistant for M.O.S.E. Chiun," he announced loudly. "Please hold for Moses." Remo thrust the phone at Chiun, who sighed loudly and touched the phone on its edge.

"Master Chiun, are you there?" Smith asked, now from the speaker.

"Yes, Emperor. Please listen to the confessions of this Russian filth."

Petyr had no idea what was going on. This pair wasn't behaving like any American agents he had ever run into. He wasn't sure what to do, but then his hand was squeezed again and he started speaking. Once again, he explained what he had done and how.

"You understand what the hell he's talking about, Smitty?" Remo asked, forgetting himself.

"I believe so. He infused carrion meat with a solution of powdered metallic binders and suspended neural toxins."

"That's the third time I've heard it and I still have no clue," Remo said.

"The meat was fed to the crocodiles in advance of the race, long enough for the particles to be absorbed into their bodies and brains, then activated in some way."

"How was this activated?" Chiun demanded of Petyr, who stammered through a fresh wave of pain. "Microwaves! Excited the ferrous metallic molecules and released the chemicals in suspension. The emitter is buried here."

Remo dug where Petyr tapped his foot, and Remo

unearthed a device in a plastic bag. "This is a prop from a bad space movie."

"It discharges microwaves!" Petyr insisted. "I swept the crocs with it this morning. By afternoon their brains were telling them they were ravenous, no matter how much they ate. They went for the runners because they thought they were starving."

"But not all the runners," Remo probed. "You wanted the Florida kid to win."

"There were seven runners who were on the do-not-eat list," Petyr offered as streams of sweat stung his eyes and dripped from his chin. "We dusted their clothes with a repellent and took our chances that one of them would come through."

"What of the kangaroos?" Chiun demanded.

"The network did do the kangaroos?" Remo said.

"Bought them from trappers a couple weeks ago and injected them with rabies," Petyr explained. "Had them in a pen way out in the bush. Couple of days ago we injected them."

Smith interrupted. "Those kangaroos were aggressive, but they weren't trying to eat the runners."

"It was just stimulants. Amphetamines, adrenaline, painkillers."

"So they were rabid, violently aggressive and unaware of their own injuries. I guess that explains it," Remo said. "Bees?"

"Remotely detonated smoke bombs with insect-specific neural stimulant," Petyr explained.

"You thought of everything," Remo admitted. "Now, who signs the paycheck?"

"The one who hired me was the foreman. I worked

with him before. I don't know his name. An American who subcontracts to skilled professionals like me."

"You must know more than this," Chiun accused. "Speak now!"

"I know nothing! I was paid half up-front, in cash. I never knew what we were doing or why. That's all I know, I swear it!"

"Were you in the U.S. a few days ago?" Remo asked. "Messing with naked people on skateboards? Using your ray gun to heat up ice skates at the Extreme Bad Babes on Ice event?"

Petyr shook his head. "Not exactly."

"What does that mean?" Chiun demanded.

Petyr gaped like a fish on a sidewalk until Chiun stopped squeezing, then he explained. "It is my technology, but I have turned it over to the foreman for a fee. He has hirelings to do the work at such events now. I do not know any more about this!"

"Who were the other six runners on the do-not-chew list?" Remo asked.

Petyr listed the names, a glimmer of optimism in his eyes. Maybe he'd survive his interrogation. Or was that unrealistic? No, they were Americans. Americans didn't kill people. Americans locked you up and questioned you again and again for weeks, but they didn't snuff you out.

"Anything you'd like to add?" Remo asked the Russian specialist.

"That's all I know, I swear."

Remo shrugged. "I believe you."

"Can I go now?"

"What do you think, dim bulb?"

Petyr's hopes crashed to the earth. Chiun made a fluid sweep of his hand, then Petyr himself crashed to the ground with tiny fingernail punctures in his forehead.

"So, Smitty, make anything of it? I sure didn't," Remo said loudly.

"You do not need to bellow for Emperor Smith to hear you," Chiun remonstrated.

"We'll work on those names. See if we can ID this foreman. What's all the noise?"

"It is Remo's respiration," Chiun explained helpfully. "Every breath he takes is like the snort of an angry bull."

"I breathe perfectly," Remo protested.

"It sounds like screaming," Dr. Smith added.

"Probably static," Remo said. "Maybe a bird on the wires." He slipped through the flap so as not to show the world the fresh corpse inside the tent. He needn't have bothered. The running and shouting guests were focusing their attention on the wriggling ground. Remo focused on the fresh air and sunshine, then became aware of Chiun falling in step beside him.

"Smitty make anything out of that nonsense about drugs and rabies?"

"He will investigate further," Chiun said with a hint of sarcasm.

The local constable and his extra security staff, hired especially for the marathon, wandered among the tents with shotguns aimed into the grass. There was a boom nearby and a voice yelled, "I got another one!" An Extreme Sports Network van rolled drunkenly onto the road, packed with bodies. More people were on top, crowding together tightly and kicking at more frantic campers trying to scramble aboard.

"Shuttle bus is overloaded," Remo observed.

The thick crowd was less terrified and more angry the closer it got to Quimby Summy's Tent City business office. His card table was strewed with the corpses of serpents, and his customers were demanding refunds by the dozens.

"You guaranteed no King Brown snakes!" shouted a man from a British sport tabloid. "Look what I found nesting in my knickers!" The writer thrust out a limp serpent with a smashed skull.

"But there hasn't been a snake here in twenty years!" Quimby exclaimed. "I can't refund all that money!"

The response from the crowd was vicious, and Quimby relented. He began processing credit-card refunds and sobbing plaintively as the queue grew longer by the minute.

"See what happens when you're not nice and try to rip people off, Little Father?" Remo said. "Maybe we should get a refund, too."

"That would be dishonest, Remo. We have seen no snakes. At least, I have not. Have you?"

Remo nudged a wriggling tree branch from under the front wheel of their rental car. "Nope," he said, carefully stowing the last trunk in the rear of the vehicle. The trunk was no longer hissing even a little.

27

The foreman was preoccupied, but he was the consummate professional. He didn't miss the drop-off by an instant. There was his contact, a local hired by an acquaintance of the foreman's. Not many people had underground contacts on New Zealand's South Island, but the foreman wasn't your run-of-the-mill operator.

The contact parked his car outside the Invercargill City Frog 'n' Firkin Café. The foreman was inside munching a quick lunch, wondering why New Zealanders put fried eggs on burgers. The contact never looked at the foreman, but he scratched the sides of his nose in the correct sequence: left once, right twice, left once, right three times.

The foreman chucked the rest of his meal and strolled to the car. The keys were in it. He drove away.

A half an hour outside Manapouri he pulled onto the shoulder of the deserted highway and inventoried the trunk. The rifle was there. The ammunition was there.

The foreman knew it would be. His contacts were professionals. He was a professional. But double-checking was the professional thing to do.

He went back to chewing on his problem.

The Russian was dead. Killed by a snakebite, apparently. Lots of snakebites going on in Jaiboru Junction—a bunch of King Brown snakes had swarmed the campground and caused a riot. Several bites, but only one death—Petyr the Russian.

There were a lot of advantages to Petyr being dead right now. He'd provided the foreman with all the microwave technology at his disposal, and the foreman really had no more use for him. Petyr being out of the picture meant one less salary to pay and one less security concern.

But Petyr being dead made no sense. Petyr was a professional, too. He worked with venomous snakes. He had been a sort of snake wrangler of the underworld. To have been killed by a snake was unthinkable. Still, Petyr was dead. Found in his tent at Jaiboru, puncture marks in his forehead, of all places, and a King Brown lounging on the cot.

"I think somebody's hot on our trail," the foreman told his employer on the secure phone when he was on the island hopper from Auckland to Christchurch. "I think we'd all be dead or captured if we hadn't left there an hour ahead of schedule."

"You're making too much of this," his employer said.

"I'm changing our strategy anyway. I dismissed the team. There's nothing for them to do in New Zealand, anyway. It's all done except for the shooting."

"Sure. Fine. Just make sure your shots are good."

The foreman curled his lip. "I'm a professional. My shots will be perfect."

The foreman didn't share his employer's lack of security concerns. Somebody was closing in on him—maybe. Usually, whenever he was in danger of being apprehended, his instincts kicked in like police sirens going off. It was a gift. Some said it was ESP or precognition or some sort of bullshit, but the foreman didn't go for that crap. He just knew somehow when somebody was closing in on him.

Right now his instincts were giving him mixed signals, and he didn't know what they meant. What he did know was that he was one step ahead of his pursuers, and he was going to stay there. That meant he had to get into the mountains, perform his sniping duties and get out.

He joined the crowds at the hotel at Lake Te Amau, then melted away unseen into the mountain trails. By midnight he had skirted the guarded posts where Extreme Sports Network's expensive long-range cameras were stationed for viewing the big event. More guards were on duty on the trail to keep unauthorized personnel from hiking up the mountain to set up their own cameras. This was an ESN event and they intended to keep it that way.

The foreman had no trouble with the guards, and he kept climbing up. The snow grew deeper and the trail was unimproved. Warning signs told him so. He didn't give it a second thought as he trudged the narrow, icy shelf that skirted a half-mile drop-off.

He found a good site, almost a thousand feet above the nearest camera station, with an unobstructed view of the vast ice wall on the adjoining mountain. The foreman began to roll snowballs.

The foreman's snowballs became a wall, and then

another wall, and then a three-sided, roofless structure. He sat inside and opened his case, assembling the cannonlike sniper rifle and tripod. There was a sound suppressor in the case, but the foreman never touched it. His target was a mile away, and he wanted every ounce of energy the weapon provided. The suppressor would decrease the force of the rounds. Besides, the walls of snow would channel the noise up and out from the mountain.

He peered through the scope until he found the little red flags jutting out of the ice wall. He had the luxury of time to line up the targets, then he fired the weapon.

28

Remo felt the plane land, but he didn't bother opening his eyes until pain shot through his elbow.

"What was that for?"

Chiun was standing in the aisle with his hands in the sleeves of his kimono. "We have landed."

"So?"

"We debark."

Remo sat up. "This is Auckland."

"Yes."

"You know, New Zealand? Australia's ugly cousin? Wisconsin down under?"

"I know where we are."

Thirty or forty people were in the aisles, unable to get past Chiun. Unlike a typical crowd of aircraft passengers, there was no pushing or shoving, no rude comments. Everyone waited in patient silence, leaving a big safety cushion between themselves and the Master of Sinanju Emeritus.

Remo sighed and followed Chiun off the 747. "I take one catnap halfway across the Tasman Sea, and you've got the entire coach section shivering in their skivvies. How was I supposed to know we were coming to Auckland?"

"I did not say where we were going. You did not ask."

"We got on a plane bound for Los Angeles so I assume we're going to Los Angeles, even if there is a short layover in the land of belching mud holes. Why're we here, anyway? The Maoris rebelling again? Just so you know, I'm on their side."

"A true Master of Sinanju does not take sides," Chiun reminded him. "We will attend another ridiculous sporting exhibition, at the request of Mad Emperor Harold. We do this without regard for the inanity of his reasoning. We don't take one side or the other. Harold's gold is good so we follow his instructions. After all, Remo, it is the gold that keeps the babies of Sinanju from starving."

"Really? Explain how that works?"

It was akin to the President asking somebody to bring him up to speed on this Constitution that people kept talking about. Remo had heard the story of the starving babies of Sinanju thousands of times.

It was the genesis story of Sinanju. Long ago, about the time that the first civilizations were coming of age in Egypt and Persia, the history of Sinanju began in a time of despair. The fisherman of Sinanju were dying of hunger, their nets coming in empty. Rather than put their offspring through the misery of starvation, the Sinanju villagers sent their babies home to the sea— which was a nice way of saying they dropped the infants into the icy bay.

These drastic times spurred Sinanju men to go out into the world to seek employment as assassins and send home their earnings to support the village.

It had been some time since the villagers had been

forced to resort to infanticide. These days every one of them would be millionaires if Chiun were to divvy up the treasure stored in the Sinanju Masters' house in the village.

Chiun ignored the gibe and stopped before a poster in the airport terminal.

"Extreme Sports Network presents the challenge of a lifetime, blah blah blah," Remo read. "Extreme athletes defy death, et cetera, et cetera. Extreme Blind Ice Climbing? Ice Climbing? Blindfolded?" As they headed for their connecting flight, he said. "Little Father, there's one thing you were right about. They *are* morons."

"Who is?"

"Just about everybody."

THE FOREMAN SAT in the men's room stall for twenty more minutes, more nervous than he had felt in years.

"You okay in there?" It was airport security. The foreman spotted a young, dark-skinned man in uniform. Just a floorwalker. On the other hand, Maoris were a perceptive bunch. The foreman knew he had to play this just right. "I'm feeling better now." He opened the stall, trying to look drained and queasy.

"A little of Te Wherowhero's Revenge, mate?" the Maori said with a smile.

"It's the wine."

"Don't like our wine?"

"I liked the first couple of bottles just fine," the foreman joked. "That's what I get for trying to drink a bunch of Kiwis under the table."

The Maori kid chuckled gently and left. The foreman shouldn't have been worried about the kid.

But something worried him. He'd been lounging in the airport terminal awaiting his flight to Los Angeles when his nerves went riot on him. It was the same warning system that had saved his ass time and again over the years, but now it was more like an air-raid siren. He got to his feet quickly, looking for the source of the danger, but there was nothing unusual in the terminal.

The attendant at the counter had announced the arrival of a flight from Sydney, and the foreman's nerves went wild. Whatever threatened him was on that flight. He looked for a hiding place with a view of the exit ramp, but something told him not to. He had to get completely out of sight or he was a dead man.

The Auckland airport serviced flights from all over the world and was designed for security. Hiding places were not in abundance, so the foreman locked himself in the bathroom stall. When the flight landed, his nerves jangled like discordant bells, and when he heard the voices of the passengers from the Sydney flight he almost did throw up for real.

"Little Father…" the foreman heard someone say, but he didn't make out the rest.

"Who is?" said another high-pitched voice, but also male.

Then they were gone.

29

"Hi, Champ!"

"Who zis?" Fred Magnum slurred into the phone as he struggled to sit up in the hospital bed. He'd spent the night pickling in painkillers, but the sunlight through the window told him night was over.

"This is Sherman MacGregor, calling from Battle Creek, Michigan, in the good old U.S. of A. Just watched tape of your spectacular win. Man, you are some kick-ass athlete."

"Thanks. Who zis again?"

"I'm Sherm MacGregor, president and chief executive officer of MacGregor Biscuit Company. As in MacBisCo. Ever hear of Extreme Nuggets? I want to put you on our cereal boxes."

Fred felt a surge of lucidity. Oh, man, this was the call he'd been waiting for! This was his dream come true! Had he blown the deal before it was even offered? "Extreme Nuggets! I love Extreme Nuggets!"

"I thought maybe you did," MacGregor said. "An extreme athlete such as yourself needs extreme nutrition, like Extreme Nuggets."

"Don't I know it," Fred agreed. "Extreme Nuggets

has the nutrition I need to get me through the most grueling competition."

MacGregor laughed. "You're a natural! When you back in the States, son? We'll sign you up. If you're interested."

"Sure am, Mr. MacGregor." Fred twisted the valve on the IV tube. Last thing he needed now was more painkillers muddling his brain.

"Son, call me Mac. All the extreme athletes call me Mac."

"Sure thing, Mac. Hold on a sec." Fred was distracted by a brief knock on the door, then it was pushed open by a man with all the confidence in the world.

"You a doctor?" Fred asked. The guy was in a sport jacket and tailored slacks. Fred had the impression he made more than any lousy doctor.

The man rested a briefcase on the foot of the bed—a briefcase of hand-polished leather with the complexion of a supermodel. He took out a flash card. It read, "Tell Mac that you will call him back."

Fred read it twice, then mouthed, "What the fuck?"

The man showed his next card. "I'm with Fence Flour Company."

Fred rolled the words in his mouth. "Fence Flour Company. Fence Flour Company?"

The next card was a picture of a cereal box—one of the most recognizable cereal boxes of all time. Oaties.

"Uh, my schedule's not final yet, Mac," Fred said to his caller. "Can I call you back when I know for sure?" He took the number and promised to call within a day, then hung up.

"How'd you know it was Sherm MacGregor on the

phone?" Fred asked the guy with the briefcase that looked as if it were made from the perfectly smooth skin of swimsuit models.

The man laughed, full of confidence. "Listen, Champ, Mac's my second cousin, once removed. I'm Fellows Fence, vice president of marketing, Fence Flour Company." The man shook Fred's hand. It was a vigorous shake, but his skin was softer and more supple than his briefcase. "Mac and I grew up together. I know how he operates."

"So how come he's kicking your ass in the cereal aisle, Fellows?"

Fence hadn't expected it, and the wind slackened in his sails. "Well, that's not quite true, is it? Look at the brand names in any supermarket in America and tell me what you see. Super Sucrose Smacks, Marshmallow Good Luck Charms, Oaties, you name it."

"Oaties Is for Pussies," Fred said, and saw Fellows Fence cringe visibly. "Don't take it personally," Fred added.

Fellows shook it off, then acted as if it never happened. "We have some things to talk about. Most importantly, there's the launch of new Extreme Oaties."

"Never heard of it."

"As I said, we're launching it and it's new, so of course you haven't heard of it. But we'd like you to be on the front of the very first boxes."

"Wouldn't that be something!" Fred exclaimed, laughing delightedly. Everybody he knew hated Oaties. Even he hated Oaties. It was part and parcel of the animosity between the traditional athletic culture and the rebellious extreme-sports subculture.

"You're famous, Fred, as of right now. But what if you had your own Oaties box? Now that's publicity! Everybody would know you on sight."

Fred Magnum had to agree with that. "But I'll get that if I go with Extreme Nuggets."

"True. But the compensation package that we're prepared to offer—"

"There's also the image problem. You know, Oaties Is for Pussies."

"This isn't Oaties, Fred. This is *Extreme* Oaties."

"For extreme pussies?"

Fellows was hemorrhaging self-confidence. "Forget all that nastiness. It's behind us. This is something new, with a whole new image. We've got a huge promotional budget, enough to drown the bad publicity."

"You mean, that with enough cash you can buy enough advertising to make people think what you want them to think?" Fred scoffed.

"Exactly."

"Man, you don't get it. We're not what you know, see? We're not pretty-boy football players or lazy-assed baseball dudes standing out in some field for three hours. We're extreme athletes. We're rebels. We hate that old-time establishment shit. We're a different breed, and you can't buy us."

"You haven't heard the price yet." Fellows Fence gave him a price.

"That's a hell of a lot," Fred Magnum admitted, "but it ain't nearly enough."

"How much is MacGregor offering? We'll beat it."

"You already did. But it's not the money. It's the

image, dude. MacGregor has the *faith.* All you got's a bunch of advertising bucks."

Fellows was flabbergasted, but he kept his cool and implored Fred Magnum to not say no, not yet. "I'll meet with you again. Soon. I may have what it takes to change your mind."

"More money?" Magnum said disdainfully.

"More money, sure, but maybe something even more convincing. I can't tell you what it is until the deal is final…"

Without the pain juice flowing into his blood, Fred Magnum's head felt cleared up. He trusted his instincts. His instincts told him loud and clear that the fruitcake from Fence was bluffing big-time.

When Fellows Fence was gone, Fred ordered up a carton of orange juice from the nurse, then tossed her out and placed a call to Battle Creek, Michigan.

"Hi, Mac. It's Fred Magnum."

"Magnum! How are you doing, kid? Man, you have got the greatest name ever! Look great on a cereal box."

"Thanks. Sorry I had to cut you short. I had a visitor. Said he was a cousin of yours."

STEPH MINCER ENTERED her boss's office to drop off some paperwork. Sherm MacGregor was on the phone. "Sure thing, Fred," he said in his friendliest voice, but he gave Steph a look that promised death, and he pointed at the door. She left fast.

Steph waited a little while. It was five o'clock, and she had stopped being a dedicated, stay-late kind of employee when her boss turned into a loudmouthed asshole. But she really ought to get these papers in front of Sherm today. What the hell? She entered his office again.

This time, he was smiling, and it was genuine. "Excellent. Man, you know it." He took the papers, signed them without looking and handed them back. Steph almost felt disappointed.

Sherm MacGregor was on an emotional roller coaster of a phone call, but all the big dips were behind him.

He had handpicked this kid Fred Magnum to win the outback marathon. The kid was on record as being a fervent supporter of Extreme Nuggets. He spouted the Extreme Nuggets sales pitch for the newspapers when he won the Pensacola Obstacle Marathon last year. He was an active member of the online Extreme Nuggets Web Site Community. Not too bright, but dedicated to Extreme Nuggets for God knew what reason—and Mac had yet to pay him dime one. The perfect spokesperson for Mac's cereal.

Magnum had delivered the unpleasant news that Fence was trying to horn in on his territory. Launching their own extreme cereal. They sent one of their bigwigs all the way to Australia to sign the marathon champion to be on their cereal boxes when the product launched in a month.

In a month? You don't conjure up a major product launch in one month.

Fred Magnum wasn't having anything to do with Fence. He had come out and declared undying loyalty to Extreme Nuggets. Mac spewed sympathetic bullshit by the barrelful. "You know I'm a true believer in the extreme athlete, Fred. That's why I created Extreme Nuggets. You people are my kindred spirits. So who did

Fence send to badger you, anyway? Was it Adam? Big guy with a buzz cut?"

Fred said something about supple hands.

"You mean Fellows?" Mac laughed aloud. "That's perfect. That's rich." It *was* perfect. It *was* rich. Fellows was exactly the wrong person to use to approach the extreme crowd.

Magnum said something about a pansy. "Right! Just goes to show you what Fence Flour thinks about the extreme athletes if they send Fellows to make their deal. How much did they offer you, anyway? Nice! Sure, I'll match it. No problem. I know you wouldn't go with Fence for any price, but if they think you're worth that much then I sure as hell think so, too."

Mac had the feeling Fred Magnum was crying. Fred Magnum was way, way too dedicated to the cause. Mac propped the boy up a few more notches with some "all in this together" platitudes. The kid ate it up.

"I always thought of MacBisCo as like, you know, like Harley-Davidson," Magnum explained. "One of them companies that is really dedicated to the people buying its stuff. You know what I'm trying to say?"

"God, yes. That's just right," Mac effused. "You hit the nail on the head. I love it. The Harley-Davidson of cereal companies! I wonder if them motorcycle boys would let us use their trademark?"

"You mean, like in TV ads?"

"Shit, yeah! It's brilliant! It's exactly the right message! Ever thought of getting into big-time marketing when you retire from professional sports?"

"It's my dream, Mac," Magnum whined through tears of joy.

30

The bellhop was a man in a pointy hat and a long, flowing white beard. The facial hair was fake. The linen robe was a dingy ivory color. The bellhop reached for Chiun's trunks.

"I got them, thanks," Remo said, stopping the bellhop before he even touched the trunks. Fingerprints on lacquer was a crime punishable by death—if it was Chiun's lacquer.

The bellhop had to be satisfied with flourishing the door for them, then he bowed low, sweeping off his hat regally.

"Thanks," Remo said, and added as an afterthought, "Ho ho ho."

The young woman at the desk wore a deep-cut gown that barely clung to her shoulders and swept to the floor. Her long straight hair was parted with a tiara, and a glimmering pendant dangled in her cleavage. "Good day, and welcome to the Middle of the Earth."

"Hi," Remo said. "I guess that means you're not Mrs. Claus."

"No," she said uncertainly. She flipped the pendant

to show him the gem-filled engraving. "Hi! I'm the Lady Galadrium, at your service!"

As she processed his reservation a band of gruff-looking maintenance workers appeared with window-washing equipment. They set to work on the floor-to-ceiling glass panels that gave the lobby a magnificent view of the mountains.

"What's up with the outfits?" Remo asked Ms. Galadrium. She didn't seem to know what he was talking about. "The janitors? Why're they dressed like that?"

She shrugged. "We go to great lengths to achieve the right atmosphere."

Remo was intrigued most by the janitors' oversize rubber shoes, which were molded to look like hairy, scabrous bare feet. One of the janitors, muttering to himself, opened a ladder and began to toil to get to the top, twisting and flopping the huge rubber feet until the fifth rung tripped him up. He toppled to the rough-hewn granite floor and lay groaning. One rubber foot was still lodged in the rungs and his real foot was only a quarter of the size, but just as hairy.

"C'mon," Remo said to Ms. Galadrium as more hotel workers hurried to block the guests' view of the fallen employee. "They Munchkins?"

"No, milord," she replied peevishly.

"Now I get it. Renaissance festival. Right?"

"No!"

"Hey, don't get snippy. I'm just trying to make sense of it all."

"As I said, sir, this is the Middle of the Earth."

"Lady, don't tell me about the middle of the earth.

I've been there. I've seen the movie. This doesn't look anything like it."

"We're doing the best that we can, sir," Galadrium said in a whisper. "And let me tell you it's not easy. They were going to sue us for using the characters from the books, so we had to change them, just a little bit, but it hurts our authenticity. But we have to have some sort of gimmick because lord knows people won't go on holiday to a place without a gimmick and the only bleeding thing we've got to bank on is that they made those bleeding movies on our bleeding mountains!"

"You're not even talking about *Journey to the Center of the Earth,* are you?" Remo asked. "You know, Pat Boone spelunks, duck gets murdered, pet store iguanas walk around with plastic spines glued on their hides?"

She pushed the key cards at him and stomped into the back room.

"Hey. Buddy." It was a mounted gorilla talking—or something with the face of a gorilla. The gorilla-faced thing was, apparently, the concierge.

"What are you supposed to be?"

"I'm an Ork. That's O-r-k, ork. Not the trademarked kind. Let me clue you in."

"I'd appreciate that," Remo said sincerely.

CHIUN EYED the man in the fake beard who was bowing and holding the front door, then perused the chain-mail-clad medics tending to the fallen janitor.

"Remo, is this some sort of poorly executed historical fair?"

"That's a good guess, but no cigar. They made some movies here a few years ago. The management's trying to cash in on it. Remember all the fuss about rings and hobbits and dragons and stuff?"

"A puppet pageant for the children?"

"Yeah. But this puppet pageant was three movies and they were each four hours long."

Chiun shook his head. "This makes no sense. What child would have the patience for it? Were these films considered to be successful?"

"Not really. That's why the theme park is in New Zealand."

"I see," Chiun said seriously, then stopped in front of a rotund, bearded bellhop with a papier-mâché battle-ax. His pendant identified him as Glomli the Dwarf. "Ridiculous!" Chiun said delightedly.

Glomli despondently pointed the way to their room and Remo went for the phone.

"Gotta call work and tell them I didn't make it in today."

Chiun sniffed disdainfully. Remo attempted to follow the directions in the hotel's pamphlet, *19 Easy Steps for Making an Outgoing Call,* then gave up and poked the special-services keys until someone agreed to connect him.

"Hi, Olaf," he said when producer Dasheway barked into the phone.

"Romeo! Where the hell are you, Romeo?"

"Some hotel in New Zealand."

"What the hell are you doing in New Zealand? We were supposed to shoot the second show today."

"Sorry. Unplanned trip."

"To New Zealand? I didn't know it was a real place. I thought it was the name of the secret soundstage where they did the movies with the gloomy smurfs."

"Friend of mine is here on business. He needed me to come along."

"Are you lying to me? Is this a ploy for more money? I'll give you more money!"

"I'll call when I get back in town," Remo said.

"I'm getting a bad vibe here, Romeo. Tell me everything's okay between us."

Remo hung up and was lured onto the balcony by the whine of servomotors. He cleared the snow off the wooden chairs and relaxed into one. Chiun joined him and they sat together in comfortable silence.

Remo thought he might have enjoyed the scenery of the Fiordland National Park, if he could just see past the fiberglass, animatronic trolls that battled continuously on the hotel grounds outside a plywood castle gate. Every hour the trolls were joined by a shabby collection of costumed warriors who charged one another for five minutes shouting badly scripted dialogue. They were hotel staff—apparently the cast included any costumed employee who could be spared from actually running the hotel at any given moment. One battle was all little people with oversize rubber feet. Another fight sequence happened while most of the staff was busy checking in a busload of new arrivals, so the only human participants were three men in rubber tree suits—they couldn't move their legs and kept falling flat on their face—and a college kid in a plastic spider suit. The trees taunted the spider incessantly. The spider's torso was shedding black foam chunks.

"Shoddy," Chiun declared.

"But distracting. I think there's some mountains behind the actors, but I can't tear my eyes away to look. They're being hard on the spider girl, don't you think? She's not the slob. It's not her fault she has to wear a suit that's falling apart."

Chiun found himself pleasantly absorbed in the farce. It was as good as whatever would be on the television, at least, and when the actors took a break his eyes wandered up to the glittering mountains. They were majestic, and this was a comfort to Chiun, who dwelled in the land of America, where fakery ran rampant. Where even nature was housed in amusement parks and treated as staged entertainment.

Wryly he thought about how far the fingers of American influence reached around the world. The clumsy vignette playing out in the snow reeked of American influence.

Chiun felt the flutter of dread touch his lungs, lightly brush his heart and fade away again. This episode was subtle enough that it escaped his attention until it was repeated, and he didn't know from whence it had come.

Chiun felt Remo become aware of his discomfort, but Remo said nothing, and Chiun allowed his awareness to reach into the mountains, into its core of ancient volcanic stone. He imagined the mountains' warm heart—a trickle of magma. It was all that remained of the magnificent burst of lava and fire that made this mountain and this land....

Somehow he felt that his imagination was steering him incorrectly. The mountain was old and cold, even to its very core. Whatever burned inside once was burned out. But there was something inside the mountain. A thrum. A rhythm.

A *pulse*. It came from the earth, from far away, carried by the hollow volcanic fluke like a stethoscope that stretched to a patient that was thousands of miles away.

"Chiun?"

He heard his name, but he sensed no urgency, and he was intrigued by his fantasy. From whence did he conjure it? What was its meaning? He imagined himself as a puff of dust that could seep into the earth until it found the hollow, strawlike fluke, and then follow it into the earth and under the ocean to the source of the pulse.

"Chiun?"

Chiun arrived at the source of the pulse, and he saw what created the pulse, and he sensed that the pulse was growing more rapid, and he wanted to shout a warning to himself, to Remo, to someone, but he was in another place, on a balcony of a hotel, a place for tourists, and the sun was hot. The air smelled of the tropic ocean. Something that did not know him was calling his name, taunting him.

"Chiun!"

"Stop it!"

He struck the thing away!

And he found himself looking into the eyes of his pupil, Remo. The sun was gone. The air was frigid. He was on a different hotel balcony before the farcical amusements and the cold, old mountain.

"Jesus, Little Father, what's the matter?" Remo was holding the old man's hand. He had caught it before the slap could obliterate the patio glass, and now he released it gently.

"It is a bad omen," Chiun said.

"What? This stupid show?" Remo laughed without joy.

"It was something I saw. Maybe just an old man's daydream."

"Maybe not. You've got me worried."

Chiun smiled, and he looked a little tired. "You are a good son."

"Cut the crap and tell me what you saw."

"There is no crap for me to cut. I tell you sincerely, Remo, that you are a good son."

Remo frowned. "Now I'm really worried. Spill it. Please."

"I don't know what I saw," Chiun said. "I meditated and felt myself in the mountain. I heard the beating of a heart, not originating in this mountain but audible there. It came from far away—that way." Chiun turned and extended a wrinkled old finger to the north-north-east.

"Uh, Chiun, we're in New Zealand. *Everything* is out that way."

"It was alive. Its heart beat with growing vigor. I recognized it—and then I forgot what I had just seen. Then I was in this place, but it was not this place. The sun was hot…and then I heard you speak. You said my name."

"Yes? I did that."

"But it was someone—it was not you speaking. My name was spoken by—" He shook his head. "It was vivid, and then gone, forgotten in an instant." Chiun was thoughtful, and he reentered their hotel room. The air was fifty degrees warmer, but neither of them took notice of it. They readjusted the circulation in their bodies to accommodate the change. Chiun descended cross-legged onto his mat and was silent, pondering his experience.

This was not the silent treatment Remo was used to—the tense silence that Chiun inflicted on him at the slightest provocation. Remo could handle that. He was used to it. He thrived on it.

But this silence was hollow. Chiun wasn't angry with Remo; Chiun was simply absorbed in his own thoughts. Remo felt lonely.

He searched out the restaurant and barged into the kitchen, inspecting the catch of the day. "Of course we have fresh fish—we are on an island!" the French-Kiwi chef exclaimed. He calmed down when Remo dumped a wad of bills in the pocket of his apron. There were some hundreds in there. Probably more than strictly necessary, Remo thought, but money was one thing he just didn't care about.

The money made the chef cooperative, however, and he even allowed himself to be micromanaged throughout the preparation of steamed fish, steamed Jasmine rice and roast duck.

"This is for an old person, yes? Someone who appreciates finely prepared food but must eat it bland?"

"Yes, something like that. But I eat the same thing."

The chef didn't press the issue, but he did slip sprigs of greens on the platters before the intruder wheeled off his dinner cart. What harm could a little touch of green do except make the plate more appetizing? He later found the parsley in his apron pocket with the money.

Chiun sat there still, as if frozen, when Remo returned, but he roused himself to eat, then stretched out on his mat to sleep. He had failed to notice Remo's specially prepared meal. Remo failed to notice that Chiun didn't notice.

He was too worried to think about much of anything.

31

Olaf Dasheway was distraught and he wasn't thinking clearly. When the phone rang he answered it—without checking the display to see who it was. Big mistake.

"It's me, Dasheway, and I'm as mad as a Mexican."

"I've got my own problems right now, Mr. Pres—"

"You stabbed me in the back and I want an explanation."

"I have no clue what you're talking about," Dasheway replied, voice dull. What was going on with Romeo Dodd? That man was the key to his comeback. That story about a trip to New Zealand was obviously a lie. He wasn't even trying to sound legitimate. The man had something else going on.

"My production schedule gets cut back, and next thing I know I'm seeing ads for this new show you're doing, *The Ladies' Man*. My show is getting shafted!"

"We're not dropping the *Slick Willy* show, just postponing production."

"But, Dasheway, *The Ladies' Man?*" The caller's feelings were hurt. "I'm the ladies' man. That should be my show. Instead they're filming me taking naps on the display beds at Sears for a cheap laugh!"

Yeah, right. Dasheway clearly recalled the reaction when they screened the *Slick Willy* pilot to a focus group. There were no laughs, not even cheap ones.

"Who cares about this guy anymore?" commented one white female in the seventeen-to-thirty age bracket. "He's more last week than Ozzy Osbourne."

"You could have at least let me audition for *The Ladies' Man*," Dasheway's caller bemoaned. "Wait! How about another *Ladies' Man—The Ladies' Men*. We'll alternate episodes."

Dasheway hung up. This guy, he simply could *not* deal with right now.

THEY WOKE together at 3:00 a.m. Remo rolled their mats around two down parkas purchased in the gift shop and cleaned of their feather filling. Exerting proper compression on the parkas flattened them into packages no thicker than a cheap paperback. That was all the preparation they needed. They went out via the patio doors, stepping off the balcony and landing lightly on the snowy earth three stories beneath. The mechanical trolls were cold and silent. The mountains were peaceful. It seemed criminal to allow the natural beauty of this place to be subverted by these noisy contraptions.

"Give me a sec." Remo found a service door under a flap in the troll's breeches and in he went.

Chiun patiently stood on the crust of snow, hands in his robe sleeves. Remo emerged from the nether regions of the troll, only to repeat the behavior with the second one.

"Was it enjoyable?" Chiun asked as they walked on.

"Very," Remo answered. "Would you like to know what I was doing in there, exactly?"

"Please do not tell me."

The ice wall was a breathtaking field of white ice, sculpted painstakingly by nature from the mountain's earth-warmed water flow. It was named the Wall of Resolution by the earliest white settlers in the region. The Maoris had a name for it, too, and they were always going on about restoring this name to the thing, but nobody could pronounce it. Well, the Maoris could pronounce it, but nobody else could pronounce it. The Maoris were always strutting around making demands as if they owned the place.

So far the name Wall of Resolution had stuck, and the Kiwi government had been trying for years to market the wall as one of the wonders of the natural world. It truly was wonderful, but there was a problem.

"It goes away," complained the New Zealand minister of tourism to the New Zealand minister of national parks. The minister of tourism was a frumpy, just-so woman who did *not* walk around in a skimpy bathing suit, thank you very much, unlike some ministers of tourism who received so much undeserved attention. "You want to make it a real tourist attraction, you figure out how to keep it from melting for three months out of the year. Nobody's going to take a holiday to see a medium-sized waterfall."

The minister of national parks proposed a bold plan to market extended holiday packages for stays that spanned the annual build-up of the ice.

"You think people are going to pay tens of thousands of dollars to sit there and watch the water freeze for ninety-eight days?" the minister of tourism demanded.

"I suppose you have a better idea?" the minister of national parks demanded.

"I most certainly do."

"Oh, God, not those idiot movies again."

"Those idiot movies, as you call them, have made billions of dollars. Billions. And those movies were filmed right here on the South Island. Where is our slice of that pie?"

"What do you want me to do, Minister? Put the hotel staff in elf costumes?"

"For starters. I've also been in contact with the Extreme Sports Network."

"Oh, God!"

"You see the difference in our thinking, Minister? You would have us invite a bevy of sedate senior citizens to look at the mountain for a few weeks. I, on the other hand, have plans to create a publicity powerhouse. I will leverage our recognition and our ice wall into something exciting and dynamic!"

"You ruin it."

"On the contrary."

"THEY RUINED IT. They took a nice ice wall, out here minding its own business, and turned it into just another obstacle of Nature for man to conquer."

"You are disdaining the industry of televised spectacle?" Chiun asked. "You premiere this Friday. Across the country and even in Europe and Australia. Probably the Chinese will show it. The Brazilians will consider it a grand farce. But the Japanese—now, they will truly appreciate your television show, Remo. They adore true-to-life farces. You will be a hero to the Japanese."

They began to scale the wall. Their fingers probed the uneven surface and found purchase among the ripples, the cracks and even in the varying densities of the ice. Where there was no firm grip to be found, they simply exerted pressure on the ice and moved the wall *down.*

"You don't sound all that ticked off anymore," Remo noted.

"About what would I be ticked?"

"You know. *The Ladies' Man.* You aren't on my case about it like you were before. Don't you care?"

"The show no longer is a concern to me. Your bluff has been seen as transparent."

"What bluff?"

"You never intended for the show to proceed," Chiun said simply. He pulled himself off the wall onto a ledge that was chopped in the ice. Remote-controlled cameras were bolted into the ice at the rear of the landing, and checkered flags were stationed to frame the image of the climbers in the shot as they made the summit. The race was still hours away and the equipment was in standby mode.

"Look," Chiun said, "you can still be on television if you desire."

"Wait just a second. What makes you think I was bluffing about the show?"

"Your behavior tells me it is a sham."

"What behavior?"

"Idiosyncrasies in your speech patterns."

"I don't have idiosyncrasies," Remo insisted.

"Unusual variations in your body language."

"I don't have body language!'

"You are bluffing."

"I am not bluffing! The show will go on."

"If it does, I will be proved wrong," Chiun said.

"You are *so* annoying when you get all agreeable." Remo unfurled the mats side-by-side and put himself down hard. He glared menacingly at the empty blackness that awaited anyone foolish enough to step off the ledge.

"Fine. You win. It was a bluff."

"Truly?"

"Ah!" Remo waved his hand at the air—a gesture of dismissal that was perfectly Chiun. They sat in silence. The cold wasn't intense enough to require the use of the un-down jackets.

"Did you remember your vision, yet, Little Father?"

"I never forgot it. Did you not listen to my description of the dream?"

"Yeah, sure. But you said in the dream you saw something and you recognized it, and then it was gone. Then you were somewhere else and you recognized something, and then it was gone. What I'm asking is, did you remember the two things that you saw in the vision?"

"There was nothing for me to remember."

"Oh," Remo said. A minute later, he added, "What?"

"I was meditating. Maybe I dreamed, and if so then what I saw was symbolic. The recognizing and forgetting—this happened two times in rapid succession. This would tell me that the act of recognizing and then forgetting is the message itself—never mind what I saw and then at once forgot."

"Oh," Remo said. "So what does the message mean?"

"I do not know."

Remo wondered if the old goat was fibbing. Chiun lied expertly.

"If what I saw was a vision, then I must take it as a directive. Perhaps I am being instructed to seek something I have yet to recognize."

Remo glanced over at Chiun, who sat in perfect stillness and composure, at one with the world. The icy breeze played with the strands of yellowing hair around his shell-like ears. The frigid fingers of wind tagged mischievously at the thin robe. Chiun was old. Older than most people ever dreamed of becoming. Great age had taken its toll on him, slowing his reflexes, sapping his stamina, maybe even reducing his intellect.

Chiun in his prime possessed magnificent stamina and skill, and even burdened with age he was a force of furious nature.

When you started out as a Master of Sinanju, you could go to pot in a big way and still be the scariest guy in town. Chiun might be slowing down in little ways, but it was nothing. Chiun was still a Master's Master.

Remo wondered if he would ever be that—one of the true great Masters. When the scrolls of Sinanju were read, would he stand out among the thousand names? Would he be great, as Chiun was great?

"There are untamed thoughts galloping about your head, Remo Williams," Chiun declared. "They are trying to push out of your face, and the cold makes your rubbery white flesh extra resilient and tending to squeak."

"I hope you're kidding me."

Chiun never even opened his eyes.

"I was thinking about the future."

"What future do you mean?"

"My legacy. My place in the scrolls. I was wondering if I will be a star or an asterisk. A standout master, like Chiun the Magnificent, or a footnote. Remo the Caucasian Oddity."

"This worries you?"

"No. I'm just wondering about it."

"You foresee my disposition in the scrolls as Chiun the Magnificent?"

"Don't let it go to your head. We both know you've got a special status. Hell, you've met Wang more than any Master who came before you. You've done a lot of good for Sinanju. You've done a lot of good for just about everybody."

"Visions and good deeds don't make for a magnificent master," Chiun said. "A great spirit, a great intellect, these make for magnificence."

"Check. Check. You're in, Chiun. Don't give me that look. I'm not trying to butter you up. I'm just thinking about stuff. How unlike me—beat you to it."

Chiun smiled faintly, then said, "Now what?"

"Now what what?"

"You have more to say. I see the words ready to spill from your tongue. You must have been thinking most intently."

"I'm done."

"We have hours of waiting still. You may as well say it."

"No," Remo said. He smiled easily, but there was no mistaking the look. Remo would say no more.

"Very well." Chiun closed his eyes in meditation

again, and Remo did, too. He thought about what he wanted to ask Chiun but would not ask.

He wanted to ask Chiun if he was getting tired.

Chiun already knew the question, and Chiun would answer it in his own time.

The production crew was up early on the day of the Second Annual Blind Ice Wall Climb. They had much to do, and the network had arranged for a big hot breakfast with fresh-squeezed juice and good strong coffee.

Then producer Aaron Presci got up to motivate the troops.

"This one is special," Presci said. "This is our biggest event all year. Biggest purse. Biggest audience. We get the most advertising, and we spend the most to make it happen. But there's something more—the Blind Ice Wall Climb was the first event that the Extreme Sports Network actually produced in-house. That means this year's event is ESN's first second annual anything. It's the symbol of ESN's pioneering spirit. The bottom line—it's gotta go perfect. I don't want to hear about problems. You have a problem, you fix it. You can't fix it, you figure out some other way of making whatever is supposed to happen happen. Breakfast is over."

The ESN crew dispersed.

"I'm getting some sort of a vibe," Presci told his assistant.

His assistant had an answer ready for him. "It's the cold. It's been kind of jarring to come from the Australian desert into winter weather."

"Next year they'll know better." Presci went to make some phone calls.

"It has nothing to do with the fact that you're a soulless tyrant without an ounce of compassion," his assistant added when he was gone.

Aaron Presci wouldn't have cared if she said it to his face. Caring about other people just wasn't what he did. What he did was produce the most thrilling extreme sporting events ever. He barely had his ass in his seat when the phone rang.

"I wonder if that's Herbert," Presci said through gritted teeth. He snatched the phone up.

"How's it going down there?" Herbert Essen asked. "Got a lot riding on this, Aaron."

"Morning, Herbert. My team is just getting into place. It's bright and early here in New Zealand."

"Any problems?"

"We had everything in place and checked out yesterday. We're ready."

"Keep me posted."

Presci knew why the network president was nervous. This was a big deal for ESN. A lot of dollars were riding on it.

The thing was, the event was ideal for television, mostly because of the nature of the ice wall. There was nothing more photogenic than the image of a human body tumbling down, down, down....

This year, for the first time, the network had cameras mounted directly in the ice wall. With any luck, somebody would fall directly into one of them—it promised to be a spectacular shot, because the autolenses had a huge range of vision and they could keep the body in focus throughout the plummet.

SHERM MACGREGOR WAS going to handle this one on his own. The foreman had put the tools in place, but now the foreman was gone. Now it was all up to Sherm.

"Come to Sherm," he said under his breath.

"The temperature's climbing, and we're climbing under the most dangerous possible conditions here today," the lead announcer explained. He was a BBC sports veteran—one of those fast-talking Brits who could sound completely amazed almost all the time. "I cannot believe that anyone would seriously attempt to climb the wall under melt conditions this severe. And yet, every climber is outfitted and ready to ascend. We go now to ground level."

In the U.S. it was the middle of the night. The climb wouldn't be broadcast on ESN-America for another twelve hours, but Sherm MacGregor had his own live satellite feed. When you're the biggest advertiser on the network, you get special perks.

The real-time data feeds from New Zealand included all the commentator cameras, all the remote cameras on the mountainside facing the ice wall, and all the climber cams, which were lipstick-size video pickups built into the climbers' special glasses.

The glasses were secured to the face prior to the start of the climb and locked on to the climber's heads. A small electric current ran through the glass and effectively blacked them out. The climbers couldn't see a thing. There was an emergency override switch on the glasses, for use if the climber felt he was in imminent danger. Using the switch resulted in immediate disqualification.

The winner's glasses would automatically become transparent again the moment he reached the top of the ice wall.

The network reminded the viewers excitedly that they at home could actually see more than the climbers could see, thanks to the climber cams. What's more, all climbers had a second cam inside their glasses, so the network could occasionally switch over to prove to the viewers that the climbers were really, truly climbing blind. This also made for a dramatic finish—the viewer could watch the glasses come on at the moment the win became official.

"Climbing this damp, slippery, dripping mass of cold stuff is insane, let alone doing it by feel," the Brit announcer stated. "But here they go."

Sherman MacGregor wanted to jump up and down in his seat for sheer excitement.

MacGregor's favorite was a North Dakota native named Cedar Dunnaway. The guy was photogenic, tough looking and not too bright. He'd be an ideal Extreme Nuggets spokesman. However, there was a woman climber who caught Sherm's eye, Penny Peppiatt. She had a cute face and a slim, strong figure. Okay, he had to admit she had the body of an unfed spider monkey, but she was cute enough. They could airbrush some boobs on her.

One of them would win today. Sherm would see to that.

The problem was the Germans. And the Swiss. And the Austrians. Sherm saw them all as arrogant loud-mouths. They'd been spouting off for months about their climbing skills. Like they had some sort of inbred ability to scale ice better than anybody else. "Mountain climbing Nazis," Sherm muttered to himself. He wasn't going to stick any of those jerks on his cereal boxes.

The problem was, they were good. They started strong and got stronger. The Swiss guy was in the lead after half an hour, then the Austrian, then the German. Out of a total of twenty-one climbers, Cedar Dunn-away and Penny Peppiatt were ninth and eleventh.

Sherm waited for his moment. He didn't want to act too soon. He'd wait and see how things fell out.

The first one to fall out came only forty-five minutes into the climb. It was a New Zealander, who claimed loudly in the media that he had the home-field advan-tage. "Nobody knows Kiwi ice like a Kiwi," he had boasted the night before.

First one toe full of spikes slipped from the ice, then his other foot gave way, and then his body landed hard against the bulge of ice over which he was attempting to crawl. He lay there, grunting over the climber cam microphone feed as he strained his arm muscles. He had to get his handheld climbing claw deep in the ice to sup-port his weight without foot support—but he didn't. The claw of the climbing hammer ripped through the ice, and the Kiwi fell. His body flipped, then slammed flat against the ice and he slid a hundred feet, gaining tremendous speed, before hitting a sharp protrusion that launched him away from the steep slope of the ice wall. He plummeted, arms and legs churning, then fell back against the ice as its incline deepened near the bottom of the wall.

That's what made the ice wall so perfect. It always formed at an angle—just a few degrees away from straight up, but just enough to keep the survivability rate high.

"That was spectacular!" the Brit exclaimed. He jogged up to the Kiwi climber, who was croaking weakly. "He's still alive! You see, as we've been saying, there is an angle to the wall. Close to the bottom of the wall, the ice juts out, quite smoothly in some places. The ice itself eases the falling climber to the bottom. This bloke's gonna make it!"

Just then the Kiwi commenced screaming. The paramedics were wrapping the V-bent shin where the bone spears protruded from the flesh. The Brit frowned at him and said into the camera, "Can we use that? Was he shouting over me?" He listened to a response in his headset. "Oh, good."

Sherm was happy when both his climbers made headway, and by hour two they were fifth and eighth. Still, there were four climbers ahead of them and making progress.

The climber in fourth was aggressive, but inexperienced. His reckless climbing got him into several tight spots. But every time he felt himself on a slippery slope he flattened out and dug in hard, then managed to get himself up and moving again.

The ice got softer in the afternoon sun and the melt became trickles. Two climbers lost their grip within minutes of each other.

One picked up a tremendous amount of speed and hit a protrusion in the wall with immense force.

"Cold fish? Let me hear the wagers!" the Brit bellowed. It was sort of a tradition the Brit started last year at the first ice wall climb; when a body was falling, the other announcers and production staff called out their guesses. A cold fish was a body that was dead before it reached the base of the wall, and everybody called out their guesses rapid-fire. Each bet was worth one U.S. dollar, and the pot was split by those who guessed correctly.

The audience at home had taken to the game. They couldn't wait for more Cold Fish games at this year's Blind Ice Wall Climb.

"Cold fish!"

"Cold fish!"

"Floppy fish!"

"Cold fish!"

The climber was, of course, as dead as a gutted trout by the time she slithered to a stop at the bottom of the wall, making her officially a cold fish. In the end there were only two floppy-fish bets among the entire production staff, so the winning pot was pretty meager.

"Uh-oh, we may have another one!" the announcer cried. "I can't believe it!"

It was the experienced climber in fourth place. He was in big trouble. He had both hammers dug into the wall, and yet they were dredging up slushy furrows. His body was creeping along faster. He pushed his toe spike in harder but it made no difference....

One claw hammer slipped free, then another, and the climber zipped down the wall.

Sherm MacGregor caught his breath as the falling climber snatched at his panic button to disable the blinders on his glasses, spotted Penny Peppiatt and made a grab for her as he flew on by. His fingers had to have brushed her sleeve, but he just kept on going.

The climber's Web cam was one of the windows on Sherm's ten-screen video feed at the moment, and it was quite thrilling to watch the white world spin violently around the plummeting climber. The camera kept working even after a sudden jolt, then another, as the body ricocheted between two ice ridges.

"Oh, tough luck!" the British announcer exclaimed. "Cold fish!"

"Floppy fish."

"Floppy fish."

"Cold fish."

Once again the cold-fish guesses prevailed, and they appeared on target as the limp body came to a halt with its face against the ice. A paramedic rushed in with a stethoscope.

"Floppy fish!" she called.

"Well, I just don't believe it! He sure looks cold to me. We'll keep an eye on that bloke just in case the medics were pulling our legs, eh?" He laughed. The paramedic gave him a churlish grin, then tended to her floppy fish.

At the halfway mark, Sherm saw it was time for him to act. The three front-runners were putting distance between themselves and the rest of the pack. Sherm's designates to win were holding on to their positions, now fourth and seventh.

He was waiting for a chance when, almost magically, he had the perfect opportunity. The Swiss climber, in the lead, maneuvered over a near vertical section of the wall. According to the GPS feeds from his devices and the GPS feed from the climber, they were within three feet of one another. To make things even better, the German in third place was now directly below the Swiss climber.

The foreman had shot the devices into the ice wall from the opposite mountain, his high-powered sniper rifle rounds burying them in the ice in the dark of night. By morning, the pits where they had entered had frozen over, making them invisible.

There wasn't much to the devices. A military-issue hardened GPS chip and tiny explosive triggered by a tiny receiver. It all fit into a sniper rifle round that was constructed to bury itself in rock, or ice, with little deformation.

The foreman had stationed the retransmitter on the opposite mountain, signaling over a satellite line to Sherm. Sherm used his mouse to click the display of the mountain, right on the round that was embedded beneath the Swiss climber.

The Swiss climber made a startled sound. The ice underneath him transformed to rubble, and he just dropped. No scrambling. No clawing. Just falling. The breath was knocked out of him by his impact with the German, and then both of them were on their way down.

"Wow! Incredible! I don't believe it!" the Brit exclaimed, and he called cold fish. There wasn't a single floppy-fish bet. And neither the Swiss nor the German was flopping.

Sherm gave the Austrian another half hour. He was sobbing manfully over the radio to the British announcer. He saluted his fallen friends and stated his intention to declare a victory for all Germanic peoples when he reached the winner's summit.

"Oh no, you don't," Sherm said, and the mouse clicked that Austrian straight into oblivion.

The Austrian froze. "Something's happening!" he bellowed into the radio.

"Explain!" the Brit demanded, but then it was over. The Austrian was on his way to the bottom. It was a long, bumpy ride, but he never achieved any of the bone-breaking somersaults and flops that killed his companions. He reached the bottom a floppy fish.

Sherm MacGregor was deeply satisfied as Cedar Dunnaway muscled his way doggedly to the winner's summit.

"Cedar, I'm gonna make you a star," Sherm said.

There was a mist leaking down from the summit, and Sherm heard several different crew voices shouting over the technical feed from New Zealand.

"It's obscuring the summit cameras. Where did it come from?"

"I don't care where it came from, just fix it."

"I can't fix fog!"

Cedar Dunnaway climbed into the mist, which became thicker around him until he had vanished from sight.

"Now the climber cams are out! Dammit, is he on the summit or not?"

"GPS says he's there, but I got no audio and no video."

"Come in, Dunnaway. You're the champ, Dunnaway! Come in!"

"How can you possibly lose all the summit cameras at the same time?"

"I have no idea. Must be something weird going on up there."

"Like what?"

"Yeah," Sherm MacGregor said aloud. "Like what?"

33

Cedar Dunnaway tried real hard at everything, all the time. He wasn't the smartest man, nor was he the most ambitious, but he was a man who tried real hard. Usually it didn't get him anywhere. The one skill that he could count on was patience. Back home, which was in Buffalo, New York, there were people who called him "the most bullheaded human being I ever met."

One time and one time only was Cedar ever given good advice. The man was the manager of the Seven-11 where Cedar was a cashier. Cedar was trying to teach himself to use a complicated cash register. He had been working on it for six hours straight.

"I've never seen anybody so determined to do anything," the manager said. Cedar took that as a compliment.

Cedar was fired. Although he eventually excelled at making change, he never became competent at other tasks as simple as facing display shelves or cleaning the frankfurter cooking machine. But the manager told him, "Cedar, you figure out the one thing that you can do that will make your life prosperous, and then you put your determination into it the way you know how to do, and then you'll be a successful man."

Cedar went home and wrote that down.

Now, it took him a while to figure out what that one thing was. It couldn't involve much thinking, so it had to be hands-on. It couldn't be creative. Cedar was not creative. He was pretty good at climbing rocks, though.

Could he make a living climbing rocks?

Well, yes, he could, if he was good enough. He could enter a contest. He could climb rocks and plastic cliffs and he could climb walls of ice. He could even get paid for doing it.

When he reached his arm over the rim of the winner's summit in New Zealand, he said to himself, "Cedar, you did try hard enough."

Then he pulled himself over the rim and the black glass before his eyes became transparent, and he was seeing a fog bank that should not have been there. Also there were two people, sitting on woven mats on the ice, who should not have been there. One was old and one was young, and neither of them looked as if he were equipped for climbing on ice.

Cedar stood himself up on the summit.

REMO WILLIAMS PULLED a tiny chip out of his pocket and rolled it in his fingers.

Chiun looked at it curiously, Remo nodded at the rim of the summit, where an arm appeared, then a man's head rose into view with a pair of face-hugging goggles that were completely black. Remo flicked the chip at the man's head.

It spun at a fantastic speed, sawing through the plastic transmitter on the head strap like a circular saw going through a foam cushion. The back half of the transmitter, including the two-inch antenna, popped off and was gone. The climber never even felt it.

"Where's the fire?" the winner asked.

"No fire. Just steam." Remo nodded at chalky-dry rock sitting in a basin of melting snow. Remo had rubbed it against another rock until the heat built up, then he dumped it in the ice where it raised billows of steam.

"We would like to ask you how you managed to win this climb," Remo said.

Cedar Dunnaway's spine was ramrod straight as he answered, "Determination."

34

Something was going on. This was not right at all. Sherm MacGregor tried to watch all his video feeds at once and flipped to other feeds, but still he got nothing useful. He was just as confused as everybody else when Copter Cam closed in on the winner's summit to airlift out Cedar Dunnaway. Cedar was standing there, looking fine as could be. Also standing there were two men, one in a T-shirt, one in a—what?—a kimono, for God's sake.

The ESN correspondent who was inside the helicopter was supposed to do an on-the-spot interview with the champion, but that didn't happen. First the two men hopped on the helicopter, and then the cameras stopped working. The two men were gone when the helicopter landed at the base of the wall.

Nobody knew what it meant, so they did their best to ignore it. Cedar Dunnaway was proclaimed champion. The other climbers were airlifted from the summit or picked off the wall. It would all be edited together into a seamless, fast-paced extreme extravaganza by tomorrow's airtime in the United States.

But Sherm still wanted to know what was going on.

He called ESN and had himself patched through to the location producer, Aaron Presci. He was their biggest single advertiser and he could do things like that.

"We don't know who," Presci said. "Maybe just some pranksters who wanted to get on TV."

"Pranksters? Come on."

"When I figure it out, I'll let you know." Presci hung up on him. Presci had to be in pretty dire straits if he was hanging up on his bread and butter, Sherm MacGregor.

Sherm could have had the man fired, but he refrained. Presci was a good, take-no-shit guy. He would find out what was going on if anybody could.

THERE WAS a message light blinking on their telephone. Remo didn't like the look of it. He was frustrated enough already. Days spent down under with nothing to show for it except a lower opinion of the human race, and now this. Whatever it was. But he knew what it was.

Chiun said nothing, just waited, face expressionless.

Remo listened to his message, and his face darkened. He phoned the front desk and asked to be connected to a number in the United States. Arizona.

The phone rang.

"It's me," Remo said.

"Son," said Sunny Joe Roam.

"Give me Freya."

A moment later, he heard Freya say, "Hi, Daddy." She sounded just a little bit frightened.

Remo spoke with her in a calm voice. It would be okay, he assured her. It would be fine. Not to worry.

When he hung up the phone, he was staring wide-eyed at the floor.

"Little Father, my daughter is afraid."

"I heard."

"I'm just enough of a big dumb jerk guy to want to go knock the block off of whoever makes my daughter afraid."

Chiun nodded. "This I understand."

Remo stood. "Going home now. You coming?"

35

Harold W. Smith watched Remo Williams with growing trepidation. Remo used his credit cards to charter a flight out of Invercargill to Auckland, then paid an exorbitant sum to charter a private aircraft to the United States, and on to Yuma. Chiun, Smith had to assume, was with him. Smith radioed the aircraft, but the pilot said his passengers refused to speak with him. Smith attempted to contact Chiun via his iBlogger, but there was no response.

Remo had set other actions in motion. A large credit-card fee was made to a specialty-vehicle moving company. A pair of drivers was dispatched to get Chiun's new travel trailer from L.A. to Arizona in time to meet up with Remo.

Smith dreaded what would happen when Remo reached Yuma, but he wasn't going to interfere.

That might get Remo even angrier, and turn a disaster into a cataclysm.

The best he could do was simply wait and watch what happened, and hope he and CURE survived it.

Meanwhile, he turned the EBE around and pointed her back to her Yuma base. It wouldn't help matters to have the spy airship hovering over the village when Remo arrived.

The EBE traveled a hundred yards, then descended to the desert floor.

"You aren't going anywhere," Smith heard some-one say.

"Freya," Mark Howard said.

Smith looked at him, standing in the door. "I asked you not to involve yourself in this, Mark."

"It is time I become involved, don't you think?"

Smith nodded. "I suppose so."

"I saw Remo coming home in a big hurry. He's ticked off."

"Yes." Smith nodded. "You sure it was Freya?"

"That was her voice."

"I had forgotten you met her."

Mark Howard made a face. "Not so much met. I heard her talk, anyway."

Smith nodded. "She's got the EBE. She'll give it to Remo. What do you think he'll do?"

"I can't imagine."

There was little more activity to watch. The aircraft landed in Yuma, on Thursday evening, and then there was nothing. Smith monitored the incoming data for hour after hour, and still nothing.

Until Friday morning.

Mark Howard called up from his rooms. "Check out the morning news show on seven. I'll be right up."

When he arrived, still buttoning his shirt, Harold W. Smith was watching the morning news show and chewing on one antacid tablet after another after another.

"This is *Good Day, U.S.A.* and we're heading back

to our affiliate in Phoenix," the smiling redhead said. "Hi, Bob!"

"Hi, Katie!"

"What's going on with that big boy, Bob?"

"Well, if you're just tuning in, here you go, folks. It's *The Ladies' Man* blimp, floating over the Phoenix rooftops!"

There it was. The EBE. A ten-million-dollar top secret U.S. military drone aircraft, drifting aimlessly over Phoenix, Arizona. Hanging beneath it was a dangling banner. *The Ladies' Man* Will Cure Your TV Blues. Tonight You Will Meet The Ladies' Man. Learn All the Man's Secrets Tonight On *The Ladies' Man."*

"I guess they want to be very sure that everybody knows *The Ladies' Man* debuts tonight on this network, Bob!"

"That's right, Katie, but let me add that this network is not responsible for the launching of *The Ladies' Man* blimp. The production company has also denied involvement in the blimp launch. Nobody seems to know who authorized this stunt or where the blimp even came from!"

"Pretty strange, Bob."

"Now, the FAA would like to find out about this because the airship appears to be constructed of a radar-invisible material! Get this—the air-traffic control over Phoenix cannot find the blimp on their radar! They had grounded all air traffic until they can figure this out."

"We'll come back to you in a few minutes for an update on this bizarre promotional stunt in Phoenix, Bob."

"Wait, Katie, something is definitely happening!" The shot of Katie in New York changed back to Bob on the street in Phoenix, then back to the blimp. Another banner was unfurling. "There's another banner opening up under the blimp, and I'm trying to make it out, Katie."

"I think it says, Call The Ladies' Man Now, Bob. Dial 1 And Hold It And Speak With The Ladies' Man Personally."

Smith swallowed an antacid tablet without chewing it. It scratched his throat all the way down, and his telephone began to ring.

ONCE UPON A TIME, Harold W. Smith had engineered one of the great telephone switching and routing achievements of all time. Smith designed it to allow Remo Williams to contact CURE with the simplest of all possible phone numbers. Press 1 and hold. Sometimes, other people pressed 1 and held it, for their own bizarre reasons, but Smith's filtering software disconnected most of them.

Maybe one out of a hundred inappropriate phone calls penetrated Harold Smith's filtering system. That was, maybe, a few each year.

Until 7:18 Eastern time on that Friday morning, when an entire nation was instructed to press the 1 key and hold it. The system was deluged with tens of thousands of calls and started getting through.

"No, Miss, this is not the ladies' man," Smith said sourly.

"You sure? 'Cause I wanna see this ladies' man in action. You think you can get me in the sack?"

"Of course not, miss."

"You willing to give it a try?"

"No," Harold W. Smith said.

"You chicken shit?"

"I am not the ladies' man."

"Hey, guess what?" she called to someone else. "The ladies' man is a chicken shit!"

"Good day, miss."

Smith hung up. Why was he even talking to her? The phone rang again instantly. The system monitor showed it had attempted to filter 24,561 calls in less than a minute.

"The system will overload," he said in sudden realization. "That much traffic will leave a surge trail."

"I'll shut it off," Mark Howard said, and jumped to his own desk.

"Don't. The end point of the traffic surge will be obvious to anyone who knows how to read the switching patterns. We have to redirect the traffic. It has to go somewhere."

"Where?"

"Anywhere," Smith said. "Just keep it in state. The trail can't diverge too broadly. It has got to be a live number."

Mark Howard's mind whirled, and he snapped out a command to the Folcroft Four. The computers dredged the recent news stories for a phone number and came up with—

"Perfect," Mark Howard said. He instituted the redirect, and the number changed, forever routing press-1-and-hold calls away from Folcroft Sanitarium.

"HELLO?" answered the United States senator.

"I'd like to talk to the ladies' man." The caller giggled.

The senator sighed. "He's not available. And you should be in school, young lady."

She hung up. The phone rang again almost immediately. "Yes?"

"You don't sound like the ladies' man," a strident woman demanded. "I wanna talk to the ladies' man."

"I'm sure you do. I'll let him know you called."

It rang a third time. "How did you get this number?" the senator demanded.

"Off of TV, duh. Is he as good as they say he is, you know, in bed?"

"Not at all, honey." The U.S. senator, D-NY, left the phone off the hook and turned on the television. It didn't take her long to land on *Good Day, U.S.A.*, with its video of a slowly spinning blimp. "Live from Phoenix," the screen said.

"...may be just a publicity stunt, but officials are alarmed that, apparently, the airship is not showing up on Phoenix air-traffic control radar. Our avionics experts have concluded that, for an airship of this size, some sort of radar-invisible composite must have been used in the structure of the airship. This raises the possibility that the airship is possibly stolen, secret military technology."

The senator's huge mouth fell open.

"Which raises some disturbing questions. Who would have the military intelligence to even know about a secret, stealth airship—and have the influence to access it?" Katie asked.

"And they'd have to be recklessly impudent. By that I mean extremely irresponsible, Katie, to use it for a television promotional stunt."

"Who fits that description, Katie?"

The senator's husband came down the stairs in his boxers and a dingy, threadbare bathrobe still bearing the great seal of the President of the United States of America.

"Mornin'. You left the phone off the hook, Hill." He settled the phone on its base. He didn't notice that his wife was red-faced.

The phone rang immediately. "Hello?" He listened, then said in a whisper. "'Course it's me! And who might you be?"

The sound of a diesel locomotive interrupted him. It was his wife. The senator was *not* happy.

36

Colonel Simonec found his flight crew huddled around the tiny portable TV on the toolbox. "Let me see!" He shoved bodies out of his way.

He hadn't wanted to believe it, but there it was on the eight-inch screen. The top-secret Extremely Big Ear drone airship, EBE 1, was drifting uncontrolled through Phoenix, dangling a banner for some TV show.

Simonec allowed his mind to leap into the future. Where did he stand? Sure, he was charged with the care and deployment of the EBE, but he hadn't ordered it on its missions. He had been forced to surrender control. They couldn't pin this on him. Right?

Simonec grabbed the TV and brought it close to his face. Something was glinting off the EBE's right flank strut. The EBE was a stealth ship, designed *not* to glint.

Simonec marched the chief of his ground crew into a corner of the bay. "Tell me you took the damn watch off the EBE before you sent it out last time."

His ground crew chief looked at him a long time without answering, but that was as good as an answer.

"Tell me you at least wiped your fingerprints off it."

The ground crew chief looked as if he were going to throw up.

So that was it. The watch was still secured to the EBE and the watch would be traceable to Simonec's ground crew. They couldn't prove Simonec knew about it, but they didn't need to prove it. Simonec was responsible for his ground crew. They'd perpetrated some act of sabotage, and that meant they must be in on whatever screwy mess had gotten the EBE into Phoenix—that's what the higher-ups would assume.

Simonec knew that somebody in the U.S. military was going to get scapegoated for this fiasco, and he knew it would be him.

KATIE ABING COULDN'T wait for the commercial break to end. "This is going to be one of our best shows ever," she told her makeup girl.

"You're kicking butt, Katie. Just don't let that jerk Bob step all over your sidewalk."

"Yeah." Katie got all shivery inside as the cameraman held up his fingers. Three. Two. One. The live light came on.

"Welcome back to *Good Day, U.S.A.* I'm Katie Abing, and it looks like the inmates have taken over the asylum! Let's go live now to New Mexico and correspondent Allison Quarberg. Allison, can you explain what we are looking at?"

"We don't know much yet, Katie. What you're seeing is apparently a custom-made recreational vehicle that is traveling the interstate at speeds of, get this, more than 120 miles per hour. Now, New Mexico State Police tell us this vehicle is already wanted for numerous state traffic violations dating from last week. We do know the vehicle is registered to a Romeo Yun-Fat, who has a Connecticut state driver's license."

"Could it be the same Romeo involved in *The Ladies' Man* stunt in Phoenix?" Katie asked.

"I'd believe anything, today, Katie."

"How far are you from Phoe—?" Bob asked.

"You're only about a hundred miles from Phoenix, is that right, Allison?" Katie interrupted.

"We're just over the New Mexico border and, in fact, the vehicle has been speeding since it left Phoenix. That was less than an hour ago."

"What a day!" Katie exclaimed. "What next, I wonder?"

HAROLD W. SMITH KNEW what was next.

Acquiescence. Surrender. Defeat. He was beaten.

Somehow, somewhere, everything had whirled out of control. How did that happen? He'd kept a pretty tight rein on things for a lot of years, and now, chaos.

Really, it had been coming for a long time. Ever since Remo became Reigning Master. Maybe, Smith thought, he ought to have paid closer attention to Remo's complaints. But it was difficult. Remo was *always* complaining.

"I accede to Remo's demands or I fold the operation," Smith said. "It has come to that."

Mark Howard nodded. "Actually, you have no choice but to accede to Remo's demands, regardless of whether you fold the operation or not," he said. "If he exposes this operation in the way he's threatened, well, the scandal will paralyze the federal government and the political parties. We can't let that happen."

"You're right." Smith sighed deeply and held his hands over his keyboard, lost in thought for a moment, as if thinking over his decision one last time.

"You've tried to control what cannot be controlled," Mark said. "I suggest you let it go."

"Ignore our security concerns?" Smith demanded, hands hovering.

"You've kept CURE secure because you've been diligent about controlling what you can, but you never could control all the unknown factors. These things were before your time or completely out of human hands to begin with. Just because you know of them now doesn't mean you need to control them."

Smith weighed the words.

"We can't control ourselves into paralysis," Mark added. "What good is that to anybody?"

"That makes good sense," Smith said. Sitting straighter, with brisk movements, he began to key in his commands.

"WE CAN SEE what appears to be a statue in the rear wrap-around windows of the Airstream," Allison reported. "It's an old man in a bright red robe, sitting cross-legged."

"That window design is certainly not original to the Air—" Bob commented, but was cut off.

"Is it a Buddha, Allison?" Katie asked.

"I think so, but quite skinny and wrinkled compared to the Buddhas I am familiar with— Something's happening. We have a U.S. Army helicopter on the scene. Man, are they in a hurry. Are you seeing this, Katie?"

"That's actually an Air Force chopper, Allis—" Bob said.

"They're attacking!" Katie exclaimed. "No. I think someone is getting out of the chopper. Yes, they're being lowered onto the RV. He's kneeling. He's knocking, I think."

"COULD YOU GET the door?" Remo called. His voice had to carry through the SUV and all the way to the back of the Airstream to the meditation chamber.

"They are not knocking on the door. They are knocking on the roof."

"Could you get the roof, then? I'm trying to drive."

"I am meditating."

The knock was polite, but it came again. "Come in!" Remo shouted.

Remo heard the roof latch crank. He had noticed the square section of the roof, but had not realized it was a hatch. The visitor tugged a few times, then knocked again.

"Chiun, it's locked. Would you *mind?*"

Chiun made an exasperated sound. "Can a man not sit and meditate in his own home?"

"OH, MY GOODNESS," Allison Quarberg cried. "It's not a statue—it's a real man. He just got up and left. Now he is back."

"We're seeing the Army agent enter the RV. Can you tell what's happening? Does the old man appear agitated? Is he being arrested?"

"No. He's in the lotus position again."

"ANYBODY HOME?"

"Up here," Remo called. An airman came carefully through the umbilical and into the SUV, crouching in the empty space of the SUV bed and eyeing the speedometer display warily. The display read 189.9 kph.

"Morning, Commander," Remo said. "Sorry for the trouble, but what a show, huh?" He glanced at the dashboard TV, showing *Good Day, U.S.A.*

"I have a phone call for you, sir." The airman handed a mobile phone to Remo. Remo took his eyes off the road for a second, thumbed a button, put the phone to his ear, then lobbed it over his shoulder. The airman caught it neatly.

"Busted," Remo declared.

"You disconnected them, sir," the airman explained. The phone twittered and he answered it. "Hello, Sergeant Samuels speaking. One moment." He turned to Remo. "They called back, sir. Please don't press anything, sir. Just talk."

Remo took it. "Hello?"

"Remo, it's me."

"Oh, you!"

"Smith," Smith clarified. "I'm ready to compromise."

"Still busted," Remo informed Samuels as he sent the phone flying. "You should hear the nonsense coming out of it."

Samuels batted it from hand to hand a few times before catching it, amazingly intact. The phone made another birdie noise.

"For you again, sir." Samuels sounded nervous.

"Okay, I'll try one more time—just for you, Admiral." Remo held it up and said, "Is it *you?*"

"Yes. It is I. Smith. I am ready to write a new contract."

"Finally. But first things first."

"What would the first thing be?"

Remo glanced over his shoulder. "Could you wait in the media room, Gunnery Sergeant? Thanks. Don't touch anything, especially my stuffed Buddha." When the airman left, Remo said, "The family comes first, Smitty. My family. My people. They're off-limits."

"Agreed."

"They don't get pestered. They don't get spied on. They don't get harassed, subpoenaed or inconvenienced, ever."

"Hands off. I understand."

"No, not hands off. Hands on." Remo declared. "We have got to be crystal clear on this, Smitty. If I come back, CURE has a new job. Protecting my people from interference by any and all government busybodies. The President doesn't bug them, CURE sure the hell doesn't bug them—nobody does. They don't even get called to jury duty. You make that happen."

"You want me to write that into the CURE mandate, Remo?" Smith asked. "I can say yes, but the President might not be agreeable."

"That's okay, Smitty," Remo said. "If you give me your word, then it's as good as being official policy, right?"

"Right. I'll give you my word. CURE will take a policy of noninterference and protection. We'll leave the Sun On Jo alone unless and until there is need for bureaucratic dissuasion."

"Which means you'll get in the muckety muck only if bad people come from the government. Right?"

"Right."

"No more cheap spy tricks."

"Yes. I have said yes, haven't I?" Smith showed his irritation.

Remo chuckled. "That blimp wasn't so cheap, was it?"

Smith sighed. "The expense was substantial, but that's a lesser consideration compared to the cleanup. The Department of Homeland Security is sure to perform an internal audit to determine what happened. They'll come to a dead end, eventually. It's going to complicate our efforts in the future."

"You'll find a way," Remo said, feeling pretty good about things.

Smith sounded less relieved. "There is still the matter of CURE security, Remo. The Sun On Jo represent a major gap in our intelligence containment structure."

"And for all the taxpayer dollars you frittered away eavesdropping on the homestead, you still think they have all this inside intelligence? Just deal with it, Smitty. Winner knows a little. Freya and Sunny Joe know even less. They'd be glad to forget all about you if you let them."

"I must, so I will," Smith said.

Remo chuckled. "You sound like you just drank lemon juice, Smitty. You know what I always say— sprinkle in a little sugar and you'll make lemonade."

"This is the wisdom of Master Remo," muttered a voice from far, far back in the RV. "Wisdom so great it does not need to be recorded in the Sinanju scrolls, for it may be found on wooden plaques in common road-side gift shops."

"It may be common, but it works for me," Remo called back.

"What?" Smith asked.

"Talking to my Buddha. That's what they called him on TV."

"Which brings us to the next subject, if you're satisfied that we're done discussing the first condition?"

"Yeah. What do you want to talk about next?"

"You've stirred up the pot this morning, Remo."

"Ain't it cool?"

Silence. "It achieved your purpose," Smith admitted finally. "I would certainly like to get you and Chiun off national television, but I'm more concerned about your second scheduled TV appearance today. *The Ladies' Man* is supposed to air tonight. And tomorrow night on another network. And Sunday night."

"I'll pull the plug," Remo answered. "Consider it done."

"I'd like to know how you'll manage it."

"Smitty, don't make me mad by questioning my abilities, okay?" Remo took a deep breath, held it, and then said with forced control, "I'm not stupid. Listen carefully, all of you. *Remo not stupid.*"

"I never said you were stupid," Smith said.

"Remo's not a genius. Remo's not good with electronic gizmos. Remo's not brimming with the wisdom of the ages. But guess what, people. Remo is not stupid."

Silence.

"Remo would just like everybody to give him the

same respect they give other people who are also not stupid. The benefit of the doubt. Even a little recognition of the fact that I do hold the title of Reigning Master of the most glorious dynasty in human history—and not by chance. For that, maybe, I deserve an ounce of respect. It's awfully hard to work with people who roll their eyes every effing time I have an original thought."

"I see your point," Smith said finally.

"I, as well," begrudged the Buddha in the back.

37

Brick Walters was snoozing in his rig. Federal law said he had a right to take a snooze because he'd been driving all night. Federal law also allowed him to park his eighteen-wheeler in the taxpayer-funded rest area along the interstate highway. Brick was a by-the-book kind of guy, and he didn't appreciate state troopers who hassled him just to show how much they mattered.

"Go 'way!" he snorted.

For the second time, somebody tap-tapped on his window glass. "Hey, in there!"

"Hey, yourself. I'm sleeping."

The next tap-tap came from the butt end of an assault rifle. The window broke all over Brick Walters, who shouted and found himself looking at a U.S. Army soldier and fifty of his buddies. They were clearing out the rest area.

"Sorry to disturb you. Please vacate these premises. Now."

Brick Walters had every right in the world to stay right where he was, but he didn't press the point. He wasn't the kind of guy to cause trouble.

The rest area was vacant of nonmilitary personnel in

a matter of minutes, and the soldiers returned to their vehicles. The gleaming silver RV hybrid slowed considerably and took the ramp, parking in Brick Walters's truck slot. The line of Army Hummers closed the gap, blocking the ramp, and half the fleet of the New Mexico State Police screeched to a halt.

"What do you mean, federal jurisdiction?" one of the troopers shouted. "This is New Mexico State and we're state law enforcement!"

More Army arrived on the scene, in Apache attack helicopters. Two monster troop transport helicopters loomed over the earth and disengaged more and more military.

"You're on national TV," the Army commander said quietly to the belligerent trooper. "You don't want to get cuffed by a military MP on national TV. You'd never live it down."

That argument made good sense. The troopers left the scene, but they made a lot of racket with their sirens, just to show those lousy Army types how they felt about it.

"SCIENCE OFFICER SAMUELS, can you give us a lift?" Remo asked of the airman, who was standing at attention in the media room.

"Yes, sir. Where to, sir?"

"Michigan," Remo said.

Samuels was a man who erred on the side of caution. He didn't know who exactly he was dealing with. This pair had just been freed from the state of New Mexico by substantial troop mobilization ordered by a general working with the Joint Chiefs of Staff. Whoever these two guys were, Samuels wasn't going to get on their bad side.

"Yes, sir. We'll get you to Michigan, sir."

Chiun was beaming.

"The meditation chamber must be working. You look marvelous," Remo said, feeling chipper.

"All this bluster arranged in our honor is invigorating," Chiun said.

Remo didn't know if Smith's grandiose intervention had been done in their *honor*, but he said nothing. He shouldered Chiun's chests and they emerged from the RV into a maelstrom of light and sound. The fleet of state troopers was departing angrily, sirens whooping and lights blazing. A gnatlike swarm of media choppers was buzzing away far over the fallow fields with two Apaches urging them along, and all around them was the diesel rumble of Hummers and the blowing chop of hovering helicopters. The soldiers formed a defense ring around the rest area, but Remo could feel their curious eyes glancing at himself and Chiun.

"Such attention. It is a pity that a Master of Sinanju must move heaven and earth to earn an exhibition of respect."

"Yeah," Remo agreed.

"I was speaking of you, my son," Chiun added.

"I know," Remo said.

"Do not let it swell your head."

"I won't, Little Father. My white head is hideously oversized already."

"You said this, not I."

Airman Samuels ushered them to a Huey with a dull, camouflage-green paint job. Chiun halted.

"I would prefer that one." He pointed to a gleaming new troop transport behemoth that sat in the sky above them, beating the air into submission with twin giant rotors.

Samuels bit his lip. "I'll arrange it."

"We may as well make the most of it," Remo said.

When they boarded the troop transport, Chiun declared, "You shall allow no damage to come to my home."

"That's what we're here for, sir," Airman Samuels assured him.

THE HELICOPTER WHIRRED away with just two passengers in its cavernous belly.

"Emperor Smith agreed to discuss a new contract?" Chiun asked.

"Yes. You want round-the-clock military escort as a part of the compensation package?"

"I suppose it would become tedious eventually."

"Right."

"And the Emperor would balk."

"I'm sure he would."

"And you intend to negotiate this contract, Remo Williams?"

"I am Reigning Master."

Chiun nodded and said no more about it, for the time being.

38

Olaf Dasheway felt his world crumble down around him. He was on the phone with the man who held the keys to his future—and Romeo Dodd was resigning.

"You can't do this," he stuttered.

"Read the terms of our agreement. Remember my waiver?"

"No." Dasheway tossed papers off his desk until he unearthed a copy of the Romeo Dodd contract. Oh, yes. The waiver. "Uh, let's see. 'If the previous employer of the undersigned Talent submits an offer of reemployment and Talent accepts this other employment prior to the broadcast of the aforementioned program *The Ladies' Man*, Talent will be absolved of all obligations and will forfeit all agreed-upon compensation.' I didn't sign this! Production companies and their broadcast licensees agree to surrender all existing physical copies and destroy all electronic copies of the aforementioned program *The Ladies' Man* that have heretofore been produced. No way! This is so nonstandard."

"You signed it."

"But, Romeo, you said you had a government job. Nobody goes back to a government job."

"I did. I'm officially a federal employee again."

"You'd rather be a civil servant than bagging hot babes and being the envy of all men everywhere?"

"The Hollywood lifestyle was too wild for me."

"You weren't here two days—give the place a chance."

"Sorry, Olaf."

"You can't! I won't abide by these terms!"

"Now, don't say anything stupid," Romeo Dodd warned Dasheway. "The federals don't want me on TV, and they'll make sure I'm not on TV."

Olaf Dasheway was rummaging noisily in his desk.

"Olaf, what are you doing?"

"Looking for scissors. A box cutter. Anything that will slice through wrist skin."

Romeo Dodd tsked. "Hold that suicide, Olaf. I have an offer to make. I know of a way to work this so *The Ladies' Man* will go on the air, as scheduled."

"In God's name, tell me how!" Dasheway blurted.

"This is what you do. You take my face out and put somebody else's face in. You can do that with computers, right?"

"Yes!"

"You can do that before tonight's broadcast?"

"Yes, if we start right away!" Dasheway cried joyfully.

"You get somebody to be the face of *The Ladies' Man* tonight, and maybe even let him continue the series. Nobody would have to know there was ever a switch—not even the networks."

"Yes. Perfect. You'll agree to that, nice and legal? Sign a confidentiality agreement?"

"Sure, I will."

Olaf Dasheway had never been on such an emotional roller coaster. Romeo bowing out was bad news, but the first episode was in the can. It would be a tremendous hit, no matter whose face was on the screen, and the networks had already committed to a full season.

"The question is," Romeo said, "Olaf, can you come up with a replacement right away?"

Olaf shot to his feet and ran out of his office, phone to his ear. A rumpled, dejected-looking man was sprawled in the waiting room. "He's already here."

"Great news."

As soon as Romeo was off the phone, Dasheway hit the speed dial. "I want Philstock. Philstock? Drop whatever you're doing and meet me at production in ten minutes. Bring a computer geek—the best you've got but he's gotta be able to keep his mouth shut. I'll explain when I get there. Yes, it's an emergency!"

Olaf barged out of his office. The sad, disheveled wreck in the waiting area glared at him, like a beaten dog expecting to be whacked with a newspaper again.

Instead, Dasheway snatched him by the lapels and dragged him to his feet, pulling him close and snarling quietly, "Do you want to be the ladies' man?"

Tears of joy trickled down the sad creature's rosy cheeks. "Yes, sir, I do. More than anything in the whole world."

"Then pull yourself together, Willy! We have work to do."

"Yes, sir!"

The pair of Secret Service agents would have chatted up the receptionist for an hour if she hadn't said, "Isn't that the guy you're supposed to be watching?"

They saw the TV producer leaving with somebody who resembled their man—it *was* him, but he had changed. He looked taller and more confident. He looked like a man who had found a new reason to live.

39

Everything was coming up roses for Remo Williams. All his pieces were falling into place. Just one more loose end to take care of, and he sure hoped it worked out the way he planned.

Of course it would work out. MacBisCo *had* to be the person or persons behind all the sabotaged games and international tensions. He had thought about this long and hard and now he was absolutely positive.

Chiun was eyeing him carefully as they proceeded along the long walk from the visitor's parking lot to the MacBisCo corporate headquarters, which butted up against the manufacturing plant. The plaque on the wall designated the factory as a historic building.

"This box of bricks is older than you, Chiun."

"Yes."

"Why are you looking at me like that?"

"Play no games with me, Remo. The air is redolent with the lusty aroma of corn. I see your eyes lose their focus, and your breathing is labored."

"No way. It's cornmeal, anyway. They make generic corn flakes here."

"The smell inspires desire in you."

"Come on, stop it."

The ground vibrated and a powerful sound came from inside. There was a pause, then it came again, every two seconds.

"Look at yourself, Remo!" Chiun cried. "Are you even aware of your actions? Or does your body open the door to this garden of sinful pleasures without your awareness?"

"I want to see what the noise is, that's all." The sound became deafening as they went through a steel door and found themselves in the hot, dim, hellishly loud factory. The air was thick with grain and yeast smells.

"I promise you, this is not getting me turned on," Remo said to Chiun.

"Can I help you?" asked a shift manager who walked over. "The tours start up front."

"Remo McDunough, D.A."

"District attorney or Department of Agriculture?"

"Me, an attorney? Definitely from the department. I was just interested in that noise. You guys stamping out tank parts or something?"

The shift manager nodded and smiled in understanding. "That's the Extreme Nugget maker." She beckoned them closer to the assembly line of whizzing boxes and pointed to a distant, looming iron press that lifted and descended, rocking the earth like the footstep of a giant. Steam hissed into the air in twenty-foot plumes.

"Takes a lot of pressure to cram that much fiber into a pea-size pellet."

"That *is* extreme. Is it safe to eat?"

"You tell me. You're the D.A."

"Oh. Yeah."

"We got some bad press, you know, when they did the tests on monkeys. The chimps would eat the nuggets, then drink water and their stomachs would burst. So now we have the chart on the back to tell you how much water is too much water, based on the amount of Nuggets you've ingested."

Chiun shook his head. "And do you consume this foodstuff?"

"No way," the line manager said.

"Remo McDunough." Remo flipped his leather ID case open for the executive receptionist in the historic MacBisCo offices. "We'd like to see Sherman Mac-Gregor. He in?"

"He's interviewing a prospective employee. It shouldn't take long. I like that name, Remo. Is it Italian?"

"Greek. Short for Remostophines."

"Impressive, Remo. I'm Stephanie. Our names together make Remostophines. Isn't that—" she rolled her eyes playfully "—kind of intimate?"

Remo was thankful that at that moment a sallow man in a perfectly neat suit emerged from the office and left quietly, trying not to be noticed.

"That didn't take long," Stephanie said. "Poor Fellows. You guys go on in."

"You want to let Mr. MacGregor know we're here?" Remo asked.

"Nah. Who cares?"

Remo and Chiun slipped into MacGregor's office and found him absorbed in his computer. MacGregor was a fiftyish, balding man with a freckled pate. Playing a video game, he made an ugly porcine chortle.

Remo and Chiun moved around the desk to watch. For a Master of Sinanju, who can walk on a powder-sand beach without leaving footprints, it was an easy thing to move silently in the carpeted office. Mac-Gregor never noticed that he was not alone.

The computer showed the Wall of Resolution, the ice wall on New Zealand's South Island, glimmering under floodlights. There was a grid superimposed over the wall, and red dots, too. The camera showed men on the wall—not climbers. They were Extreme Sports Network technicians. It looked as though they had been dismantling gear on the winner's summit, but now they were hanging off the rim on safety cables. One of them was limp, with a bloodied head. A chunk of the rim was missing above them.

The second worker was clawing at the ice with his fingers, but without the hammers and cleats of the professional ice-climbers, he kept slipping back until finally he seemed to dig his fingers into the ice out of sheer force of will and dragged himself with painful effort to within reach of the shattered rim.

The red dots were now directly over the struggling man, and Sherm MacGregor cackled nastily. He moved the mouse onto the red spot, and then his finger applied just enough pressure to the mouse button to change the blood flow and whiten his finger.

He never finished the click.

"Wow, they are coming up with the coolest stuff these days," Remo said, holding up the thing with the dangling cord that had just been in MacGregor's hand. "What do they call this game?"

MacGregor found his voice. "Who are you?"

"What do they call this game, Little Father?" Remo asked.

"A mouse."

"I'm kidding. I know what a computer mouse is. But this game of yours is so realistic. Now, that's new to me."

"Get out of my office, whoever you are," MacGregor said loudly.

"Chill, Sherm. Can I call you Sherm?" Remo put a hand on MacGregor's shoulder and pushed down just as MacGregor stood up. MacGregor lost that battle. Then Remo adjusted MacGregor's spine, which stopped functioning. "So, what's very cool about your game is that it looks just like this place in New Zealand we visited a few days ago."

Sherman MacGregor was chilled by this little bit of trivia—it frightened him more than the fact that he was now paralyzed below the neck.

"New Zealand's kind of a stupid place. They have this great scenery and they put in cheesy attractions so visitors can't see the scenery. I guess they do that everywhere, not just New Zealand. But they had this stupid contest in New Zealand, just like on your game. They have people who climb up a big frozen waterfall, blindfolded. Stupid, right? And the one who gets to the top of the ice floe first is the winner. But we found out something shocking."

The younger, dark-headed man was talking like a goofball and would have been underdressed even on casual Fridays at the office, but there was something a lot more serious on his face. "Do you want to know what we found out, Sherm?"

The younger man was not acting goofy anymore, and the look on his face was deadly. In those eyes Sherman MacGregor saw the glimmer of destruction. This man was something extraordinary.

"What did you find out?" Sherm asked.

"The contest was rigged."

"Oh."

"We were in Australia a week before that. Another stupid contest. And you'll never believe what we learned."

Sherm's mouth was bone dry. "Rigged?"

"Yes. The stupid Australian contest was rigged, too."

"Don't forget the shameless unclothed ones," the old man added.

"That's right. Sedona. Would you believe they roll down hills, on their backs, in their birthday suits? It's fascinating for all of ten seconds, and then, yech. But somebody rigged that one, too. A big difference though. Nobody was killed in Sedona."

The glimmer of destruction flashed in those horrific eyes again, like the beacon of purgatory. "Lots of people died in Australia. A few corpses in New Zealand. Montana was a slaughterhouse."

"Montana?"

"Don't tell me you don't remember Montana," Remo blazed. "When you go and snuff out the lives of a dozen-odd skydivers, just to give your man the competitive edge, the least you can do is remember the contest."

"I didn't have anything to do with it. Any of it."

The lie was transparent even to MacGregor. Remo sneered. "I was there. I was a part of that jump, Sherm. I smelled the bodies burning."

"Let's talk this over," Sherm suggested.

"We are talking it over."

"Could you make it so I can move?"

"Absolutely not. Let's talk about the Drake Passage. I see your confusion. The Drake Passage is a body of water. If you go out the door, turn south and walk and walk until you can't walk any more, that's the Drake Passage. It goes around the tip of South America and a bunch of guys in sailboats took the passage on their way around the world. Another dumb-ass contest. Only somebody started offing the guys who were winning the race, and when they reached guy number 3, somebody got rid of the killers. That somebody was me. Now is it ringing a bell?"

"The Around the World All by Yourself sailboat race," MacGregor admitted.

"See, I've been cleaning up your messes for months."

"It was the foreman who committed the crimes, not me. He was the one who hired the hit squad to take out the sailboat racers."

"Explain, Sherm. What was that supposed to accomplish?"

"I wanted the guy in fifth place to win. He was a young guy, real enthusiastic. A go-getter. He was supposed to be on boxes of Extreme Nuggets. But they called the race off. So after that, me and the network, we decided there should be a standard policy that all competitions must continue despite injury or loss of life. Canceling was a big financial hit for everybody."

"ESN's not in on your little scheme," Remo said. "They're heartless bastards, but they're not the ones committing murder."

The accusation had been ready to fly out of Mac-Gregor's lips—at least ESN could take some of the blame. But these killers already knew the truth. Why was he so helpless? Why wasn't he fighting back?

Because Sherman MacGregor would do anything to *not* unleash the destroyer that dwelt like a malevolent spirit in this man. This man knew how to kill in ways MacGregor could only dream of.

"Please take me to jail," MacGregor said.

"So, is that how you did it? You'd pick a candidate, engineer their victory, then recruit them? Wouldn't you get them for less if you struck a deal before they won?"

"Didn't want to be associated with them prior to the win. Didn't want it to look like I had foreknowledge. Don't I get my rights read to me?"

"Who's the foreman?"

"I don't know."

"Where is he now?"

"I don't know his name. He's a free agent. He claims he's never been caught. I was in Mexico City hiring mercenaries and he approached me. All I have is a phone number."

40

Mrs. Mikulka was having a chat with young Mark's lady friend, Sarah, a lovely girl. The phone interrupted them.

"Hi, Mrs. M. It's Romeo. I need to talk to Dr. Smith. Would you believe I lost his phone number?"

Mrs. Mikulka pursed her wrinkled lips. "Oh, Romeo, of course. I will put you through to Dr. Smith."

She buzzed the call through, then hung up, a curious frown. "You know, you would think he would have memorized Dr. Smith's direct line by now. That Romeo has been a good friend of Dr. Smith's for so many years. But I've always thought he might be a little flighty."

"Romeo?" Sarah asked deadpan. "Like on *The Ladies' Man?*"

Mrs. Mikulka tittered. "Can you imagine *that* Romeo on some TV show about, you know, seduction? I don't think so."

"He's not a ladies' man?"

Mrs. Mikulka made a face. "I think he spends all his time waiting on his father, hand and foot. He's very devoted, I'll give him that. But he's no ladies' man."

DR. SMITH SWITCHED the call to a secure line as Mark
Howard penetrated the encryption code guarding the remote control of the explosives in the ice wall.

"Cleverly done," Howard admitted. "There's an Extreme Nuggets Web site hosted in New Zealand by
MacBisCo. It gets pinged from Battle Creek ten times
a second. The commands for the explosives get to New
Zealand masked as a ping, then go over standard phone
lines to a transmitter mounted on the mountain face
across from the ice wall."

"I see," Remo said.

"You do?"

IN MACGREGOR'S OFFICE, the computer window
showed the two technicians being helicoptered off the
winner's summit. The one who had climbed back to the
summit was treated at the scene by paramedics. The
other one got just a few moments of attention with a
stethoscope, then his face was covered.

"So, what did you win today, Sherm?" Remo demanded. "Or was that just you having a little fun?"

MacGregor looked at his lap.

"Well? Was it fun after all?"

MacGregor didn't answer.

"Let us render this device unusable," Chiun said impatiently as the helicopter left with the technicians.
"Cornmonger, if I detonate the little booms far away,
they will forever after be harmless. Is this not so?"

"Right," MacGregor said.

Chiun reattached the mouse and unceremoniously
clicked the cursor on the remaining red spots. The ice

bulged and cracked where the last charges went off, and all the red spots turned to black *X*s.

"I have never seen a more cowardly way to kill," the old Master of Sinanju declared.

"Now we call the foreman," Remo announced. "You ready to track him down?"

"We're ready," Mark Howard said from the phone speaker.

Remo used the speed dial on MacGregor's mobile phone—just click, click, nothing to it—and held it to the ear of the cereal magnate.

Sherman MacGregor tried to relax, to make his voice natural when he talked to the foreman.

The line rang, and rang, and stopped.

41

The foreman dropped the stack of blue jeans and tube socks. The moment his mobile phone started ringing, the fear had come. They were close to him. They were on to him. They were *calling* him.

He looked at the phone display. It was Sherman MacGregor calling. They had caught the son of a bitch. He'd squealed and fingered the foreman.

These people were something out of the ordinary. The foreman had been in close scrapes before, but he never had the feeling of fear that he had right now, and that he had when he cowered in the toilet in the Auckland airport.

He didn't know what they looked like, but he knew what they sounded like. Two men, and one of them called the other one Little Father. The one who was Little Father had a high-pitched, almost a singsong, voice. They were terrifying. If the foreman lifted the cover on his mobile phone, those two, or whoever they worked for, would immediately pinpoint the foreman in the All-Mart in Baton Rouge, Louisiana.

The foreman slipped the battery off the back of his phone. The shrill screech of his nerves immediately dissipated.

They were calling from Battle Creek, Michigan, but they might have all sorts of resources at their disposal. The foreman forgot about his new clothes. He just left, fast.

He drove out of Baton Rouge and didn't stop until he was into Alabama, where he purchased rubbing alcohol at a truck stop. He rubbed down the phone with the rubbing alcohol, then burned it on the roadside with the rest of the alcohol.

He got in his car and drove for hours, then burned the car, too, in the bay of an unattended do-it-yourself car wash in St. Louis. He walked through the night until he reached a bank on the opposite side of the city. His safe-deposit box was there with papers for a new identity.

But he was still the foreman. That's all he ever really was, no matter what the paperwork claimed. The foreman was famous and yet the foreman was like a shadow. He was too good, too clever, too gifted with his own special sense of self-preservation.

He could never, ever be caught.

42

"He's in Baton Rouge," Mark said. "He disabled the phone. Must know the jig is up."

"We have what we need from the MacBisCo networks," Smith added. "Once Sherman MacGregor's software is made public, it will be clear who was behind the ESN game fixing. That should dampen the international saber rattling."

Remo hung up the phone. "Guess we've no more use for you," he announced.

"You have two great faults," Chiun said. "You are an insidious cornmonger and a despicable coward."

"I deserve jail," MacGregor said sincerely.

Remo grimaced harshly. "You deserve something more...what's the word I'm looking for, Little Father?"

"Extreme?"

"Right."

"Showy?"

"Maybe."

"Ostentatious?"

"I prefer poetic."

"Your brand of poetry comes from the walls of public washrooms."

"Please arrest me," Sherman MacGregor pleaded.

"Can we tour the factory?" Remo asked.

Chiun's eyes went wide. "No, Remo, don't do this."

"Listen to him!" MacGregor urged.

"He is an incurable corn addict," Chiun explained. "His very dreams are of the saccharine sweetness of the harlot vegetable, corn."

"I'm not an addict," Remo said. "I haven't had corn in years and never dream about it."

"You speak of corn in your sleep like you would speak to a lover."

"Now you're making up stories, and I don't want to visit the factory to munch on cornmeal," Remo said, putting an arm around Sherm MacGregor's shoulders and walking him out of the office. The building was silent. It was 5:25 and nobody cared enough to work late anymore. "We won't go near the corn, I promise. What I want to get a closer look at is that Nugget compressor thing of yours. We saw it earlier and I can tell you, that thing really is extreme."

"Oh, lord," MacGregor gasped.

"A waste of time," Chiun squeaked.

"But poetic," Remo said.

43

They were at Folcroft in time for a late dinner. It felt almost good to be back there. Almost like coming home.

But not quite that nice, really. Folcroft wasn't home. The sterile condo in Connecticut wasn't home. Chiun's monstrous recreational vehicle wasn't home, either.

Remo didn't know what home was, but for now, Folcroft would do. There were things to take care of. A new contract to negotiate. A parrot to interrogate.

"It's the bird from Union Island," Remo said. "What's it doing here?"

"I know not," Chiun said truthfully, regarding the bird curiously.

They had been to the Caribbean vacation spot called Union Island months and months ago. Chiun struck up a conversation with one of the tropical birds in the open-air aviary in the resort lobby, only to find out that it didn't belong to the hotel. It had simply flown in one day and made itself at home.

When Remo and Chiun left, the parrot followed them to the airport. Remo was sure Chiun planned on taking it with them back to the States, and he didn't want another pet. Chiun's pets were always a disaster for Remo.

But they left the island without the bird, and Remo forgot all about it.

"Are you certain it is the same bird?" Sarah Slate asked.

"Yes, it is the same," Chiun said in the gentle voice he reserved for two humans on the planet: Sarah Slate and Freya. "I recognize the pattern in its pupils."

"It sure looks like it made the flight from the Caribbean to New York," Mark Howard said. "I'm surprised it survived the journey."

"Yes," Chiun agreed.

Remo was getting impatient. "Hey, Chiun, what's going on? Don't you find this a little weird? It's a big purple bird that flew thousands of miles to find you at a place it has never been before. That's not usual."

"Nothing about the bird is usual," Sarah said. "I think it's intelligent."

The parrot chose that moment to recite a limerick about a woman with angina, as well as other interesting anatomical novelties.

"That's intelligent? That's not even very funny," Remo pointed out.

"Waste not my time," Chiun said to the bird. "Speak to me your message if you have one."

The bird demanded food.

Chiun sounded like a spinster schoolmarm. "I hope you have not crossed the eastern coast of this continent simply for trail mix. I do not have trail mix, I do not consume trail mix and I shall not take the responsibility of providing you with trail mix."

The bird was silent. Sarah presented it with a palmful of nuts and dried fruit, which the parrot picked at. Then it fluffed up and sank down on the chair back that was its perch.

"I guess it's taking a nap," Sarah said sheepishly. "It said those things, Chiun. Really."

"Of course, I do believe you. And it shall say those things again, and when it does I shall consider the words. Until then, what more can I do?"

As they left the suite, the bird flapped across the room. Chiun gave it a glare. The bird flapped away frantically, just before it touched the old man's bony shoulder, and settled instead on Remo's.

"You inviting yourself over to live with us?" Remo asked it.

"Bring the trail mix," the bird said. It wasn't a request.

MARK HOWARD BROUGHT over a chair, as there was no furniture in their suite that offered the bird any kind of a perch.

"Polly's not staying on Remo's shoulder, got it?"

The bird ignored him, but flapped to the chair back when it arrived. Its sprained leg seemed to be getting stronger, and it hunkered down for a nap.

"Chiun," Remo said, "I need to know something about one of the old Sinanju Masters. Something that is not in the scrolls."

Chiun's look was a mixture of delight and suspicion. "You have searched the scrolls?"

"The ones we have with us," Remo said. "But I'm sure it's not in any of the histories I've read."

Chiun was still suspicious.

"It's about Yeou Gang's sleazy reputation. How come it was forgotten in just one generation? I mean, was there a war or some catastrophe that wiped out all the kings and emperors of the time?"

Chiun was quietly surprised that Remo had seen this missing detail in the story. "There was no catastrophe," he admitted.

"So, what did Yeou Gang do? Hire an image consultant?"

"He trained one," Chiun said reluctantly. "His pupil knew of his shame, for Yeou Gang did not hide it. His pupil was Yeou Gang the Younger, who was more wise than his father yet bore him a great respect, for the shame of Yeou Gang the Elder had forged in him a deep passion for the tradition of Sinanju. Yeou Gang the Younger resolved to renew the esteem of Sinanju, and to do so while his father lived. He accomplished this while undergoing his Rite of Succession."

The Rite of Succession was one of the two major ritualistic undertakings by Sinanju pupils. The first, the Rite of Attainment, made the Sinanju pupil a Master of Sinanju. The Rite of Succession made a Master into the Reigning Master. Officially, this was the position of highest rank in the Sinanju tradition. When Remo went though the Rite of Succession and was named Reigning Master, he became, theoretically, the Sinanju boss. Which meant he had authority over any other Masters that were still living. But this was only a theory.

But during the Rite of Succession, Remo had been ritualistically presented to all the global leaders and had engaged each nation's most skilled assassins. The battles were ceremonial in nature, but they were battles to the death. The result of such an exercise was that all the world's most powerful rulers were made to know of the skills of Sinanju. The ceremony also decimated the ranks of the world's skilled assassins and thus made the Sinanju Masters even more in demand.

Remo's Rite of Succession was one of the most efficient in all of Sinanju history. Prior to the development of air transportation, the rite would last for years simply due to long travel times.

"Yeou Gang the Younger went first to the palace of Saras, a Harrapan king, where he easily defeated the greatest warrior that was pitted against him. As Yeou Gang the Younger and his father took their final tea with the Harrapan court, the young Master heard one member of the court use a disparaging word in references to Yeou Gang the Elder. The young Master silenced the one who said the words, on the spot. This was somewhat of a surprise to the Harrapan emperor."

"I guess it would be," Remo agreed.

"The one who was silenced was the emperor's aunt," Chiun explained.

"Even more of a shocker."

"Yeou Gang the Younger stood before the emperor's court and declared that he would suffer no insult. The husband of the slain woman protested, saying that she was repeating words that were common in the kingdom. Yeou Gang slew the husband, too. This was cause for alarm in the court, and there were those who called the young Master impetuous and murderous."

"Uh-oh."

"Yeou Gang the Younger suffered them not to live,

and the emperor called for his royal guard to put a stop to the decimation of his friends and family."

"Uh-oh again."

"Soon there were more bodies than living men in the court of this emperor. After the soldiers were dispatched, Yeou Gang the Younger asked the court if there were others who wished to repeat the foul disparagement they had heard of the great Sinanju house, or if there were those who felt they might someday be tempted to repeat such disparagements."

"Any hands go up?"

"None," Chiun said. "Yeou Gang the Younger then informed the fawning emperor that he would return to the kingdom at some unspecified future time to question the court about rumors regarding the great Sinanju assassins. The emperor understood perfectly. As soon as the Masters departed, the emperor made the defamation of the Sinanju masters a crime punishable by death. Yeou Gang the Younger repeated this performance more than one time during the seven years of his Rite of Succession journeys, but word spread well enough even in those days."

"Yeou Gang the Younger was a real player," Remo said.

"The shame of his father was wiped away. Sinanju prospered. The Harrapan king so feared the return of Yeou Gang the Younger he moved away with his court and allowed his power to wane before he again faced Yeou Gang the Younger."

"I love a happy ending." After a while, Remo asked, "How do you feel?"

The old man's eyebrows popped up. "What manner of question is that?"

"C'mon, Little Father, I'm not asking you how you're doing today. I'm asking you how you feel. How do you feel physically? How do you think you will feel a year from now or five years from now? Do you feel like you can keep going in, you know, this capacity?"

Chiun considered his answer. Or maybe he was considering the question, but he answered eventually. "I feel strong, Remo Williams. I feel good. But sometimes I feel my age. Does this worry you?"

"I don't know. The Masters of Sinanju can live for decades more than other men. But you've already done that."

Chiun smirked. "Don't count your inheritance yet, my son. I think I will last for a few more years."

Remo tried to sound lighthearted. "What makes you so sure? You have some sort of secret?"

"Perhaps."

"Age-defying skin cream? A specially formulated Vitamin E supplement that actually reverses the cellular damage of age?"

"Yes. The first guess was correct. It is a skin cream."

"And that's the straightest answer I'm getting, right?"

"Yes."

"You gonna turn me on to some of that skin cream?"

"Not while I still live. But after I am gone, you may open up my last will and testament. Paper clipped inside you shall find the business card of the housewife who peddles my cosmetics. She is the source of this life-extending skin cream. She is quite intelligent and resourceful—so much so, her company bestowed upon her a pink car."

"Must be really expensive skin cream, but worth every penny. You look *marvelous*."

"You are an unskilled liar, but I appreciate your efforts. I shall prepare tea for us." Chiun rose gracefully to his feet.

"Sounds great," Remo said.

"After which, you shall prepare dinner."

44

It was an uncomfortable group that gathered in the morning for the wrap-up.

"I wish I could tell you that international strain is easing as a result of the exposure of MacBisCo," Harold Smith said. "It seems to have hurt rather than helped—although America isn't the only target anymore."

"Who, then?" Remo asked.

"Who isn't?" Mark Howard responded. "The Germans and the Swiss and the Austrians are furious with one another, but they're allied against the Kiwis and the U.S. Everybody is mad at the Australians. All of Europe is mad at the U.K. China is ticked off at Russia."

"You lost me. What do China and Russia have to do with the extreme games?"

"Nothing, and that's odd," Smith said. "There are significant tensions building around the globe, and now that the games aren't there to keep the pot stirring, conflicts are emerging randomly."

"It's like everybody wants to pick a fight with everyone else," Mark Howard said. "I don't like it."

It was an odd turn of phrase. He stared determinedly at his computer screen.

The corner of Smith's mouth turned down thoughtfully. "Let us hope it does indeed die down in the coming days. I see no reason why it should not. Master Chiun, has the bird said anything noteworthy?"

"Not as yet, Emperor. The creature will make his purpose known when the time is right."

"Have you come to any conclusion as to who may have sent him?"

"No person sent him, Emperor. Of this I am confident."

"I see. Remo? Shall we begin our renegotiations this morning?"

"Smitty, you look beat," Remo said. "Maybe tomorrow. Get some sleep. I wouldn't want to take advantage of you."

"Isn't that what you've done?" Mark Howard asked without animosity. "Exploit your position of strength to force the issue."

"I guess so. Isn't that what all negotiations are about?"

"This is not the lesson of Sinanju," Chiun responded hastily. "Bargaining from a position of strength is acceptable, but violating your contract to achieve it is inexcusable," Chiun maintained stoically, and a little sadly.

"What, me? A Sinanju Master? Violate a contract?"

Chiun looked at his protégé's smug expression. "Of course you did."

"No, I didn't."

"Remo," Dr. Smith said in irritation, "whatever I have agreed to, I agreed to it because you did violate our contract. There's no argument there."

"Yes, there is," Remo said. "I read the contract. My understanding of the contract is that the Master of Sinanju is to perform his duties to previously set standards. I did that. You wanted us to go to the nude luge. You wanted us at the ice skating babe-a-thon. You wanted us in Australia and New Zealand. I was there for you."

Smith was aghast. "You weren't. You told me you quit. You refused to do what I asked you to do. You can't disobey orders and expect that to fulfill your contract."

"I always have," Remo said without concern.

"Previously set standards of performance?" Mark Howard asked.

"You got it, Junior."

"That is a juvenile interpretation or our agreement," Chiun spit. "Here I must side with the Emperor, Remo. You may not ignore the finer points of the arrangement."

"I followed the arrangement as I understood it. I did my homework. I read the thing, and more than once. It hurt worse than eighth-grade algebra, but I did it."

"You obviously didn't," Smith said. "You misinterpreted much of it if you honestly believe you followed the terms."

Remo set his mouth hard, then stood up abruptly and opened the door with a whoosh of air. "Hey, Mrs. M. Got my package?"

"Yes. Here you go, Romeo."

"Don't get up." Remo bounded out and was back in a moment, the door crashing shut behind him. It was a FedEx box, which he scalpeled open with his extralong fingernail, withdrawing a heavy roll of rich parchment and a stapled, ragged stack of photocopies.

"My copy of the contract," Remo said, holding up the photocopies and fanning them. They were scribbled on every page with rows of question marks, dense boxes of Hangul scribbling and four-letter words blocked out in boxy Superman-style lettering. "What a bitch. I gotta hand it to you, Smitty, Little Father, this is the most god-awful pile of mumbo-crapola ever put together by man or machine. You two ever want to make real money, you could form an insurance agency."

"But what is this?" Chiun practically shrieked in dismay. He had the roll of parchment and was spinning through it at lightning speed.

"That's my interpretation."

"It is Hangul, mostly!" Chiun exclaimed. "It is on parchment. The penmanship is *legible.*"

"G'wan," Remo said.

Chiun landed the parchment heavily on the desk before Harold W. Smith. "It is nearly perfect." He was smiling. Remo was as red as a stoplight.

"Your notes are in Hangul?" Smith asked.

"Not my notes, Smitty. The contract."

Chiun beamed. "Yes!"

"What are you saying?" Mark Howard demanded.

"The clause of intent," Chiun announced proudly. "My son, Remo—" Words seemed to fail the old man.

"*This* is the contract, Smitty. I wrote it up, based on my understanding of this mess of malarkey." Remo flicked the photocopy.

"No. That is the contract. It is what Chiun and I agreed to."

"Chiun and you agreed to it, Mark Howard signed onto it, I'm somehow obligated to it. Yeah, it's a real unique humdinger of a heap of vicious circles through loopholes. I never did get the whole picture in my head but I could understand it in bits and pieces, and that's what matters. Because you put in a clause of intent. Smart move, Little Father."

"I did not foresee this, however."

"The clause of intent was designed to prevent loopholes, not create them!" Smith said angrily. "It says that the contract language cannot be manipulated to create unforeseen concessions of Sinanju authority. It was designed to prevent unintended transfers of obligation. Remember the fiasco when the Russian usurped the Sinanju contract years ago? That's what prompted Chiun to ask for a clause of intent. The only reason I agreed to it was because every other contingency was so minutely spelled out that I did not see how it could be used against me."

"But you also agreed that the decision about what was and was not intent was up to the Master of Sinanju," Remo Williams said.

Smith stopped talking and slumped in his chair. Chiun smiled like an angel. Mark Howard shook his head and stifled a grin.

"That would be me," Remo said. "You can look at who's bossing around who and make your own decisions. Chiun can write whatever he wants in the House of Sinanju scrolls. The real truth is what Sinanju tradition says, and Sinanju tradition says I am Reigning Master. I'm the one who decides what the intent of this is. And I did. I read it. Every word, every page, three times. Then I read it again, and I transposed what the intent was onto these pages. I don't mind telling you, it was the most bloody awful experience of my entire life, and I've been through some shit."

Remo stopped to listen. Despite outward appearances, Smith's heart still beat regularly, so he went on.

"So you see, Smitty, *this* is the official contract between the House of Sinanju and CURE."

Smith nodded very slightly.

"And I did not violate any of it," Remo stated. "Got it? Chiun?"

"Yes, I see." Chiun's hazel eyes looked as if they would soon start dancing around the room for sheer pleasure.

"Smitty? Junior? Whichever one of you I'm supposed to really be reporting to? You getting any of this?"

"I get it, Remo," Smith said, sitting forward with sudden animation. "I've been had."

"You have not."

"I can't even read this document."

"Here's the English version." Remo slipped another stack of handwritten pages out of the box. "Read it. You'll see. No violations by me."

"The public exposure?" Smith demanded defensively.

"Never happened. Never intended it to."

"The disregard of orders?"

"Never worse than in the past."

Smith waved one hand dramatically. "I can't accept any of this."

"The fact is, the only one who broke the terms of the contract was you, Harold W. Smith. You violated the parts about interfering with my extended family. It wasn't just a little violation, either. It was outrageous."

"Egregious," Chiun corrected.

"Right," Remo said.

"Therefore, the Master of Sinanju has the right to void the contract entirely at this time."

Smith grew still again. "You have me there."

There was a potent silence in the old office at Folcroft Sanitarium.

"Answer me this," Smith said. "You have all this, and still you wanted the contract renegotiated? What more do you want?"

Remo rolled his eyes to the water-stained ceiling tiles. "Christ Almighty, Smitty, you were at the meetings. Some authority to do what's right when I know I'm right and you're wrong. Remember Humbert Coleslaw? What a pickle you would have saved the government if you'd listened to me and focused CURE on getting rid of that bad apple early on. Plus, a life. Accumulated vacation time. This stuff is not in the contract, my version or yours. Some, I don't know, independence?"

"Self-determination," Mark Howard said.

Remo smiled. "Exactly."

45

Smith went for his afternoon walk, despite the chill. He was tired, but needed the exercise. At his age, deterioration could set in fast when you became sedentary.

"Hiya, Smitty," Remo said from a bush where a man could not possibly have been standing, but Remo was suddenly there.

Smith raised his eyebrows. "Hello, Remo."

"Didn't mean to startle you. Chiun and Sarah are doing an all-day blog-huddle and I got sick of their gossip. They're like, so junior high school."

Smith smiled slightly. "Sarah is very young," he said.

"Sarah's not as bad as you-know-who." Remo fell in step beside Smith, more relaxed than Smith had seen him in—he couldn't remember when.

"Decide what to do about her yet?" Remo asked.

"There's nothing I can do."

"Guess not."

Smith still carried his tension with him like a backpack full of bricks. "There's too much history behind this organization, Remo," Smith said. "In the early days, it was simpler. There was just the three of us,

Chiun, yourself and me. It was easier for me to control CURE's security."

Remo looked at the old man and smiled easily—a genuine look without the smart-ass edge that Smith was used to now. "Smitty," Remo said, "don't you *get* it?"

"No," Smith said. "Honestly, I don't."

Remo nodded thoughtfully, then said, "There has *always* been too much history behind the organization because there's too much history behind Sinanju. Too much for you to know, too much for me or even Chiun to know. I don't understand what brought CURE and Sinanju together in the first place, but as soon as that happened, bam, you've got five thousand years of history. You think CURE's been manipulated and used by some unknown force, you should try making sense of the lineage of Sinanju Masters. First, they all came from the same gene pool that spawned Chiun and they have the dispositions to prove it. Second, they've all got Korean names. Third, they've been tossing around in the winds of fate since forever, even if they won't admit it."

Smith scowled. "Are you saying that, whatever it is that pulled CURE's strings is the same thing steering the course of the Sinanju Masters all this time?"

"That's right."

"So CURE was incidental in the grand scheme?"

"Exactly. Make you feel better?"

"No," Smith said, his old head shaking. "It doesn't make me feel better, Remo. Still, I suppose it makes it clear that I'm not going to find out who or what this guiding force is. As far as the history goes, I suppose you are correct. I've never truly admitted to myself how widespread was the knowledge of Sinanju. Sarah is evidence of that, and she was an individual that we just happened to associate with in the course of events...."

Remo smiled. Smith was sour.

"Or maybe we didn't just happen to," Smith said. "Maybe she is here for a reason. To save your life."

"Or to become manager of vermin control at Folcroft." Remo shrugged. "Or something else. Who knows?"

"What else?" Smith said sharply.

"I don't know," Remo said, suddenly on the defensive. Why was he suddenly on the defensive? "I said I don't know. How should I know?"

"I thought maybe you knew something I didn't."

"About Sarah? Honest Injun, Smitty, I don't have a clue about the fortune in her cookie. What were you thinking?"

"I was thinking protégée."

"Oy. No, thanks. She's too smart. It'd be like hanging out with Lisa Simpson for twenty years. Besides, Chiun would want to retire if I got a trainee. I think I'm going to stick with old Moses for a while."

"How long is a while?" Smith probed.

"Chiun was in his eighties when I started on the long, annoying road to Reigning Master," Remo said, smiling. "Eighty sounds like a good age to take on a lackey."

Smith nodded, hearing the ringing bell of irony in Remo's words. Indeed, eighty wasn't old, not to a Master of Sinanju. To any other man, to Smith, eighty was the twilight of life.

Harold W. Smith abruptly laughed. Out loud. "Huh huh huh!"

"What? What?" Remo demanded.

"I don't think I'll be around when you're eighty years old, Remo," Smith said, with a rare glitter in his eyes. "That means your protégé is one problem I won't have to deal with."

"Who says my protégé would give you problems?" Remo asked indignantly.

"Huh huh." Smith stopped walking and wiped his eyes with a starched handkerchief.

Remo scowled. "Before you bust a gut, remember I didn't *promise* to wait for eighty. I could be walking down the street tomorrow and spot some Korean kindergartner with fast reflexes."

"So, you're a traditionalist," Smith observed. "Chiun took an atypical protégé, while you're thinking of going with the standard Korean child."

Remo shook his head. "I never thought of it like that. Me the Master who sticks to the Sinanju tradition while Chiun's the one who breaks all the rules of Sinanju protocol."

Smith looked at him hard. "You are of Sinanju village."

"Hey, not me."

"You are. Remo, don't you get it?"

"Get what?"

Harold W. Smith smiled. "You, too, came from the gene pool that spawned Master Chiun. You have the disposition to prove it."

Remo Williams never thought of it in those terms, never so clearly. Now it was perfectly, obviously true.

"Wow. That's amazing. That's incredible. Christ, how'd I miss that all these years? I really am a Sinanju Master, even so far as being—what are they? Obstinate? Argumentative? Cantankerous?"

Smith nodded. "Those are all pretty good."

Remo chuckled. "Me. Remo. A village elder. What a kick in the pants. What a revelation."

"Maybe, for you, that revelation was the final step," Smith suggested. "Maybe at this moment you have become completely the Reigning Master of Sinanju—master of the tradition, of the village, of the heritage."

Remo nodded. "Yes. Yes, Smitty. That's one of the wisest things you've ever said to me. It's exactly right." Remo could feel the new understanding roiling around his brain. Maybe he'd never get a handle on it, but just knowing it was enlightening. *He had the personality traits of the Sinanju bloodline.*

"Think I'll enjoy being obstinate and argumentative and cantankerous to the end of my days?"

"Haven't you always enjoyed it?" Smith asked half-seriously.

Epilogue

"He is awake."

Remo opened his eyes and found the bird standing on the floor near his mat, looking right at him.

"He is awake," the bird said again.

"That's a self-fulfilling statement, bird. Saying it makes it true."

"He is awake."

"Try saying this—*he is asleep. Night.*" Remo attempted to make the words a reality, but the parrot didn't cooperate. Remo heard it shifting nervously from good foot to bandaged foot and he looked at it again.

"What are you worried about?"

"He is awake."

"You want a cracker or something?"

The bird launched into another limerick.

There once were some nasty, loud boys
Who spent their time playing with toys
The worst of the pack
Was a scoundrel named Jack
Who woke HIM with all of his noise.

Remo thought about it. "I know it's dirty, but I still don't get it."

Chiun emerged from his room with trouble lines engraved in his flesh, and he strode right up to the hyacinth macaw.

"Say it again, bird."

"There once were some nasty loud boys…" The bird recited the limerick again.

Chiun's jaw trembled, like the face of a very old man.

"Little Father?" Remo asked.

"Him. He is awake. It is the warning the bird came to deliver, Remo. In his ancient city beneath the pacific seas he is no longer dreaming. Remo, he is awake!"

Remo's alarm heightened. Chiun might be easy to irritate, but not to frighten, and right now he looked frightened. "Who is awake?"

"Him," the bird squawked.

"Him." Chiun nodded.

"Does this have something to do with Jack Fast?"

"The worst of the pack," the parrot repeated.

"We never should have left him there," Chiun said. "I knew what that place was when I read the markings on the stone with my fingers."

Remo struggled to catch up. "You mean the underground river mouth where Jack Fast went in? Is that the place we're talking about?"

"One of the communication channels. A speaking tube, transversing the crust of the earth."

A speaking tube doing something through the earth. The concept collided unpleasantly with the concept of an ancient city under the Pacific Ocean where something was no longer asleep. Remo had dived the Pacific various times, but the memory of one dive haunted him still.

"Chiun, during my Rite of Attainment—"

The old man and the purple bird cocked their heads at him, wordlessly scolding him to silence.

"Yes, my son," Chiun said. "It is him, but at that time he was sleeping. Now that he is awake, who knows what he might compel us to do."

DANCING WITH THE DEVIL

Don Pendleton's Mack Bolan

Devil's Bargain

Alpha Deep Six. Wetwork specialists so covert, they were thought dead. Now this paramilitary group of black ops assassins and saboteurs has been resurrected in a conspiracy engineered somewhere in the darkest corners of military intelligence. Their mission: unleash Armageddon.

They've got America's most determined enemies ready to jump-start the nightmare, and the countdown has begun. Mack Bolan is squarely in charge and his orders are clear: abort the enemy's twisted dreams.

If Bolan survives, then it gets really personal. Because Alpha Deep Six has a hostage. A Stony Man operative...

Don't miss this special 100th episode,
available January 2005 at your favorite retailer.

Or order your copy now by sending your name, address, zip or postal code, along with a check or money order (please do not send cash) for $6.50 for each book ordered ($7.99 in Canada), plus 75¢ postage and handling ($1.00 in Canada), payable to Gold Eagle Books, to:

In the U.S.	In Canada
Gold Eagle Books	Gold Eagle Books
3010 Walden Avenue	P.O. Box 636
P.O. Box 9077	Fort Erie, Ontario
Buffalo, NY 14269-9077	L2A 5X3

Please specify book title with your order.
Canadian residents add applicable federal and provincial taxes.

GOLD EAGLE®

GSB100

Black Harvest

*Available March 2005
at your favorite retail outlet*

Emerging from a gateway in the Midwest, Ryan Cawdor senses trouble within the well-fortified ville of a local baron, whose understanding of preDark medicine may be their one chance to save a wounded Jak. But while his whitecoats can make the drugs that heal, the baron knows the real power and money is in the hardcore Deathlands jolt. And where drugs and riches go, death shadows every step, no matter which side of a firefight you stand on....

In the Deathlands, tomorrow is never just another day.

James Axler
Outlanders

EVIL ABYSS

An ancient kingdom harbors awesome secrets...

In the heart of Cambodia, a portal to the eternal mysteries of space and time lures both good and evil to its promise. Now, a deadly imbalance has not only brought havoc to the region, but it also threatens the efforts of the Cerberus warriors. To have control of the secrets locked deep within the sacred city is to possess the power to manipulate earth's vast energies...and in the wrong hands, to alter the past, present and future in unfathomable ways....

Available February 2005 at your favorite retail outlet.

Or order your copy now by sending your name, address, zip or postal code, along with a check or money order (please do not send cash) for $6.50 for each book ordered ($7.99 in Canada), plus 75¢ postage and handling ($1.00 in Canada), payable to Gold Eagle Books, to:

In the U.S.	In Canada
Gold Eagle Books	Gold Eagle Books
3010 Walden Avenue	P.O. Box 636
P.O. Box 9077	Fort Erie, Ontario
Buffalo, NY 14269-9077	L2A 5X3

Please specify book title with your order.
Canadian residents add applicable federal and provincial taxes.

GOUT32